The Perfect Bow

Samirah Zaman

Paperback ISBN:978-1-7393407-4-2

Ebook ISBN: 978-1-7393407-5-9

First paperback edition: May 2024

Cover art by: Saima Begum

Playlist

Labour – **Paris Paloma**

I Lost Myself In Loving You – **Jamie Miller**

Chaotic – **Tate McCrae**

The Climb – **Miley Cyrus**

Costume Party – **Lauren Duski**

Make It To Me – **Sam Smith**

If I Were A Boy – **Beyonce**

History Of Man – **Maisie Peters**

Salute – **Little Mix**

Pretty Hurts – **Beyonce**

Enough For You – **Olivia Rodrigo**

Avijog – **Tanveer Evan**

Dil – **Shreya Ghoshal**

Jaan Ban Gaye – **Asees Kaur**

Madhanya – **Rahul Vidya & Asees Kaur**

Ro Lain De – **Amitabh Bhattcharya**

Suraj Hua Maddham – **Sonu Nigam**

Do Anjaane Ajnabi – **Udit Narayan & Shreya Ghoshal**

Aaye Ho Meri Zindagi Mein – **Udit Narayan**

E Hawar Parpar – **Raj Barman**

To all the women who are fighting the invisible battle —
I see you. I hear you. I'm with you.

But most importantly, for Rahima.
Whose strength knows no bounds, and whose hope ignites us all.
May the seeds of love you sow, multiply in your garden and blossom in the paradise that awaits you.

Chapter One

My mother always said I never gave her any trouble and her pregnancy passed with ease. After an eight-hour labour, I came out with a soft cry, almost afraid to disrupt those around me. While my mother cried happy tears and the doctors tended to her, my father cradled me in his arms and whispered the *Adhan* in my ears.

He stared down at me with wonder in his eyes as he imagined what my life would be. Who would I be? What achievements would I call my own? How many days did he have with me before he was forced to give me away?

My grandmothers were the first people to see me after my parents. My Dadi, *paternal grandmother,* offered a tight smile. "It's good to have a son first."

My mother bit her tongue and lowered her gaze.

But not my father. "*Why?* What can a son do that my daughter can't?"

"Provide."

My dad stroked my cheek and, with strong conviction, said, "My daughter is going to be the best. She *will* become my pride and joy."

In my culture, having a son was seen as a victory. A son meant no worries because a son could never let his parents down. A son never leaves his parents. A son could never be a failure. But my soft father was not once disappointed with a daughter. He shouted the news with pride.

"A daughter is a blessing," he would say. "My daughter is going to fulfil the duties of a son, but even better. Just watch."

And such expectation required a name to go with it.

The tale goes he searched every baby name book, spoke to every *Imaam* and took suggestions from his large extended family. But nothing was good enough for his precious little girl. Then one night as he lay in bed, staring at his five-day-old daughter, a soft whisper came to his ear.

Sumayyah.

The next morning he asked the Imaam, "What does this name mean?"

The middle-aged man looked at him with a wide grin. "This name has a very beautiful meaning, Bhaisab. It means pride, exalted, unique, high-above." He paused. "*Special.*"

My father's heart knew in that moment that this name was destined for his first-born child. Because he knew, no matter what life threw at her, she was going to be everything he dreamed of. She would be his pride and joy. She would be extraordinary. He knew she was going to live up to her name.

"Sumayyah Rahman," he uttered.

Without a doubt, he knew his daughter was going to be completely and utterly *perfect.*

Chapter Two

Much to the disappointment of my Dadi, two years after I was born, my mother gave birth to another baby girl; *Nafisa*. My parents weren't disappointed, and I was ecstatic to have a baby sister. I became Nafisa's shadow; always just one step behind her. As the years went on, I learnt to be the perfect older sister: vigilant, protective and loving.

Nafisa was my first best friend. Our contrasting personalities never got between us. While I carried worry at my core, she was a free spirit. I spent my Saturday mornings following my mum around the kitchen learning to cook, as she slept until mid-afternoon. Our quiet evenings were spent with me perfecting the skill of sewing while she lost time in video games. I was studious. She was creative. I was reserved. She was outspoken. I laughed quietly, and she roared with happiness.

But I never made a note of our physical difference until one summer day as we played out in the garden.

Nafisa kicked her legs, splashing water on my face.

My eyes screwed shut as my hands came to protect my face. "Nafisa!" I whined. "Amma will shout if we ask her to add water again."

Despite my scolding, she laughed. "Abba will give us more water."

She wasn't wrong. My father rarely denied us anything, as long as it was reasonable. That was how we were in our garden, under the sun, in an inflatable paddling pool.

"Abba isn't home," I reminded her.

She shrugged her shoulders and closed her eyes.

I let the water run through my fingers before causing little ripples with water droplets. I was so mesmerised by the water I jumped when my grandmother let out a scream.

"What are they doing outside?" she screamed in Bangla.

Nafisa jumped up just as my mother came to the garden door. "Kitha oiseh?" *What happened?*

My mum's question was ignored. Instead, my grandma grabbed me by the arm and hauled me back inside my house, dripping wet. My mum hurried off to find a towel before I soaked her kitchen liner. In the meantime, Nafisa became the next victim of my grandma's assault.

"Nani!" she moaned as she was pushed through the door. "What?"

She frantically shook her head. "No sun. No good you," she explained in her broken English. *Translation: don't go out in the sun. It's not good for you.*

"What's wrong with you?" my mum asked, as she roughly towel dried us. "You scared me."

At seven I was bi-lingual in English and Bangla, but at that moment I wished I couldn't understand the words that came out of her mouth.

My grandma's face twisted in disgust as she glanced at me, but her expression intensified when she looked at Nafisa. "Do you want two black children? You can't do anything about this one," she gestured to Nafisa, "She came out with her dad's colour, but this one," she jutted her chin toward me, "At least, protect her colour. The sun will turn her ugly."

"Maa!" my mother groaned. "Stop."

She pulled the achaal of her sari tighter around her head. "Am I wrong? Do you want her to be darker?"

My eyes strayed to my sister, who for once didn't have a smile on her lips or a snarky comeback. Her eyes were cast downwards. But even at that young age, I knew I had to protect her from their harsh words. I grabbed her hand and led her away from the conversation my mother and grandmother were having about the twenty-year-old family friend who had no marriage proposals. They attributed it to her skin colour.

The door opened with a slow creek as I crept into Nafisa's room. She didn't notice me coming in as she stared at her reflection. I wondered what she saw when she looked at herself. Like me, did she see her beautiful smile? Was she hypnotised by her chocolate brown eyes? Did she know how envious I was of her luscious curly locks of hair? *Did my sister know she was beautiful?*

"Nafisa?" I called softly.

She hummed faintly without looking away from her reflection. Her slight frame stood in front of the mirror, even when I went and stopped next to her. A tear slipped down her cheek.

"Why are you sad?" I asked.

She swiftly brushed her tear away. "I'm not."

I thread my fingers through hers. "Nani is old."

"Nani is white. Like you. And Amma."

I never gave much thought to the colour of my skin, let alone hers. And I never loved her any less because of this difference. "You're beautiful."

"Nani said I'm ugly."

My heart pinched with pain for her. "Ignore her."

"You're beautiful, Afa." The endearing Bangla title for sister turned that pinch into something harder. "I want to look like you."

"And *I* want to look like *you*," I fired back. I squeezed her hand. "Actually, I want to *be* like you."

Her eyes regained a glimmer. "Really?"

I wrapped my arms around her. "Yes. You are perfect the way you are."

We hugged for a few moments longer than normal before we went down for dinner. At seven years of age, I naively thought my words would be enough for my sister. But we never forget the words others throw at us. They embed themselves into our skin, that we wear like scars.

Perhaps that's why over the years, I often caught my sister staring at her reflection in disappointment.

Chapter Three

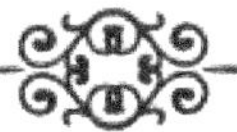

"I still can't get over this new look," Zoya said as we left our French class.

Trying to hide my insecurities, I rolled my eyes. "It's not that big of a deal. It's only a hijab."

Halima hummed in agreement. "I think it looks good on you."

"I didn't say it looks ugly. It's just..."

I stared at my friend, waiting for her to finish her sentence. "Just what?" I probed.

"A change," she finished. "Wasn't starting secondary school a big enough change?"

She slipped into the school toilets and into a stall before I could answer. As Halima also relieved herself, I took in my reflection. I had worn the hijab before when attending my Arabic lessons. My mum was adamant about me adopting wearing it daily as she did. Every day she would remind me she wore it from the age of six. She reiterated Islam encourages the covering of a woman's hair and body. She said she dreamed of her daughter observing the practice. And I was not one to disappoint my mum.

"A new school was the perfect time to wear it," I explained as Zoya washed her hands.

"Okay, but don't be surprised if the boys aren't interested in you."

Halima nudged our friend. "Shut up, Zoya. Just ignore her."

I laughed at my friends. "We've been friends since nursery. Do you think I'm an amateur in dealing with her?"

Zoya wrapped her arms around my shoulders. "You know I love you."

We stepped out into the corridor as large groups swarmed past us. We went from being the eldest in primary school to the little fish swimming amongst the sharks in secondary school.

"You don't have a choice."

Her light brown eyes lit up with mischief. "I'll forget about you once I make new friends."

"Never!" Halima declared.

We wove through the crowds until we found the canteen. With food on our trays, we scanned the room for a corner to tuck ourselves into. From the day we met, we were inseparable. Our teachers encouraged us to make new friends, even separating us into different classes, but every break and lunchtime we found one another in the playground. Our games turned into conversations filled with laughter and secrets we only shared with one another. I found a sisterhood in my friendship, and I melted from relief when we all got into the same secondary school.

"There's this really cute boy in my English class," Zoya said.

"Boys are," Halima finished her sentence by gagging.

"Your dad would be angry if you were talking to a boy," I warned my friend.

"He should have forced me into an all-girls school then," she shrugged.

"He tried," Halima muttered.

"And God still gave me a place here," she laughed.

Zoya's dad had one fear for his daughter: a boy would 'corrupt' her. Her father had a reason to worry she would be run amuck with boy attention because Zoya was nothing short of beautiful. With almond-shaped hazel eyes and a tall, slim build, she was what most boys went after.

Halima was petite with a curvier build. Natural curls framed her sweetheart face exquisitely. Her round eyes, full lips and filled out body were every boy's fantasy. She was stunningly gorgeous.

Compared to my friends, I was simple. I was neither tall nor short. Before wearing the hijab, my long, dark hair swayed behind my back. My brown eyes were plain and naïve. My legs were too skinny and my arms too long. I was the invisible girl, but I didn't mind.

"Hey!" Zoya called out to a girl who walked past us. "Do you want to sit with us?"

Halima and I shared a look of wonder. We never invited people to sit with us, preferring to enjoy our own company.

But the girl stopped and gave a smile of relief at Zoya's offer. "Yes, please!" She slid into the seat next to Zoya and opposite Halima. "I don't think we've met."

"This is Rani," Zoya said. "She's in my form class. This is Halima and Sumayyah."

I offered a hello with a polite smile. "How are you finding the first day?"

"I keep getting lost," she laughed. "And I have no friends to figure out this massive building with."

I frowned, feeling sorry for her. "Didn't anyone from your primary school come here?"

She shook her head. "I moved here from Manchester. I don't know anybody."

The day was daunting, despite having Zoya and Halima here with me. I couldn't imagine starting a new school in a new city where I didn't know anyone. "You can always sit with us," I offered.

Her mossy green eyes were filled with gratitude. She offered us all a smile. "Thank you."

And there, tucked away in the corner of a busy school cafeteria, a friendship of three blossomed into four.

"How was school, Maya?"

My dad's nickname for me never failed to make me smile. I took at a seat at the table with my steaming plate of rice and chicken curry. "Good."

"Good teachers?"

"Nice teachers."

"Aisha!" my dad called. "Get me water."

I looked at the short distance between his seat and the sink. I kept quiet as my mum came running from upstairs to meet his request. She placed the glass in front of him before scurrying away.

"I made a new friend."

"School not for friends, Maya. You be the best. Number one."

There it was. The two phrases my dad drilled into me like a mantra. I had to be the best. I had to be number one. Second best was not enough. I loved my dad. He invested heavily in me to ensure I never settled, yet at times I longed for him to recognise the difficulty of being the best.

He took my silence to continue in his broken English. "I come to this country and have nothing. I work hard my whole life. I don't want for you. I want you to be okay. Word hard now, Maya. Enjoy later. Life is very hard. Abba has *khoshto." Hardship.* "You be number one. You be happy." *If you are number one, you will be happy.*

"I am happy, Abba."

He shook his head. "Happiness come later. With good job and husband and children. When you this, I happy."

Once you have achieved perfection, only then will I be happy.

Chapter Four

THE WORDS IN MY biology textbook blurred as Rani and Halima laughed together. I looked over at them, splayed out on Rani's bed, while I cram studied for my upcoming GCSE mock tests. The mere thought of the tests caused anxiety. My grades would determine if I was smart enough to pursue the doctor route. If I got anything less than the top grade, I'd need to find another dream.

I bit my lip as I thought about what else I could do if I failed. While other children had big dreams of being an astronaut, or president, my dreams were tied to becoming a doctor. I spent all of secondary school proving to my dad I could do this. Because I will. *I have to.*

"Put the book away!" Rani groaned. "Come and have some fun with us."

After school, we all made the short walk to Rani's house. Well, all except Zoya.

I glanced up at the clock. "Give Zoya a call. She said she'd be here by now."

Four years of secondary school built Zoya's confidence to lie to her parents. More often than not, when her parents thought she was *studying* with us in Rani's house, she was out with a boy from school.

The practice meant we had mastered it, but the lie hinged on Zoya returning at the right time. She was cutting it close today.

Rani waved me off. "She'll be here. At least Uwais makes an effort. All Ravi does is flirt with me. Do you think he likes me?"

I turned back to my textbook as she recalled every interaction she'd had with the new boy who started four months ago. She was utterly infatuated with him. She was convinced he would be her first boyfriend. The same could not be the same for Zoya. Every few weeks, she had a new love interest, despite knowing her family would never approve of her dating. Part of me wondered if she did it just to rebel.

Just as I picked up my phone to call, her name appeared on my screen. I put the phone to my ear. "Where are you?"

"My uncle saw me and called my dad."

Ice filled my veins, and for a moment, it felt like my heart dropped to my stomach. "Where?"

"The park." She was gasping for her breath. "Meet me at ... the... park."

I slammed my book shut, capturing the attention of my friends. "What did you say?"

"That I was with you guys, obviously."

"What happened?" Halima asked, already sitting up.

"She got caught," I deadpanned. "She said to meet her at the park," I relayed with a shrug of my shoulders.

"Shit! What do we do?" Rani jumped into action. "We need to run. Let's go!" She grabbed her jacket and raced out of her room and down the stairs.

Halima and I followed suit. I was still shoving my books into my bag as we raced down her street towards the park.

"Which side of the park are you on?" Rani asked, on the phone to Zoya. A few seconds later, she nodded. "Okay. Two min—"

She suddenly halted with wide eyes.

I followed her line of gaze. The pounding in my chest had nothing to do with the mini marathon I just ran. In the short distance, Zoya's dad climbed out of his car and headed towards the park. My skin tingled with nerves. If he found her alone, I feared what he would do to her when she got home.

I snatched the phone from Rani. "Run as fast as you can to the Leisure Centre side. *Now!*"

"Good idea," Halima muttered. "But how are we going to get past him?"

The soft wind whipped through the small circled we formed in the middle of the street. "Let's go in from the opposite side. Hope you girls are wearing comfortable shoes."

I closed my eyes and made a quick prayer to God that we found her before her dad did. After that, we said nothing as we ran like it was *our* lives that depended on it. Maybe it did because we all knew what would happen to Zoya if she were caught. Every few minutes we checked to make sure we were all together and exactly eight minutes later we saw Zoya hiding behind a tree. And she was alone.

Halima pushed her hard. "I hate you."

Despite the harsh words, Zoya fell into her arms and thanked us repeatedly. "I owe you guys."

I was angry at my friend for putting us in this position, but at that moment, my relief trumped anything else. "Why were you so close to the edge of the park?" I scolded.

"We were about to leave and my uncle drove past."

"What will you tell your dad?" Rani asked. "He knows it was a *boy*."

I tried to come up with a viable answer. I was so engrossed in my thoughts that at first I didn't notice the troublesome glint in the eyes of my friends. When I did, I groaned. "What do you want me to do?"

"Hijab into turban style and then," Halima shuffled out of her coat and handed it to me, "Hood up."

It would have been futile to argue with three headstrong people. So I made quick work of restyling my hijab and swapping coats with Halima. "How do I look?"

Rani scrutinised before nodding. "Good enough to pass as a boy at a quick glance."

We threaded our arms and walked as a powerful unit through the park, as though we weren't on the edge of a cliff ten minutes ago. That was the thing about a friendship like ours; it didn't matter how scary life got, we always knew we weren't alone. That's why when Zoya's dad yelled her name when he spotted us, she didn't panic. She knew we wouldn't sell her out. She knew no matter what; we had her back. It's why, despite the close call, she never stopped lying to her parents. Because she knew we would always protect her.

But we couldn't have known our protection would only last until a month before her eighteenth birthday.

Chapter Five

The school had done a fairly good job of turning the gym hall into a prom scene. Streamers hung low, fairy lights twinkled, and pop music blared through the speakers. The far end had tables with platters of food and jugs of drinks. The teachers who were forced to chaperone were talking amongst themselves with a bored expression. My friends and peers were on the makeshift dance floor, laughing and twirling away.

Halima and I sat on the sidelines and watched everyone enjoy our final night in school. Our exams were over and while everyone celebrated the milestone, I was worried about the results. I needed top grades in everything if I wanted to get into the sixth form and take the five academic subjects I had chosen. Exam season was filled with study sessions with my friends and late night cramming. My dad forbade my mum from getting me to help around the house. To him, this was a crucial step towards becoming a doctor and housework was secondary.

"Why are you so glum?" Halima asked.

I smiled at Halima, the only other friend of mine who didn't have a date. Rani and Ravi were officially dating and had been for six months. They were smitten with one another, and determined to make their love last, they enrolled at the same college. Zoya also had her boyfriend with her for a year of sixth form. Nine months ago, she met Adeel, a sixth former who was the year above us. She surprised us all when she never lost interest in him. The two of them left their partners and stalked towards us.

"Why don't you come and dance with us?" Rani pouted.

I vehemently shook my head. "I don't dance."

"Even if I say please?" Zoya pleaded.

"Sorry," I smiled. "You guys look beautiful."

My dress wasn't new. It was a forest green dress I had worn to my uncle's wedding during the Easter holidays. Rani's dad bought her a dress just for the event. The orange mermaid dress clung to her body, making her look a few years older than the sixteen years she was. Her mom braided her hair and twisted it into an elegant bun. She was lucky enough to have a professional do her makeup. Zoya wore a long dress her cousin let her borrow. The light green material complemented her fair skin, and she looked like a porcelain doll. Using the limited makeup Rani bought with her, she applied her makeup in the school bathroom and had makeup wipes ready to remove it before her dad picked her up. To all our surprise, Halima wore a vibrant red A-line dress. It was a rare occasion where she showed off her curvy figure. But instead of flaunting her body, she stayed hidden in the dark with me the entire night.

"I feel like a princess," Rani gleamed. "Ravi said I look sexy in this dress."

I tried to imagine a boy saying that to me. Unlike my friends, I hadn't been batting off boys. I wondered if Zoya was right; *was it because of my hijab?* My mum was delighted I was never caught in a tangle of boy drama. She always said good girls don't date; we are to let our parents find us suitable partner. It didn't bother me because I was too focused on my studies, but occasionally, when my friends would talk about the boys who showed an interest in them, I wondered why I never had stories of my own to share.

I looked around the small circle we formed. Sadness squeezed my heart as I realised this may be the last time we would be together for a while. We were going from spending five days a week together to occasional meetups. While Zoya and I were staying in our school sixth form, Halima and Rani were attending two different colleges.

"Where did five years go?" my voice carried my sadness. "I can't believe this is the end."

Halima gave my hand a squeeze. "We're still going to be best friends."

"And talk *all* the time," Zoya added.

Rani wrapped her arms around us. "Nothing will change."

I looked down at our hands as we held onto each other like a lifeline. For prom, we were eager to wear something matching. With our different styles and taste, we decided on something small and neutral. Tied on each of our wrists were silk ribbons that matched our individual dresses. It was a last-minute effort after spending weeks unable to agree on an item. But as I eyed the ribbons, I felt overwhelmed with emotion. It was a symbol of unity and individuality. The token represented our friendship and solidified our everlasting bond.

I zoned out of the conversation and stared at my bow. The lopsided loops caused an itch in my brain. I had tried enough to get it right, but it somehow always ended up *wrong*.

"Earth to Sumayyah!" Rani called. "Did you hear anything we just said?"

"Sorry," I squeaked.

Halima frowned. "What's wrong? You've had a lost look on your face for ages."

I held up the wrist with the bow. "Why isn't it right? The bow is never perfect, no matter how hard I try."

The girls' lips curled into smirks, but Zoya was the one who spoke. "Why does it matter?"

My eyes narrowed. "Look at it. It's..."

Rani cooed and squeezed me tight. "Our little perfectionist."

When my frown never disappeared, Halima tried to make me see reason. "Isn't that the whole point of a bow? It's never meant to be symmetrical."

"Yeah," Zoya added. "I think I read that somewhere, too."

I knew I was getting frustrated at something trivial, but it was the principal. No matter how many times I tried, I could never get it right. What if that signified my future? I was terrified of what waited for my future. What if I couldn't keep up with the milestones in the next few years? What would I do if I failed? I had no backup. My dad envisioned a life for me I doubted I could live up to.

"Mine has to be," I bit out.

"We need to get you smiling. Get up," Rani demanded. "You *are* going to dance with me."

I offered a smile. "There! I'm smiling."

Zoya rolled her eyes. "It's just a silly ribbon. Don't let it get you down. And like Halima said, there's no such thing as the perfect bow."

Chapter Six

"Sorry I'm late!" Rani exclaimed as she rushed to the table. "My lecture overran. Have you guys ordered?" She dropped to her seat and tried to catch her breath.

With hunger on our minds and commitments that awaited after this, we quickly ordered our food and started our first face-to-face catch up since university began six months ago.

"I'm so glad we could all make it," Rani squealed. "I can't believe how many times we had to reschedule this."

Zoya rolled her eyes. "Sorry girls. I hope you never do, but if you get a mother-in-law from hell, you'll understand."

Rani scoffed and shook her head. "That won't be me. Ravi says his mum is *so* chilled out. She won't care what we get up to."

"Lucky you," she retaliated dryly. "My mother-in-law is everywhere I turn." Zoya wasn't shy about berating her mother-in-law. While she was nice, she expected Zoya to be at her beck and call.

"How did you get out today?" Halima asked.

"She's gone to Pakistan for a few weeks."

"Freedom!" Rani cheered with a laugh.

Zoya's annoyed expression didn't budge. "Hardly. Idris is still here and with his mum gone, he's basically become my child. He's a twenty-six-year-old man who is incapable of washing his own dishes."

"Was he okay with you meeting us today?" I asked, worried about the repercussions if he wasn't.

She waved my concerns away. "He said he wants me home before he gets back from work."

Zoya gave us the shock of our lives in March 2010. We were all worried about her when her family found out about Adeel and took her to Pakistan on a one-way ticket. She had no way to speak to us, so we were forced to patiently pray and wait for when she returned. Two months after she left, she called us and asked to meet up. Desperate to see our friend, we rushed to meet her in a local park. The joy and relief quickly faded when she revealed her marriage to Idris. She said he was seven years older than her and treated her well. He was settled in England, but travelled to Pakistan often. When we said our goodbyes, each of us had unshed tears in our eyes because we knew she was trapped in the prison her father created for her.

"Have they stopped pestering you about having children?" Halima asked.

She rolled her eyes. "No. It's like an everyday battle with him *and* them. I got the coil put in without telling him. Maybe if he thinks I can't have children, he'll divorce me."

I wondered if that was her actual plan. Despite her statement that her marriage wasn't entirely negative, her unhappiness was unmistakable. Her life had become the four walls of his house and her company was his family.

"Maybe it wouldn't be so bad," I offered. Everyone's eyes were fixed on me. "It's not like they'll let you work. Maybe a baby would force him to move out. And your time will pass."

She sighed. "Can we talk about anything but my sad life? How are you guys?"

"I met someone," Halima blurted out.

Rani's hands slammed down on the table. "Someone call the papers! Halima Akter has a boyfriend!" We all laughed with Rani.

"He's not my boyfriend. He's just..." A soft smile overcame her face. "He's nice and sweet."

"Does *he* have a name?" Zoya pried.

"Nazir. I met him at uni. It's still early days but you guys know me ... I've never been interested, but he's just different."

The blush on her cheeks made me grin. "I'm happy for you. I hope he treats you with all the love you deserve."

"Just make sure his mother isn't the wicked witch from the west," Zoya remarked, making us all snicker.

Rani sighed with a dreamy smile on her face. "Everything's the same old with me. Studying and loving the pants off Ravi. But forget about me." Her eyes turned to me with a devilish glint. "I want to hear all about *you* and Mr Going-To-Be-A-Doctor Ibrahim."

My cheeks felt warm at the mention of my university friend. He was handsome, spoke gently, and had big dreams, just like me. But most importantly, my parents would approve.

I took a sip of my water, hoping to calm my nerves at the interrogation about to take place. Eventually I settled with, "There's nothing to tell. We're just friends."

"Friends my ass," Zoya laughed. "You're blushing at the mention of his name."

"He's a nice guy, but I'm sure he doesn't like me." *If he did, he'd be the first guy to show any interest in me.*

"Such a liar!" Rani screeched, earning stares from nearby customers. "He's *always* finding a reason to message you. I say go for it."

Shaking my head, I said, "You guys are crazy." Just as my words came out, my phone pinged with a message.

"And who's that?" Halima teased.

"It doesn't matter. I'm having lunch with my friends."

Ibrahim slid into the seat next to me despite the lecture hall being half-empty. "Hey. I messaged you," he said.

I placed my notebook in front of me. "Sorry, I was out with my friends. Is everything okay?"

The lecturer walked in, disrupting whatever he was about to say. "We can talk after class."

The lecture dragged as I stressed about the looming conversation. What if he didn't want to be friends anymore? Or worse, what if he wanted *more*? *Was I ready for that? Did I want a relationship? Was I willing to lie to my parents?* I tried to focus on the lecture, but couldn't stop myself from stealing glances at him. Ibrahim caught my gaze a few times but only offered a tight smile. My notes were illegible and as the minutes ticked by, my heart raced even faster. I wasn't sure if I wanted time to go faster or slower. I started to mentally prepare a response for any potential scenario.

Once we were dismissed, Ibrahim suggested we find a quiet spot in a coffee shop. He offered to pay for my drink and then, *finally*; we sat. He looked the opposite of me. His lips were curled into a smile and his fingers pushed his hair back in a casual move. He relaxed into his seat before speaking. "My family is quite religious."

My eyebrows furrowed. "Okay?"

"And I wouldn't want to lie to them."

I swallowed hard. "Okay."

He rested his forearms on the table and leaned in closer. "I really like you, Sumayyah. You would fit perfectly into my family. You're smart and beautiful, with good morals, and I think you'd make a wonderful wife."

Wife?

My eyes widened as I realised where this was going. Of all the hundreds of scenarios I imagined, this was not one of them. "Where are you going with this?"

"You're a good girl, and I wouldn't want to disrespect you by asking you to be my girlfriend. Let's skip all that and get married."

I choked on my drink at his abrupt statement. I absolutely wasn't ready to get married, especially to someone who I hardly knew. Our conversations over the past six-months revolved around university. I didn't truly know him. And there was the obvious: I had just started my career journey.

"We're only nineteen. We have so much studying to do. I want to be a doctor."

He shrugged. "So do I. Who's saying we can't study while being married? How great would it be to have someone support you during this? We'd understand one another in ways others won't."

"Ibrahim..." I looked away as I tried to verbalise my apprehension.

"Would you rather be in a haram relationship?"

My eyes widened. "No! Of course not! But this would be easier on you because you're a man." My thoughts went to Zoya and what her life became after marriage. Pressure from husband, in-laws, and societal expectations for babies. "As much as I want to be a mother, I want that after I've achieved my goals."

His boyish smile made my heart flutter. "You're studying Medicine. Contraception exists."

My cheeks warmed at the thought of contraception. "I don't know, Ibrahim. You're nice and I'm sure you'll make a good husband, but we barely know each other."

"Generations before us didn't even *see* their spouse until after the *Nikkah* and they were perfectly fine. We can get to know each other with time." He took a deep breath. "This is too much. I don't want to pressure you. I just know how I feel and I don't want to be tempted to commit a sin. Why don't you talk to your mum and see if she would be open to the idea?"

I carried those thoughts with me all day. I wondered what my parents would do at the prospect of getting me married. My parents had my life planned out; education, career, marriage and then babies. What if I wanted to rearrange the plan a bit? Would they like Ibrahim? I know they'd respect him for wanting to do this the right way. He didn't want to sneak around and to me, that was worth a lot. He would support my dreams of being a doctor because he wanted the same thing. He would understand the late nights and struggles of managing a family with a demanding career.

By the time I sat down with my mum late that evening, I knew this was worth discussing. "Amma?"

"Ji?" She spared me a glance as she folded her laundry away.

"Can we talk?" I asked in Bangla.

"Kitha?" *What?*

As I told her about Ibrahim, I saw the disappointment intertwined with the fear in her eyes. No matter how many great personality traits I shared about him, the look never left her face. She didn't need to say what she was thinking because I knew what was coming. "If he was a good boy he would do this the right way by speaking to your father. Decent boys don't make friends with girls."

"Amma—"

"No!" she shouted. "What would people say when they hear you're getting married this young? People will talk and say it's because you were nafakh." *Dirty.* "They will think you are like those English girls."

Tears brimmed in my eyes at her harsh words. I couldn't help but wonder if that was what she thought I was doing. My mum never wanted me to go to university. While my dad pushed me into studying to become a doctor, my mum worried families wouldn't want me in fear of being '*too educated*'.

"But you and Abba know that isn't true."

"Sumayyah!" she snapped. "This isn't right."

I stood up and stared at her. "Why? It's not haram to want to get married."

She stared at me from head to toe. Suspicion filled her eyes. "University friend?" she asked sarcastically. "You kids think you're smarter than me. If you just met him, why are you so angry?"

"Because!" I looked away from her, trying to find the words to explain this is something *I* wanted. Perhaps my love for Ibrahim wasn't immediate, but it could grow. It would be nice to have someone to understand the pressures of this field. If I was too tired to help around the house, he would understand. If I had a hard day at work, he wouldn't force me to socialise with the guests that give us a surprise visit.

The tears in my eyes softened her hard exterior. "This is your life. I want you to be happy. Getting married young isn't easy. It's hard to make a marriage work." She looked lost in her thoughts before she shook her head. "This boy won't fit in with this family. He is too modern. He will have female friends his whole life, and then what will you do? The world will dismiss his wrongs and shame you from letting him stray. Let this go and study."

I let out a small laugh. "Wow, Amma. You never wanted me to study. You were the one that started talking about marriage when Zoya got given a husband. And now look at you."

"You have a luxury here. What will you do when he wants you to serve his food?"

"He's not like that! He's studying to be a doctor like me."

This time, she laughed. "They're never like that at the start. Then, before you know it, he expects breakfast and lunch and dinner. His mum needs you to scrub the floors. His dad doesn't like you working. His brother gets married and then you have competition. After a few months, you are expected to give a grandson, and if you don't, you hear about it for the rest of your life. *That* is the life of a Bangladeshi bou." *Wife / daughter-in-law.* "Your life becomes his life. Your job is to lie down and give him what he wants. Is that what you want?"

"What should I do then, Amma? Never become a wife? Or never become a doctor? Either way, I don't win."

She hums under her breath. "Now you understand the life of a woman."

Chapter Seven

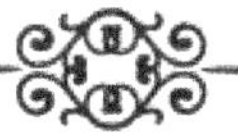

I paced around the room as the muffled chatter from downstairs was intertwined with laughter and the clinking of cutlery. I paused in front of the mirror and eyed my reflection. At twenty-five, I had finally grown in my features. My sharp nose finally looked like it belonged on my face. My round eyes felt in proportion to my face. And I had mastered the coy smile. Today my brown eyes reflected the nerves I felt.

My fingers brushed over the heavily embroidered sari my mum draped onto me. According to my mum, the mint green outfit and matching hijab wouldn't wash me out. The colour wasn't my preference, but today mattered to her because a groom had come to see me. My parents were eager to meet him and his family. He was handsome, educated, and hailed from a reputable family and place in Bangladesh. When his marriage CV was presented to my parents, they gleamed with joy at his prospects and were quick to arrange today's meeting.

My mum lectured me about giving him a fair chance. According to her, I was being too picky, especially for someone who was hard to give away. Her biggest fear came to life when she heard somewhere that families were rejecting me because I was too educated. She sobbed that night and muttered to herself about how she warned my dad about these consequences. She was eager about this new boy and had practically declared he was the one – all based on a piece of paper.

When the door swung open, nerves surged in my throat, but it turned out to be Nafisa. "Chill, Afa! It's only me," she laughed.

I moved from the mirror to sit on the bed. "Have they finished eating?"

She shook her head as she closed the door and took a seat next to me. "The women are just finishing up." She eyed me cautiously. "Why are you so nervous? You've done this three times already."

No amount of practice can take away the feeling of anxiety as a family judge you in a brief hour. They examine your body. They make note of how you speak and what you say. The home you live in is judged by them. They analyse family dynamics. All the while eating a feast and still walking out the door offering nothing. I hated the whole idea of a *dekha dekhi.* But alas, this was the norm in my culture. If me and the potential groom agreed to move this forward, my family would soon be in his house to project the same judgement on him and his family.

My fingers twisted. "One day you'll understand."

She let out a scoff. "No way! I'm finding someone for myself."

My thoughts went back to four and a half years ago when a younger Sumayyah approached her mum about Ibrahim and her harsh reaction. As I closed my eyes, I could envisage Ibrahim's face as I told him I didn't feel that way about him. He was a good guy. He accepted my answer and kept a distance from me. We graduated the summer just gone and only a week later, he celebrated his one year wedding anniversary.

I held my sister's hand. "Whatever is written for you will come. This isn't so bad."

She raised her eyebrow at me. "Tell that to your face. Just tell them if you're not interested."

Nafisa knew I had tried. I asked my parents to give me just two more years to finish my foundation years as a doctor, but my mum went into a meltdown about how I was getting too old and eventually nobody would want to marry a woman past her prime. After weeks of pleading with my dad, she got him on her side and eventually me, too.

"I want this. I am ready for marriage." I knew how to cook and clean. At the start, it would be difficult, but I would eventually learn how to balance marriage and work. It didn't matter when I got married, this would be the predicament.

"But you'll be marrying someone you don't know."

"It's not like I'll be marrying him tomorrow. I'll get to know him."

Nafisa frowned. "Don't you want to love him?"

Love. Would I ever love him? Maybe. It was possible.

"Of course I do. People can fall in love after marriage in the same way they can fall out of it."

She held my hand and placed a kiss on my row of knuckles. "Very true. I hope you have all the magic and love in your marriage. You deserve the perfect happily ever after."

My heart raced in my ears as I made my way down the stairs. The voices turned to a hushed whisper as I came into view. Per both my grandmother's instructions, I kept my head bowed and a solemn expression on my face.

"Brides don't smile," my grandmother scowled after the first family left.

My mom came and stood next to me and with a proud smile, she introduced me. "Amar furi, Sumayyah." *My daughter, Sumayyah.*

"Assalmualaikum," I greeted softly.

My mum walked me through the living, to an empty seat on the sofa. I kept my head down as a few of his family came over to greet themselves.

A younger girl took the seat next to me. "Hi!" She was perkier than all of them. "I'm Haniya. I'm his sister."

I peered up at her. Her eyes were filled with excitement and a warmth I never received from the previous sister-of-the-groom that came to see me. "Hi. It's nice to meet you."

"You must be feeling so nervous," she awkwardly laughed.

"A little," I answered honestly. "Did you eat?"

"Your mum is such a good cook! My mum made me leave the table by shooting daggers. I'm definitely going to get a lecture on etiquette on the way home."

A genuine smile graced my lips. "Sounds like something my mum would do."

She bumped her shoulder against mine. "Sounds like a match made in heaven."

Our conversation was interrupted by her mum, Anjuman. She looked a few years older than my mum. She didn't match my vision of an evil-looking woman. Like her daughter, there was a softness to her I liked. She complimented me on my outfit and asked a few questions about my studies. The next forty minutes went like that — small talk with strangers who could potentially become my new family. Despite how nice they were, my nerves never left because the biggest event remained; meeting *him*.

My Bhabi, *sister-in-law*, Masuma, was the one to lead me to the second living room. She closed the door behind us and I finally felt like I could breathe. "How was it?" she asked.

I used my hands to fan my face. "Did you feel this way when we visited you?"

Masuma married into the family eighteen months ago. While her husband wasn't my biological brother, but first cousin from my dad's side, we had the relationship of real siblings.

She laughed. "Yup! You'll be fine. Are you ready to meet your maybe-future husband?"

"No," I squeaked. "How do I look?"

She rolled her eyes with a laugh. "Fine. I'm going to tell them to bring him." She placed her hand on the door handle before stopping. With a playful smile, she said, "Don't worry. I'll put my earplugs in, so ask him whatever you want."

My cheeks warmed in embarrassment. While she was gone, I took a seat on one end of the three-seater sofa and fixed my posture. I heard his voice before I saw him. I couldn't hear the joke that made my Bhabi laugh because I was swooning over his deep, smooth voice. It felt like my body was encased in velvet. I kept my head down as he walked past me to the other side of the sofa and took a seat. Masuma closed the door and took a seat on the other side of the room.

"Asalamualaikum," he said.

"Wa alaikum salaam." I felt the burn of his stare.

Silence descended upon us as he studied me. *Was he trying to see if he was attracted to me?* "Do I get to see your face?" he teased.

I bit back my smile. I slowly lifted my face and finally turned to see him in the flesh. My first thought was *pictures did not do him justice.* The first thing I noticed was his grey eyes. They reminded me of a cloudy day, where the sun hid behind them. His dark hair looked softer than mine and I almost asked him about his haircare routine. I should have looked away, but I couldn't stop shamelessly staring at him, even when his fingers nervously stroked the end of his beard. When he broke out into a smile, my heart swooned. A smile like that belonged on the front cover of a magazine. His broad shoulders shook as he chuckled.

"What's funny?" I asked.

He shook his head. "This is awkward for you, right?" He was the first suitor who voiced my thoughts. The other three men were obnoxiously confident. But he was different.

"Very. How do you I decide if you're my life partner in thirty minutes while my Bhabi eavesdrops?"

We both glanced at her just as she snapped her head in the other direction.

"Ask me anything you want and I'll answer honestly."

All the other times, the men led the conversation, asking questions about my ability to fulfil my duty as a wife and daughter-in-law. I was never presented with the opportunity to ask the questions. That's why I blurted out, "What's your favourite cereal?"

His eyebrows raised in surprise. "You can't beat a bowl of Cornflakes. *With* sugar and cold milk." He paused. "Can I ask you one?"

I nodded. I expected a question about working after marriage or how many children I wanted. That's why I was surprised when he asked, "Pineapple on pizza; yes or no?"

No matter how hard I tried, I couldn't stop the smile. "A hard yes."

With a groan, he stood. "Damn. Let me tell my mum it's a no." We both laughed in unison. He resumed his seat. "If that's a nonnegotiable, I can pick them off."

"Or you could learn to love it," I suggested. Enjoying the flow of the conversation, I asked another random question. "Favourite place you've travelled to?"

"Australia. How about you?"

"I haven't travelled much," I answered honestly.

His grin exuded youthfulness. "I'll take you travelling after marriage."

The conviction in his voice took me by surprise. "You're awfully confident."

"No. I'm Yousef Hasan."

If my mother witnessed the laugh that burst out of me, I would have been lectured for hours about it. But Yousef didn't care. If anything, it made him smile wider. "That was a terrible dad joke."

"I have more, if you're interested."

As our eyes met, I realised he brought out a different side to me. This Sumayyah wasn't timid. She wasn't afraid to laugh. She wasn't worried about sitting perfectly or afraid to say the wrong thing. I wondered if waking up to those grey eyes forever would make me happy. To those unfamiliar with my culture, and even some within it, the idea of envisioning a life with someone you recently met seemed absurd. But this is the purpose of the day. Marriage is not solely dependent on love. Compatibility also matters. Maybe I wasn't marrying for love, but for stability. Maybe I was choosing a partner based on a tick box. *But who said love can't come afterwards?*

"Do you spend your Friday evenings writing your jokes down?" I asked.

"No. Friday I play football with my friends. What do you do for fun?"

The next thirty minutes went like that. We asked questions about the small things, ignoring the big questions we were supposed to ask. Yousef shared the little parts of him that most people don't think about. And he attentively listened when I shared tiny fragments of me. By the end, he wasn't just the handsome engineer that his CV bragged about. He was a real person.

We stood up when a knock came at the door. We shared one more silent look.

"It was a pleasure meeting you, Sumayyah."

"You too, Yousef."

He looked nervous for the first time. "There's no pressure for you to decide right now, but I hope this isn't our last interaction."

Before he left the room, I said, "You didn't ask about the other stuff."

His eyebrows furrowed in confusion. "What stuff?"

My eyes flitted to Masuma, who was still pretending she couldn't see or hear us. "You know ... working, living arrangements, kids; that stuff."

"My priority is finding a life partner. Everything else is secondary. Who knows where life will take any of us? If we're not compatible, why do those things matter? If you have the right significant other by your side, everything else in the world seems insignificant." He smiled at me once again. "Besides, we'd have the rest of our lives to figure that stuff out."

Chapter Eight

I smiled whenever I spoke to Yousef. It could have been an ordinary conversation about the weather, but I would grin from ear to ear even though he couldn't see me. Our parents didn't want us seeing each other in person alone, so we made the best of what we had over the last seven months. From the day we both said yes, Yousef called me every single day. Our conversations were ordinary. We shared mundane details about our day and key moments from our past. We were four weeks away from being husband and wife. The wedding was fast approaching and while our families were getting ready for a wedding, he and I were preparing for a marriage.

"I think we need to have a serious conversation. Do you have a few minutes or are you running late?"

I looked at my dashboard. My friends and I were all gathering in Rani's flat in three minutes, but I wasn't ready to hang up and from the tone in his voice, I don't think I could have hung up. "I've got time. Is everything okay?"

"With the wedding getting closer, I just thought we should talk about contraception."

For the first time since our parents had put the ban on seeing each other, I was grateful. My cheeks instinctively warmed and my eyes bulged out of my head. “What about it?” I squeaked.

A moment passed before he spoke. “Did you want me to sort it or are you…” he trailed off. When I never responded, he tried again. “What I mean is, did you want to use condoms, or were you thinking about the pill?”

I concealed my gasp with a cough as the word condom echoed in my head. Of course, I knew we needed something in action, but I hadn’t considered that part and he had never mentioned it before. Nobody had ever seen me naked before. I hadn’t even shared a bed with anyone since I was six, other than the occasional guests who would come and stay in my house. His question was a reminder that I’d be sharing a bed with a *male* in a few weeks.

I cleared my throat. I was being ridiculous. I was a doctor for God’s sake and sex was basic human biology. There should have been no shame in talking about it with my future husband. But twenty-five years of being made to feel shamed for even *knowing* what sex was, wasn’t easy to wash away. My culture had a clear stance: women don’t talk about sex. It’s not our place.

Yousef let out a soft laugh. “I’m just as clueless as you. I know I’m not ready for a baby.”

I let out a breath of relief. “Me too.” Putting on my doctor persona, I sat taller, hoping it would provide my voice with more conviction. “Obviously, a condom would be the safer option.”

He paused. “Yes.” His response sounded incomplete, almost as if there was a ‘but’ he held back. I waited to see if he would complete his thought, but he didn’t.

"Yousef?"

"Let's talk tomorrow," he finally said. "Have fun with your friends, almost-wife."

I felt unsettled about leaving the conversation incomplete. I wanted him to finish his thoughts, but I also didn't want to push him before he was ready to open up about what was bothering him. "I will, almost-husband." After I hung up, I took a few deep breaths. Pushing the topic to the back of my mind, I exited my car and made my way up to Rani's flat. I rang the doorbell and waited.

"Hi!" Rani said as she pulled the door open. "What took you so long? You're never late."

I couldn't say anything because when I walked into her living room, my eyes widened with shock and my heart warmed with love. The most elegant bridal shower has been set up. Pink, white, and gold balloons hung from the ceiling. The hardwood floors were littered with confetti and the small dining table had sweet and savoury dishes set out.

"This is beautiful!" I gleamed.

They rushed over and engulfed me in a group hug. I squeezed my friends tight, hoping they understood how much I appreciated them.

"I know it's not much—" Halima started to say, but a light slap on her shoulder from me stopped her.

"Don't be stupid! This is perfect. I love it."

They led me over to the sofa, where we all got comfortable. "I know a big party isn't your thing, so I thought to keep it low-key," Rani said.

"Just you, your girls and food," Zoya added.

"And presents," Rani winked.

The room echoed the roars of our laughter as we took a trip down memory lane. I held my stomach as a stitch formed.

"Those were the days," Halima said wistfully. "They seemed so hard at the time, but I'd do anything to go back to the simpler times."

"Can you believe three out of four of us are married?" Zoya said, as if she couldn't believe it.

Truthfully, part of me couldn't believe it. Very few are lucky to have friends that carry them through their lives. I remembered the days when we would talk about marriage and children as though it were a lifetime away.

Halima and Nazir got married two years ago. Her wedding was elegantly extravagant. Nazir gave her the wedding most women dream of and when his eyes fell on his bride, he smiled as though he won the lottery. Halima was no different. She couldn't go longer than an hour without calling her husband. I was happy for my friend. For someone who swore to never fall in love, she fell the hardest.

"What is your best advice for the new bride?" Rani asked.

My two friends fell silent as they tried to come up with their answer.

Zoya answered first. "If you want to remain happy, make sure you have something for yourself. It's easy for your marriage to become your entire personality. Don't lose yourself in your marriage."

"Mine would be ... set the expectation from the start. If you don't like something, say it when it happens. Because if you let it go, he'll think it's okay even when you tell him it's not."

A heaviness rested on my chest at their answers. I expected answers like 'don't go to bed angry' or 'make him pick up his socks'. Their answers made me worry about the trials that may lie ahead. What would make Yousef and I argue? We hadn't so much as disagreed on something. Our understanding was mutual, but would it shift once we started living together? What if my mother was right all those years ago? What if he becomes someone else entirely?

Rani must have also felt the rise in tension before she jumped up from her seat. "Presents! You're going to love what I got you."

I spent the next ten minutes opening gifts from Zoya and Halima. There were a few pamper gifts mixed in with couple gifts ranging from mugs to bath towels. I hesitated before opening Rani's gift. The playful glint in her green eyes warned me of trouble.

I was right to be worried. Carefully wrapped was a book on *sex positions.* I stared at her with wide eyes. "Oh, my God!"

"You'll definitely be screaming that in four weeks!" she laughed, with the others joining in. "I have one more. This one is more practical." She handed me another parcel, but this one was much softer.

Pulling the wrapping apart, I revealed a black satin robe with lace running along the hem. "Thank you?"

Rani rolled her eyes. "Your husband will be thankful when you slip that over your sexy lingerie."

That familiar burn of embarrassment made an appearance. I wasn't the type to put underwear on to seduce my husband. I wouldn't even know how to do that. I'd never bought anything fancier than plain t-shirt bras and full briefs. As I looked at my friends, I knew they were the only people I could ask for advice. As close as I was to Masuma, I was too mortified to ask her for bedroom advice. But I could ask my friends. All of them had lost their virginity. They could tell me what to expect. They could tell me what to do. I wanted Yousef to enjoy his time with me. Intimacy is an important part of marriage, and I didn't want to fail him.

"What is it like?" I blurted out. "I mean..." I swallowed my embarrassment. "I've never even kissed someone, and now I'm going all the way. I'm just a little nervous."

"That's totally normal!" Zoya reassured.

"He mentioned contraception today and I couldn't even talk about it through the phone!" My groan came out muffled as I covered my face. When I looked at my friends again, I shook my head. "I'm twenty-five. I've studied the human body! Why does this topic make me feel like this?"

"Because we're taught that it's a disgusting thing," Rani remarked with an eye roll. "It's a crime that women enjoy sex, but we like and need it as much as men."

"Men talk about it openly because it's a trophy for them," Halima added. "The act is for them. We are just the toys."

Zoya scoffed. "Got that right. My first time was uncomfortable, and I was glad he was done fast."

I winced at her brutal honesty. "But it gets better, right? I mean, you've had a baby."

Zoya welcomed her first-born son, Karim, just over a year ago. "I guess. It's just like my wedding night. I just do as he asks."

Oh.

"He wanted sex on your wedding night? But you barely knew him," I said. Although we hadn't spoken about it, I assumed Yousef and I would wait before we had sex. I wanted to be comfortable around him before sharing my body.

She shrugged. "He didn't care. For him, it was his right. Our bedroom door barely locked before his pants were down."

Needing someone to reassure my assumption was right, I turned to Halima. "How about you? Did you wait?"

She shook her head. "I wanted to collapse from exhaustion, but Naz was all over me. I was so out of it that it was just something I did."

Rani gave her a pointed look before looking at me with sympathy. "It will mean more to you because it's with someone you waited for. Don't sweat it."

That was easy for her to say. I wondered what I would do if he wanted sex on the first night. Would I say no? *Could* I say no? Technically, we would be married and there would be nothing to stop us. He'd undress me out of my wedding gown and his eyes would feast on the body that belonged to him. A good wife wouldn't turn her husband away, especially on such an important night.

"Sex is always awkward the first few times," Rani continued. "You will grow comfortable with each other. You'll learn what he likes and vice versa. It's not something logical, it's emotional."

Halima let out a laugh. "I have to disagree. To most men, it's all physical."

Rani nudged her elbow into Halima. "We're trying to calm her," she muttered.

"Let's not set some crazy expectation for her. Are you telling me sometimes Ravi doesn't pound into you just to get himself off?" She arched her brow as she waited for an answer.

"That's all Idris does," Zoya answered instead.

Rani offered a sheepish smile. "Okay! Fine! Sometimes it is like that but—"

"No buts," Halima intervened and turned to me. "I'm sorry, but it is the truth. I'm sure he'll be gentle in the beginning, but eventually it's just an end to a means. Sex becomes to feel like a chore."

I shook my head. "No. I refuse to become like that. If it becomes like that, I won't do it." Sex was not a meaningless thing to me. It's two bodies intertwining and two souls connecting spiritually. It's an act of love, not indifference.

Halima's sad smile was haunting. "Yes, you will. Because eventually you'll understand in our culture marriage isn't a partnership. It's a man's world and you'll do anything to keep him happy and satisfied."

Chapter Nine

"How are you feeling?" Nafisa asked as she joined me in my bedroom.

"Like I'm sweating through every pore."

My Islamic wedding, the *Nikkah,* was about to start in ten minutes. Today I completed my half with my family and Yousef's immediate family present. And tomorrow, on our wedding day, he would complete his and then we'd be married.

"You'll be fine, but dad is already bawling his eyes out."

My dad had been crying since the wedding had been set. Every fall of his tears triggered the same reaction in me.

My mum burst through my bedroom door. "Good. You're ready." She perfected the pleats in my sari before standing up. "Make sure you don't say *kabool," I do.* "too quickly. Wait a minute or two."

I was given this advice a few times already. For a woman to say *I do* that quickly was an embarrassment on her part. It meant she was too eager to leave her parents' house. She came across as shameful.

"Okay. Are they here?" I asked.

My mum pursed her lips. Tears welled in her eyes as she avoided looking at me. "Yes. They're here to take my daughter from me."

"Amma?" my voice cracked. "I don't want to go. I don't want to leave my home."

She cupped my face. "This home was only ever temporary. Since your creation, I prepared for this instant. My daughter will no longer be mine."

"I'll always be here for you."

She stepped back and brushed her tears away. "There's a new life waiting for you. Go and be a wife. You've had enough freedom to work. It's time to build a home and family."

My tears didn't stop falling as I finished packing the last of my belongings into suitcases. I brushed my tears away as Masuma came into my bedroom.

"All done?" she asked.

I remained on the floor and looked at the room that felt empty despite my furniture remaining. All elements of my existence were packed away, ready to take into my new home. "All done. Will Bhaiya," *brother*, "take it tomorrow?"

She sat on the floor opposite me. "Yeah. We'll come a little after the wedding. How does it feel?"

The Nikkah was more difficult than expected. Even if my mother hadn't told me to wait before consenting, the word wouldn't have left my mouth so easily. Marriage meant leaving my family behind. My maternal grandmother's word about Yousef's family becoming my priority kept echoing in my head. I realised I wouldn't be coming home to my family, but his. When I was having a tough day, I couldn't hide in my room. I would have to put on a smile and mingle with his family. Life as I knew it was about to completely change, and I was due to live with strangers as of tomorrow.

And nothing, not even Yousef's *'hi, wife'* text, could take away the bout of sadness I felt.

"Scary."

"It is scary at first, but you'll adjust. The first few weeks might be filled with tears, but you'll see they're nice people. You'll learn their routines and find a new one for yourself. Ask your mother-in-law if you're unsure. And nothing says you can't influence their lives."

"What if they're not?" I swallowed the lump in my throat as I finally gave a voice to my biggest fear. "What if *he's* not nice?"

"Then you talk to him and figure out a middle ground. Marriage is built on communication and compromise."

The tightness in my chest didn't let up. "What if that's not enough? What if he doesn't understand me?"

Masuma took my hand in hers. "Then you come to us and we will help you. Just because you're married doesn't mean you stop having a family. You're just extending it."

I bit down on my lip to stop my cries. "But what if I'm not happy? What if they're horrible? What do I do?" I begged.

"You *try*, Sumayyah. It won't be all roses and rainbows. You need to understand that. You will argue with him and you'll probably butt heads with his mum. That is part of the package. But if it becomes unbearable, then you tell us and we will get you out."

A chill washed over me. The hairs on my arms stood alert. "Divorce?" I whispered.

"Nobody gets married to get divorced, but it exists for a reason. Always try to make your marriage work. You'll need to make sacrifices, and he will too. Divorce is a last resort." She plastered a smile onto her face and shook her head. "Why are we talking about something so horrid the night before your wedding? I actually came to talk about tomorrow night."

I looked away from her to hide my coy smile. I expected this conversation. The bride's Bhabi traditionally has the conversation with her about the morning after the wedding night.

"Do we really have to?" I groaned.

"Don't worry! I'm not going to tell you what goes where," she laughed. "Just remember that the morning after you have to shower before you can pray. My advice is to get up early and change your bedsheets before anyone else is up. Fold the dirty sheets away and wash them when the house is quieter. You're expected to make tea for everyone in the morning, but get dressed before you do. Your mother-in-law might want you to be in your sari before you go down, but just ask her or get him to ask. Make sure you salaam everyone when you go down."

I felt the urge to get a notepad and write all the things expected of me. I feigned confidence and nodded my head. "Okay. I got it. When will you guys get there?"

"Your dad said around midday. His cousins might come to help you get ready."

"I remember when we did that for you."

"You'll be okay, Sumayyah. We're only a phone call away."

I stared down at the ground as a fresh wave of tears came. "I don't want to go," I admitted. "I'm not ready."

Masuma shuffled closer and wrapped her arms around me. “We’re never ready to go. We’re never ready for marriage and the hurdles it brings. But it is the written rule for us women, and we are strong enough to do it. They are lucky to have you. You are going to be the most loving daughter-in-law. Most importantly, you are going to be the perfect bou.” *Wife.*

Chapter Ten

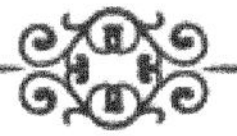

My dad sobbed as he helped me into the car. "My daughter is gone. My daughter is gone."

I wrapped my arms around his neck as I wailed into his shoulder. "Abba. Don't make me go," I cried louder than him. "Don't let me go."

"Let me see my daughter one last time," my mum begged.

As my dad tried to let go, I couldn't find it in me to release him. My dad had dedicated his entire life to me. He built my expectation of love so high; I wondered if anybody could compete. I wasn't ready to let him go. But he wrested away and let my mother have her moment. Through the blur of my tears, I made out the tears that soaked her skin. I squeezed my mum tight. She could hardly speak through her sobs and every moment with them made it harder to breathe.

She placed a kiss on my forehead. "Go. Live your life. Amar kham shesh." *My work is finished.*

Just before they closed the door, Nafisa wedged her way in. She tilted her head as she stared at me. She wiped away her tears. "So, you're leaving me?"

I grabbed her hand and squeezed. "Take care of them," I got out between my cries. "Promise me."

Her head fell into my lap as she cried. Gone was the sister who, in the morning, screeched anytime someone came too close to her, afraid they'd ruin her outfit, hair, and makeup. She cried on me like the two-year-old who fell in the garden and broke her arm. When that happened, I stayed with her and nursed her back to health. This time, I was the one who hurt her by leaving.

"I love you, Nafisa."

She couldn't respond because she was pulled away, and the door was closed. Within minutes, we exited the car park and were on the way to my new life.

Yousef said nothing. He remained a sturdy figure on the other side of the car. He silently handed me a tissue, which I gratefully accepted. The car fell into a sad silence as I tried to pull myself together. The day wasn't over. I still had to hide my sadness and sit with his family.

"Do you need anything?" he finally asked.

I needed to put my tear-streaked face back to perfection. "Can you hold my mirror while I fix my makeup?"

He gave me a soft smile. "Anything for you."

After I finished fixing as much as I could, we sat in silence. Yousef slowly reached out and held my hand. It was an odd feeling. After seven months of speaking, this was our first intimate moment alone. His hand felt warm in mine. He held it with such strength, it almost felt reassuring that I wasn't alone.

"You're going to see them tomorrow, and I'll never stop you from going to them."

Going to them. My parents' house was no longer my home.

"Thank you."

My head and neck were throbbing from the weight of my intricately embroidered dupatta. My skin was itching from the fabric of my dress. I had been in this dress for almost ten hours and I was ready to rip it off. My ankles ached from the heels and I could feel the straps digging into my swollen feet. I just wanted the day to be over.

"How long do you think we'll be downstairs with your family?"

"Not too long. Why?"

I let out a breathy laugh. "I'm tired and dying to get out of all this. My scalp is aching from this tight bun."

"Did I tell you that you look beautiful?"

Our eyes met. The lights from the lampposts flickered on his face, but his grey eyes were bright and alive.

"Many times during our photoshoot," I reminded him.

He lifted my hands to his mouth and tenderly kissed the back of it. "One more time won't hurt then." He smiled. "You look beautiful, my wife."

"Thank you, my husband."

And for a moment, I forgot about the heartache of leaving my family behind. For just a moment, I believed I would be okay.

When the chauffer parked outside his house, we were asked to wait a few minutes before entering. My heart raced again as I prepared to see my new home. While my parents had approved and Yousef had shown me pictures so my family could gift furniture, I had never seen it in real life. What if it was tiny? Or dirty? *What if it never felt like home?*

Before I was ready, my passenger door opened and his mum greeted me with a wide grin and a tray that carried sweetened milk and mishti. It was Bangladeshi tradition to 'sweeten' the new daughter-in-laws mouth with milk and Indian sweets. I didn't have the stomach for either. She offered a spoonful of the dessert which I reluctantly accepted. My stomach was turning with nerves. A chorus of *Alhamdulillah* was shared amongst his family.

Haniya helped me out of the car. "Welcome to your new home."

"Thank you."

Before I knew it, Yousef stood beside me, facing his front door. The house was adorned with lights and loud chatter travelled from inside. Yousef stepped inside first before turning to me and taking my hand. Hand-in-hand, we walked past the guests. I didn't know where we were going, but I had no choice except to blindly follow him. We ended up in a marquee out in his garden.

Everything was a blur. I couldn't take in the details of his home. I was directed to a seat in the rear of the tent, right in front of the stage. One glance at all the unfamiliar faces had my head bowed down in fear. Yousef sat next to me talking to, who I assumed were his cousins. Every few minutes he would ask if I was okay, which I nodded because what else was I supposed to do? Let out the scream that was building inside me? All I wanted to do was hide in my old bedroom and burst into a loud cry.

The next two hours were spent taking pictures with his extended family. He introduced me to everyone, but I couldn't grasp any of their names or faces. All I could focus on was trying to accept that all these strangers were my new family. I smiled politely and thanked everyone for their gifts.

"Can I get you anything, Bhabi?" Haniya asked. Hearing that title bestowed on me felt strange.

"Some water, please."

She nodded, but before she could walk away, Yousef called her.

"Tell Maa we're tired. Your Bhabi has been up since six and it's nearly two in the morning."

I turned my head to look at my husband. The request wasn't for him. He was comfortable and happy, surrounded by his family. I was the only one who wanted to leave. I almost hugged him, but remembered where we were.

Thankfully, when Haniya returned, it was with water and the news that we could head up to our bedroom. Yousef led the way up two flights of stairs. The handrails were adorned with flowers and lights.

"This is so pretty," I said to Haniya.

"Thank you for appreciating them! Your husband called it a waste of time and money."

"Ignore him."

Haniya's name was screamed from somewhere downstairs. She huffed and excused herself.

Yousef and I stood outside our bedroom door for a moment. With a small smile, we locked eyes. "Welcome home," he whispered. He twisted the handle and led us into a dimly lit room.

As expected by tradition, his sister and sister-in-laws decorated the room with candles, lights, and petals. A small tray table was laid at the foot of the bed with two champagne glasses and an imitation alcohol bottle. My lengha skirt dragged with it the petals that lay on the floor. He shut the door behind us. The furniture gifted by my father was built and in place. The bed was transformed into a four-poster bed with poles and draped in soft white fabric.

"Do you want to get changed?" he asked.

"My bags aren't here yet." I opened my bag to call Masuma, but there was a knock at the door before I could grab my phone.

"Sumayyah? It's Bhabi."

Instant relief filled me at the familiar voice. When Yousef opened the door, I practically strangled my Bhabi. Somewhere in the midst of my laugh, it turned to cries.

"Save something for me!" Nafisa joked as she joined us with a few bags in her hands. Yousef took them from her before she fell into my arms. Her sniffles caused an ache in my chest.

When Masuma's husband, Abdul, and his brother Mahmood came into the room with my suitcases, Yousef excused himself and gave me some time with my family. We waited for the door to click shut before any of us spoke.

"How's mum and dad?" I asked.

"They're okay." Nafisa smiled. "Obviously they're sad, but Sasa and Sasi are with them. When we left, Khala was dishing out mishti."

I nodded and let myself believe her. "That's good."

"How are you?" Abdul asked.

I looked around the room. "Okay. I'm really tired. He's got such a big family."

"His sister seems really nice," Masuma said. "Much nicer than..." she pointed at Nafisa.

"Ha-ha," she retorted sarcastically. "She'll never replace me."

"What time are you guys coming tomorrow? Please come early."

"Your dad said everything needs to be ready by eleven-thirty."

"Please don't be late," I begged.

A soft knock at the door silenced us. Yousef popped his head around the door. "Maa is saying you have to come and eat."

"We're not hungry—" Abdul started to say, but Yousef cut him off.

"It wasn't a request," he laughed. "You know how it is."

Masuma smiled and placed her hand on her husband's shoulder. "Why don't you three go? Let me just help Sumayyah with getting her stuff out." The couple shared a look before he nodded.

Yousef led my two cousins and sister out of the room. Once they were gone, I locked the door. "I feel like I'm dying, Bhabi. I want to be naked under a cold shower."

She chuckled. "Not long left now. Do you need any help with your dress and hair?"

"I'll wait until my mother-in-law confirms there's no more people and pictures."

"Okay." She pointed at the two large suitcases. "Leave those for now. Everything you'll need for tonight and tomorrow is in this bag." She held up a smaller suitcase. "Your mum ironed the sari, but it might need a quick steam. Ask Haniya to do that tomorrow."

I didn't care about the clothes for tomorrow. I was only worried about one thing. "Are my parents really okay?"

"They're okay. They knew one day they'd have to give you away."

"And Nafisa?"

"She'll get used to it. Stop worrying about them." She looked around the room. "They did a good job with your room. Very romantic," she teased.

I followed her gaze until it fell onto the bed. "I'm too tired for romance."

"There are no rules on what happens tonight."

My thoughts went back to my friends. "I've heard otherwise."

"It's the first time you guys can be with one another. There's nothing wrong with wanting some intimacy."

"What if he wants all the intimacy?"

"You don't want that?"

I shook my head with confidence. "Not tonight."

"Just tell him. He'll understand."

"What if he doesn't?"

The playful smile on her face provided some ease. "Then send him to get you some water and pretend to fall asleep before he comes back."

I laughed with her and called that Plan B. All too soon; I was saying goodbye to my family with promises of seeing them in less than twelve hours. It was almost three in the morning and I was close to collapsing.

My mother-in-law knocked on our door. "It's late. Get changed and go to bed." Her soft tone was reassuring.

"Would you like me to wear my sari when I make breakfast? Or should I wear a kameez?"

Her quiet laugh scared me. "Don't worry about that. You get some sleep and rest. I'll make breakfast. You get up slowly and get ready. I've told everyone to come for lunch, so you guys can get rest." She took my sari for tomorrow and said she would iron it for me. She left, the was door locked, and we were alone.

I took a seat on the bed and lifted my skirt to finally free my feet from the prison of my heels. Yousef kneeled before me and slowly unbuckled the straps. I let out a sigh of relief as the blood flow resumed. He spent a few minutes massaging my feet, and I almost fell back and asleep, but the burn of my scalp was too hard to ignore.

"Can you help me take the pins out of my hair?"

After unpinning the dupatta and head jewellery, I unwrapped my hijab and laid it next to me.

Yousef climbed onto the bed behind me and removed the black clips that were woven into my hair. We spoke about the day and our favourite parts. It felt like we were talking about a distant memory. When my hair was finally free, I ran my fingers through it and massaged my scalp.

Yousef's hands met mine as he took over. "You have beautiful hair," he complimented.

I realised it was the first time he had seen my hair. "It's an ugly, giant mess right now." I closed my eyes as his fingers worked magic. "That feels so good. Can I fall asleep like this?"

His laugh was a gentle melody, pulling my eyes closed. "I suggest some pyjamas first." He hesitated. "Did you need some help with your dress?"

On instinct, my thighs clenched shut. Helping me would mean seeing me in the fancy underwear I bought. While I wasn't planning on being intimate, I didn't want him to put off my ugly plain underwear. "Yes, please. This corset top is crushing my organs," I joked, hoping to ease the tension that suddenly filled the room.

We both climbed off the bed. Yousef stood behind me and patiently waited as I slipped the bangles off my arms. Once I was done, he slowly pulled the strings that held my top together. As the fabric loosened, my core tightened with nerves. What if he didn't like my body? Or worse, what if he wanted to explore it tonight?

"Done." His warm hands pulled the fabric from my body until it dropped to the floor. Our eyes met in the mirror. His eyes never strayed past my face. "Do you need help with your skirt?"

I shook my head. "It's okay. Why don't you get changed, too?" While his clothes were much more comfortable than mine, he had been wearing his embroidered sherwani since early afternoon.

"Do you want me to get changed in another room?"

"No. It's okay." I turned around and pulled at the strings holding my skirt up. The heavy fabric fell to the floor and pooled around my legs. The diamonds scratched my skin as I stepped out of it. I turned around to grab my pyjamas. My eyes landed on a half-naked Yousef. He paused, looking as alarmed as me. My gulp could be heard loud and clear.

"Sorry, I—"

He cut me off. "It's fine. We're married. Seeing each other like this is part of the deal," he mused.

My fingers twisted together as I mentally went over the speech I prepared. "I know what's expected tonight, but I don't think I'm ready for that."

Anything else I had to say fell away as he walked towards me. We stood in the middle of our bedroom, dressed in only our underwear.

Yousef gently pried away my twisted fingers and held both my hands. "There are no expectations tonight, Sumayyah," he whispered. "I never once thought tonight we would do more than share the space on our bed."

My heart felt like it caved at the genuine look in his eyes and tone of voice. "Are you sure?"

His hand cupped my face. His thumb brushed my cheek. "I've never been more sure of anything else except the decision to marry you."

"How lucky am I?" I asked with a smile.

"*I'm* the lucky one. You wrote my name on your palm in henna, but Allah wrote your name next to mine long before we were both in this world." He placed the lightest kiss on my temple. He repeated my question. "How lucky am I?"

Chapter Eleven

My eyes burned from the lack of sleep. Panic swarmed with my blood as I didn't recognise my surroundings. The low whistle of breathing forced me to turn around to see Yousef soundly sleeping. I took a moment to appreciate the face I'd see each morning. I smiled to myself, knowing I wouldn't be disappointed. I fiddled with the two rings nestled on my finger. Yousef got me the perfect ring. Admittedly, I sent him at least ten versions of the same style. The diamonds looked bright against the dark henna stain on my hands.

Creeping out of the bed, I quietly rummaged through my bags to find my hairbrush. I had gathered my toiletries, ready for a shower, when Yousef's deep rumble made me jump.

"It's a bad omen for the husband to wake up the morning after alone in bed." His hair was in an array. He rubbed his eyes, reminding me of a young child.

"Did I wake you?"

He yawned. "Why are you up? What time is it?"

"It's only eight. Go back to sleep."

"Are you planning a great escape?"

I couldn't help but laugh. "No. I wanted to shower."

He threw the covers off himself and stood up. As he stretched, his t-shirt rose, and I looked away. "Let me show you how the shower works."

With a grateful smile on my lips, I followed him to the room next door. Thankfully, we had a small bathroom on this floor. The stand-in shower was easy to use and Yousef left me alone with my anxieties for the first day in his home.

"Are you okay?" my mum asked as she came on the phone.

"I'm okay. How are you and Abba?"

"Tikh asi." *We're okay.* "What are you doing?"

I was sitting on the bed in my robe, and my hair wrapped in a towel. Yousef wasn't in the room when I returned after my shower. I thought it would be a good time to call home. "I need to get ready."

"Has your hori," *mother-in-law*, "woken up?"

Very faintly, I could hear voices travelling from one of the floor below. "I think so."

My mum sighed. "Get dressed and make her tea. Why are you sitting like a princess?"

"She said she didn't want me to make tea," I explained.

She huffed. "They all say that. Don't give her a reason to complain. Put a kameez on and go down. Make sure you cover your hair."

Was she right? I ignored Masuma's tea advice after last night, but maybe I was mistaken. Maybe my mother-in-law said that to test me. Today I had to prove my worth.

"Okay. What time is everyone coming?"

"Your in-laws said for lunch."

"I wish I could see you and Abba."

While my family was invited, it was a tradition that the bride's parents didn't attend. They would come in a few weeks with an official dawaat, *invite*, from Yousef's family.

"You'll be home for *firah* the day after tomorrow. Sintha khoris na." *Don't worry.*

My mum rushed to wrap up the conversation, worried my in-laws were waiting for me downstairs. I pulled on the first Asian attire I could find that didn't need to be ironed. My wet hair was pulled into a bun and covered by my hijab. With my heart in my mouth, I descended the stairs, towards the voices.

"Bhabi, did you need something?" Haniya asked as I reached the bottom of the stairs.

"No. I just wanted to help make breakfast." I walked with her towards the kitchen.

"You don't have to do that! There are so many of us to help mum."

"It's okay." I stepped into the dining room where the men and women gathered. "Assalamualaikum," I greeted with my head slightly bowed.

"Wa'alaikum salaam," they returned.

"Sumayyah, kitchu lagehni?" *Do you need anything*, my mother-in-law asked.

"I wanted to help you make breakfast," I replied in Bangla. "Would anybody like tea?"

A middle-aged woman came over and hugged me. She looked at my mother-in-law as she said, "Already so lucky."

"Alhamdulillah," she replied. "We're okay. You go and get ready."

"Are you sure?" I asked.

She nodded. "Go. Yousef is bringing your breakfast up."

I thanked her and left the room in search of the kitchen. Yousef was pouring milk into a steaming mug. "Do you need some help?"

He looked startled at my presence. He let out a laugh. "Why did you come down? I was going to bring breakfast to you."

Taking slow steps towards him, I stopped by his side. "Please let me help with something. I feel utterly useless."

Checking behind me to see if anyone was watching, he wrapped his arms around me. "Enjoy it because by next week you're going to be picking up my socks and wet towel from the floor."

"Okay," I whispered. "Let me help you take it upstairs, at least."

He pretended to give it some thought. "All right."

"Are you ready?" Yousef asked as he waltzed into the room.

His aunt added the last pin to my sari and took a step back to admire her handy work. "Perfect." She smiled at us before leaving us alone.

Yousef closed the door and turned to me with a playful grin. "I can't believe you're my wife." His slow steps sped up my heart rate. "Can I hug you?" he asked when he was before me.

Instead of answering, I wrapped my arms around him. "I don't want to get makeup on your clothes," I squeaked when he squeezed tight.

He pulled back and stared at my face as if he couldn't believe I existed. "I don't care."

I playfully slapped his chest. "You're being silly. Let's go. Our guests are waiting."

"Ours," he repeated. "I love the sound of that."

With a foolish smile, we headed to the garden where the guests awaited in the marquee. A round of applause followed us as we took a seat at the stage area. I scanned the space and my heart almost burst when I saw the familiar faces of my family. The urge to run to them was so strong, but before I could move, they came rushing over. Yousef shuffled over as I stood up to greet them. Their words merged into loud chaos, but I didn't care. I wanted to save this feeling of completeness in a jar and save it for the days of missing home that I knew were coming.

My family bought with them a range of food items ranging from sweet to savoury. I laughed as Nafisa stuffed food into Yousef's mouth. Yousef was a good sport and laughed with me. I tried to make the same effort with his family, but it was hard when I knew nothing about them. They all reintroduced themselves, and I tried to remember their names. Yousef was the first male cousin to get married, which made me the eldest daughter-in-law of his family. That meant pressure to be the best.

When the tradition of the *maas khata* started, my cheeks burned with embarrassment. It was a small skit where the husband brings home a fish for his new wife to cook. It involved putting my poor acting skills into practice before taking pictures with said fish. I worried about getting blood on my clothes as we posed with the fish, but my mother-in-law reassured me she'd be cutting and cooking it. We rushed out of the marquee to wash the smell of raw fish off our hands.

I was drying my hands when Yousef's aunt came over with laughter on her lips.

"Are you ready to cook it?" she joked.

I opened my mouth to answer, but my mother-in-law jumped in. "No! She doesn't need to cook."

"I can help," I offered.

"It's okay. I'll teach you another day."

Something about her tone pricked my skin. Why would she assume I didn't know how to cook?

My eyes flitted to Yousef, who was finally washing his hands. I wondered if he would correct his mother by telling her I could cook a fish curry. I knew he knew because we had spoken about it. But he was too busy scrubbing his hands.

"Maa," I began. "I know how to cook a fish curry."

Her knife stopped mid-cut. "That's good. We'll try it another day."

I tried to smile, but she was still dismissing me as if she didn't believe me. "You've had my cooking," I reminded her, "when you came to see me the first time."

She waved me off. "I'm sure you helped your mum."

I looked at Yousef again, who was now listening. "Ji naa," *no*, "I cooked the whole curry."

She nodded her head and smiled. "That's good. Your mum had time to teach you these important skills."

What does that mean?

My eyes narrowed at Yousef. He looked uncomfortable, but remained silent. If he wasn't going to say anything, I would.

"Why wouldn't she have time?" I asked.

At last, she sensed the tone in my voice. She plastered on a smile and waved off my concern. "Mai, I didn't mean to upset you. I just meant..." She looked at her sister for help, but none was offered. "You're an educated girl. Girls in this country study and don't learn how to take care of the home and family. I struggle with my Haniya too; she's too busy with exams and has no time to help me. When her exams are finished, I'm going to teach her."

"She has a bhabi now! Her bhabi can teach her!" her sister jumped in to ease the tension.

Yet, the nagging feeling in my chest remained. "I'll teach Yousef too," I added.

The two older women laughed. "Boys don't need to learn these things."

"Why?"

Yousef stepped towards me. "Sumayyah," he muttered as a warning.

"He has you," his mum explained. "You're going to take care of him."

The storm in my eyes met the pleading in Yousef's. He wanted me to back away. He wanted me to stop talking. He wanted me to show respect to his mother, even though she was wrong. I felt tears burning in my eyes, but I nodded.

My smile was forced. "Of course. What else am I here for?" I left the kitchen and headed for the stairs.

"Sumayyah. Where are you going?" Yousef asked as he followed behind me.

"I need to go to the bathroom. I'll be back."

He didn't believe me, but left anyway.

As I walked up the stairs into the safe confines of my bedroom, I realised my new truth.

It was okay for Yousef to *just* be one thing; the breadwinner. But that wasn't good enough when it came to me. When she said she would teach me, she wasn't talking about cooking a curry. She meant she was going to teach me how to be her trophy daughter-in-law.

Chapter Twelve

I closed my eyes and tilted my head towards the sky, enjoying the feeling of sunshine on my skin. As my legs moved, the water from the private jacuzzi swished between them. It was a relief to have time for myself. There were no surprise guests or small talk with my new family. It was just me, Yousef and the sun in Bali. It was day two of our honeymoon. We spent day one catching up on sleep and taking a walk around our hotel. After washing off the sheen of sweat that covered us, we fell asleep within minutes.

This morning we visited the mall and were due to have dinner on a cruise ship. Yousef wanted to visit the markets, but I was too exhausted to do anything else, so I compromised and we were on our balcony, relaxing. Yousef launched himself into the water, but I sat on the edge, dipping my legs in.

"Feeling relaxed?" he asked.

I sat straight and smiled. "Yes, but I could use a nap. It feels like all the wedding rush has finally caught up."

His broad shoulders and bulging arms looked smooth with the tan he had already caught. His torso was bare as the water bubbles around him. I paused to admire his handsomeness.

His yawn mirrored my emotions. "Same here. It's like I was running on adrenaline and this is the crash. You know, it's much more relaxing *in* the water?"

I looked down at my t-shirt and leggings. "I didn't pack for swimming."

"Who comes on holiday without swimwear?"

My eyebrows arched. "Did you want other men leering at your wife?"

No matter how many times I heard it, his laugh never failed to make me smile. "Good point." He looked around our secluded balcony. "Nobody can see us. Just get in." He held his hands up in fake surrender. "I'll keep my hands to myself."

I bit my lip to stop my laugh from breaking out. Yousef and I were still yet to mark that milestone in our marriage. The past two weeks took such an emotional toll on me that the physical aspect was pushed aside. He had been nothing but patient and I waited for the day he ran out. But it never came. Most nights, I was asleep before he climbed into bed. Between hosting for the extended families that seemed never-ending and the cooking and cleaning, I was exhausted by the evening.

The words my mother-in-law said the day after my wedding still echoed in my head. She hadn't mentioned it again, nor did she speak to me like that again. Maybe Yousef said something after my departure. I never asked. In fact, we never spoke of it. It was brushed away like it never happened. But I wouldn't forget it. It pushed me to prove that I was more than capable of being both educated *and* a good wife.

I shook my head at him. "Fine." I slowly lowered my body into the warm water. The bubbles pulsated against my skin, soothing my aching bones. "Happy?"

He stretched his arms until his fingers intertwined with mine. He pulled me towards him until I was standing in front of him. "*Now* I'm happy."

I wrapped my arms around his neck. "I thought you were going to keep your hands to yourself?" I teased.

Yousef placed a gentle kiss on my forehead. "Sorry. Can I push my luck and get a kiss?"

With a shy smile, I nodded.

That was a milestone we had mastered.

I grabbed Yousef's hand like my life depended on it and ignored his chuckle as I did. "You try to climb on board in heels!"

He wrapped his arms around my waist. "Where are you going to fall?"

He had a point, but I wasn't about to give in. "I could fall and roll off board."

"I wouldn't let go."

The swarm of butterflies in my stomach was so strong, I almost stumbled. While Yousef spoke with the hostess at the front, I couldn't keep my eyes off him. His smile was calm. His eyes were alive. He was perfect. And he was my husband.

We were led to a table near the edge of the desk. The square table was covered with a crisp white cloth. A single rose sat in a crystal vase and next to it a flame flickered. Like a true gentleman, Yousef pulled my chair out for me before rounding to the other side and taking his seat.

The deck was alight with fairy lights. I looked at the other couples who prepared for a romantic dinner with their other half. I peered into the night beyond the rail. The night sky was indistinguishable from the water. It was hypnotising to watch the waves crash. The evening brought a pleasant break from the blazing heat. The slight breeze cooled my clammy skin and brought with it a fresh peace of mind.

With a cool flute of a soft drink in hand, I turned to Yousef. "Isn't it crazy we didn't know each other a year ago and now we're married and on our honeymoon?"

"It feels like I've known you my whole life. Do you think that's crazy?"

I shook my head. "No. I feel like the same way. And then you say something crazy like how much you hate brownies and I remember I married a complete lunatic."

"I can get used to the pineapple on pizza business. I draw the line at brownies."

"Let's hope there are brownies for dessert. More for me!"

"I checked. It's cheesecake."

As our laughter ran with the wind, our eyes met. Being with Yousef made me feel whole; as if my whole life I wandered the world missing a part of myself I didn't know was missing until I met him.

"What do you want most in life?" I asked.

When he was in deep thought, his fingers twisted the small hairs of his beard. His eyes glazed over and past me. His eyebrows furrowed as he thought of a genuine answer. He cleared his throat. "I want to be happy."

"Everyone wants to be happy," I remarked. "What would make you happy?"

He answered without missing a beat. "A family."

His answer brought a smile to my lips. Becoming a mother was important to me. We both knew we wanted to wait a few years before starting our family. I was worried Yousef wouldn't want to wait until I finished my training, but he reassured me he that, he too, had career goals and wanted to enjoy being just a couple for the foreseeable future.

"How many children do you want?"

"At least two; a boy and girl." He sipped his drink. "How about you?"

"If I had a daughter, I'd want to give her a sister. Nothing beats having a sister." A sad smile appeared on my face.

I missed Nafisa, and I knew she was lonely at home. While we spoke almost daily, phone calls couldn't replace sitting in bed with her. I never thought I'd miss nagging her to wake up and help me around the house. I missed listening to her vent about her day. Haniya was sweet. She was there to help when I needed it. She accommodated to me, but she couldn't replace my sister.

"Our daughters would be so beautiful, like their mother." He winked at me. "Who knows, maybe this time next year we'll be curled up in bed with a baby of our own."

I clamped down on the inside of my cheek as I dwelled on his teasing. *It was a joke, right?* "I thought you didn't want to try for a baby right away?"

He thanked our waiter as he placed down our appetisers. Yousef didn't answer me, too busy cutting into his scallop. "This is so good," he said. He stopped chewing when he saw I hadn't moved. "Why aren't you eating?"

I picked up my fork, yet made no move to eat. "Only two months ago you said you didn't want to start a family right now." Panic was filling me. I had one year left of my foundation years. I had to choose a specialty, which meant another minimum of three years. Babies came after that in my plan.

He shrugged his shoulders. "I'm not saying *right* now, but maybe in a few months." When he looked at me, it was like nothing else existed. "I can't explain what you've done to me, Sumayyah. I want to love every part of you until my last breath. So yeah, maybe my plans have changed since we got married. But it's only because the love I have for you is too much for one person to bear. I need a million versions of you to love."

The burn started in my toes and crawled up my body until I was wrapped in the warmth of his affection. With ease, the word *love* slipped off his tongue, reassuring me I made the right choice in marrying him. The depth of his commitment to me made me feel weak sometimes. I couldn't grasp that someone could love me with such depth. But I was loved, and it was a fulfilling feeling.

At the same time, I heard Zoya's advice about not losing myself in my marriage. I needed to hold on to myself and the dream job I was still working towards. I wanted to give my husband all he yearned for, but I also owed it to myself and my dad to become the doctor I had worked hard to be.

"I love you too, Yousef. But I also need you to understand I've got an education I need to complete first."

He slowly chewed. "What if you did both?"

It wasn't just work I had to consider. I had barely unpacked my belongings in his house. We were still in the early stages of getting to know each other. *Hell,* we hadn't even had sex yet, and we were discussing conceiving.

Letting out a deep breath, I said, "Let's enjoy our honeymoon and get settled back into normal life first." Desperate to change the subject, I asked, "Are you excited about going back to work?"

"It's going to be weird not spending every second with you. I think I'm going to miss you."

I let out a laugh. "*Think* you're going to miss me? Try again, husband."

He reached across the table and took my hand in his. "I'm going to miss you, wife. When are you back to work?"

"Monday. I'm already tired just thinking about it."

"How often do you work night shifts?" he asked as we waited for our main course.

"Just a few in the month. Is that going to be a problem?" I made it clear before we got married that nights shifts were compulsory and out of my control.

The shake of his head offered me the same reassurance he gave when I brought it up before. "No. Work is work." He paused. "But that would have to change after we had children."

This was not said before we were married.

"Why?"

For a moment he looked surprised, as if he hadn't expected me to ask such a question. "Because you'd need to be home with the baby."

I let out a laugh. "I'd be on maternity leave for the first year. Did you think I'd pop out a baby and go back to work?"

Yousef laughed with me. "Of course not, but even after a year, how do you expect to leave your baby at home?"

"*Our* baby wouldn't be home alone," I pointed out.

"You can't expect my mum to look after our baby at night."

There was that prickling feeling again. "I wasn't talking about your mum. *You* would be home. *You* would be the father. I'm sure you're capable of looking after your own child for a few nights a month alone."

The tension could be felt, and Yousef softened. "Sorry, I didn't mean to offend you. I just assumed you would change your work patterns."

"Would you change yours?" I retaliated.

"A baby doesn't need his father around as much as he would need his mother."

I didn't want to argue with him while on our honeymoon. I didn't want to argue with him about this ever. I studied my whole life to become a doctor. I sacrificed enjoying my childhood to make sure I made it to this point. I wasn't going to throw it all down the drain.

"I agree, but a child still needs its father."

"And I'd be there." Yousef let out a sigh. "I'm not asking you to stop working entirely, Sumayyah. I'd never expect that." Something in his tone made it clear that he wasn't saying his whole truth.

"But you would *want* that?"

When he swallowed hard, I knew I'd hit the nail on the head. "In all honesty? Yes, I would want my wife to stop working after having children. It would be hard to do both. Being a mother is a full-time job. But I know how much your career means to you. When the time comes, we can see what works. It's pointless discussing this when we're not even close to trying."

"Why didn't you tell me that before?" I asked.

He tilted his head, and he finally shared the same look of dread I felt. "Would it have stopped you from marrying me?"

His question stumped me. I didn't know if it would have changed my mind. He wasn't asking for the impossible. He wasn't asking for anything unusual. His request was the norm for our culture. Most women didn't work.

"No," I eventually answered.

"Then why does it matter?"

I lowered my gaze. "I guess it doesn't." I was beginning to understand just how important a family was to Yousef and as I sat there and listened to him talk, I noticed he never had the same spark when he spoke about anything else. "You'll be okay, right? If we didn't have any babies for the foreseeable future, you wouldn't be unhappy?"

His smile eased my anxiety. "As long as I have you, I am content."

Chapter Thirteen

The loud squeal could only belong to one person; *Rani.* She garnered the attention of the other customers as she ran towards us. We all stood up and hugged our friend tighter than we normally would. Rani stooped and spoke to Karim in the silliest voice. The joy on Zoya's face was unbeatable as her son laughed at the faces Rani pulled. Next to her, in his pram, Nadim slept peacefully. Zoya welcomed her second son into the world four months ago. He was a perfect replica of this brother, but according to Zoya he was twice the work Karim was.

Rani eventually took her seat. Her grin was wide, and she was bouncing off her seat. "How are you guys?"

I looked at my other two friends in confusion. "How are *you*?" I asked. "You look like you're about to burst."

She let out another squeal. "Okay. I was going to wait, but..." She turned her hand upside down and flashed an enormous diamond. "Ravi proposed!"

We were all out of our seats again, hugging and congratulating her. Finally, after a decade, it was time. When we settled down, she shared all the magical details of her proposal. It sounded like something out of a movie, not that we expected any less from her.

"Ravi did well," Zoya praised.

Rani admired her ring. "I know! I really wanted to tell you guys in person, so I'm over the moon we finally found time to meet up. How is married life treating you guys?"

"Marriage? I'm basically running a daycare at this point," she joked. "Nobody can prepare you for two. I'm always tired. I don't even have time to poop anymore."

"You look good," Halima said.

While Zoya was still stunning, she had aged the past year. Her second pregnancy wasn't as easy as her first and it didn't help she had a toddler to look after as well. Admittedly, she looked exhausted, but I admired her strength and appreciated her making the effort to meet us.

She rolled her eyes. "Liar, but I don't have the energy to argue with you."

"You're doing amazing," I reassured her.

Zoya ran her fingers through Karim's hair before placing a kiss at his temple. "Thanks guys. I love my kids, but I miss normal human interaction."

"So no more kids?" Halima laughed.

She vehemently shook her head. "God, no! I really want a permanent solution, but Idris says he wants one more." Zoya fell silent. As her eyes darted away, I caught the tears that brimmed in her eyes. Her watery smile broke my heart. She wiped away the tear that fell. "I love my kids, but I didn't even want a second and look where I am. I'm up all night with a crying baby, while my husband sleeps soundly. I spend my mornings cooking and cleaning. My afternoon goes by feeding everyone in that house. And now that his brother and his wife live with us, it's even worse. My evenings are spent pampering after my husband. By the time I climb into bed I feel like I'm on the edge of shattering, but my husband wants adult time. And then the cycle begins again. I crave some time for myself. Does that make me selfish?"

We all shook our head. "I would be alarmed if you *didn't* want that," Rani reassured. "It's fine to be happy with just two. Hell, I don't even want one."

This was a known fact about Rani. While she made a fuss over the babies around her, she didn't yearn to be a mother. She was content with work and Ravi. That was enough of a life for her.

Zoya hugged her son tighter. "Ignore me. I'm just hormonal. How are you, Halima?"

Halima bit her lip and gave us an awkward smile. "I actually have some news myself, and like Rani, I wanted to tell you in person."

"Spit it out!" Zoya pushed.

"I'm pregnant."

As she smiled and my friends let out yet another scream, I couldn't help but feel something was off. She didn't shriek the way Rani announced her engagement. Halima's demeanour was apprehensive, as if she was testing the waters.

Regardless, I smiled for my friend and gave her a hug. "How far along are you?"

"Just past three months. It doesn't feel real guys."

"Was it planned?"

"We're weren't trying, but we also weren't *not* trying, if you know what I mean."

Rani winked at her. "Got it. Well, I'm thrilled for you! Are you hoping for a boy or girl? I totally see you as a girl mum."

"I think the world has enough men, don't you agree?" she asked.

And then it was all eyes on me. My friends waited expectantly for my update, but there was nothing to share. One year of married life had flown by. There were no monumental moments. Life had been nothing but ordinary. Yousef and I went on two holidays after our honeymoon. On most days, we were working, and there were rare nights he spent alone as I cared for my patients at the hospital. I spent my days off helping my mother-in-law around the house or running errands with Haniya if she were home. I ate dinner with his family. We spent an hour watching TV in our bedroom before we fell asleep. Life was ... mundane.

I shrugged. "Nothing to report. Life remains the same. Work, husband and in-laws."

"How is Yousef? Is he still treating you like a queen?"

Admittedly, there was no more of him bringing breakfast to bed, but that was because I always woke up before him to make sure I could help his mum. If his mum spoke out of turn, he wouldn't speak back to her. But he was still thoughtful and sweet. I would often catch him staring at me and then he would smile in a way that made my heart burst and tell me I'm beautiful. When winter came and I was on a late shift, he would put a hot water bottle on my side of the bed so it would be warm when I got in. He would push me to extend my visits to my parents' house, even though he missed me and his mum would grumble about it. So while he wasn't perfect, he was a good husband, and I did love him very much.

"He's everything I prayed for," I answered. "He tries his best."

Rani pouted. "You two are just adorable. And I can't wait to have *all* of you at my engagement dinner in a few weeks. Is that understood?"

The question was pointed at Halima, who struggled to get Nazir anywhere. She put her hands up in surrender. "I'll try, but no promises."

Yousef came up behind me. His arms wrapped around my waist and he buried his face into my neck. "Hi. I missed you," he mumbled.

I couldn't help but chuckle. "I was only gone for the weekend."

He pulled me back with him until he fell back onto the bed. I rolled off him and laid beside him instead.

"How are your parents?"

"Good. They asked about you and were wondering when'd you pop down to see them."

He took my hand in his and kissed my knuckles. "I'll go soon."

I rolled my eyes. "You say that all the time. I live with your family. Whenever your extended family turns up unannounced, I sit and socialise with them even if I've just finished a shift. My parents live less than thirty minutes away. It wouldn't kill you to call them once in a while."

"I'll call them tomorrow," he promised.

"Good. The same way I look after your parents, you should do the same for mine," I reminded him.

"It's different because you *live* here."

I pulled my hand out of his. "Exactly. I left my parents alone to be here with you."

Yousef let out a soft sigh. "Firstly, they're not alone. Secondly, you say it like it's a punishment."

Irritation burned in me. We'd had conversations like this before. It seemed no matter what I said, he never understood my side. It was late. I was tired and missed him, so I didn't feel like arguing with him. "When you hog the blanket, it feels like punishment."

And there it was: my favourite smile. Relief made his shoulders sag, knowing that there was no disagreement on the table tonight. "How are your friends? Did you have fun with them today?"

"Yes. It was really nice. Rani's engaged. We're going to her celebration dinner in a few weeks. And Halima's pregnant!"

His brief gasp caught me off guard. "Really?"

I nodded. "Yeah. I was surprised too, but she has been married for three years now."

"We've been married a year already."

Yet another recurring discussion; babies. Yousef was eager to start trying, worried about our age and the odd sense that he was missing out; especially after his best friend Jameel had a son a few months ago. But I wasn't ready. There were times I felt like I was still an alien in his house. I was still adjusting. I was still learning things about Yousef. I was still trying to build my career. It wasn't the time for us to have a baby.

"We've been married *only* a year."

He gave me a playful smile. "Still deciding if you love me enough to stay married?"

I ran my fingers through his hair before trailing them down the side of his face. "You know I love you, but you have to understand how hard this year has been for me. My entire life was uprooted."

"But we're settled now," he argued.

"Yousef," I pleaded. "Can we not do this now?"

"Do what? I'm just wondering why you're not ready."

"I've already told you," I snapped. "I'm just about to start my speciality training. I've already changed my plans to accommodate to yours." I muttered the last part, but it was still heard.

He sat up. "What's that supposed to mean?"

He knew what I meant. When we discussed my specialty training, Yousef questioned why I needed to study more. I wanted to train to become a medicine hospital consultant, but that meant another minimum of seven years of training. Even though I reassured him we could start a family at some point during that, he argued it would cut too much time out of our marriage. The back and forth lasted for a while before I gave in and chose to train as a GP. The specialty lasted only three years, so we reached a compromise. I'd undertake a shorter training, but we would only start trying for a family after I had completed it. That didn't stop him from bringing it up often.

"Nothing." Not wanting to discuss it any further, I stood up and starting getting ready for bed.

"Sumayyah—"

"Stop," I cut him off. "It's easy for you to want a baby. You're not the one that will be pregnant for nine months. You're not the one whose body will grow and change. You're not the one who will have to give birth. It will be me that has to stop working. It will be me that gives up sleep and showering and eating. Your life will go on as is."

"That's not true. I would be there the whole way."

"But you won't because you'll be working or going out with your friends. People won't expect you to be there."

Yousef sat up and gave me a pointed stare. "I'm talking about myself. Who cares what people expect or say?"

"Me; I care because they won't be talking about you. You'll have a baby at home but be out living your life and that's okay. But if I did that, I would be a neglectful mother. You can just be Yousef and that's enough for people, but it's not enough for me."

His eyebrows furrowed and hurt shone in his eyes. "What's that supposed to mean?"

For once, I met his stare. "It means, how am I supposed to believe that you'd be there the whole way? I got married and done *everything* you or your family have asked me to do. I did it without asking questions because that's what a good wife and daughter-in-law does. All I wanted in return was for you to show a fraction of reciprocation to my family. We've been married for a year already," I said, throwing his own words back at him, "And you still haven't learnt how to be a good son-in-law. But what does it matter, right? As long as your wife is the perfect *bou*."

Chapter Fourteen

The restaurant's private room had a table running from one end to another. The warm lights made it feel intimate, despite the large crowd that had already formed. Zoya called my name. With my fingers intertwined with Yousef's, we made our way over to her.

"Hi!" She pulled me into a hug.

"Hey. Is Halima here yet?"

She shook her head. "They're running a little late." She nudged her husband. "Idris, say hello."

Her husband looked up from his phone and nodded at me before shaking Yousef's hand. Idris was a handsome man. His green eyes were adopted by both his sons, but while theirs were bright and alive, his were darker and unimpressed. His medium build and height were perfect for Zoya. Looking at them standing side-by-side, their sons in their arms, they seemed like a picture-perfect family.

"How are you, Yousef?" she asked.

He gave her a polite smile. "Alhamdulilah, very well. Congratulations on your second baby. How is motherhood going?"

Zoya's smile was impenetrable. "It's everything I wanted. I hear you're the perfect husband. Our Sumayyah is very lucky."

Yousef's arm wrapped around my waist and pulled me closer. "I believe I took her from you more than a year ago," he joked.

The two of us laughed. "She'll always be ours first," she retaliated.

"Zoya," Idris cut in. "Let's sit."

She bowed her head and headed for a seat. We followed behind her.

Rani's parents came over and thanked us for attending. Her mum was emotional at giving her only daughter away. Rani was the third eldest sibling, but the only daughter of the five. Her parents and siblings spoilt her with love and affection. It was probably why she demanded such love from Ravi.

I waved at Halima as she stalked in twenty minutes later with Nazir on her tail. Nazir was easy to spot in a crowded room with his towering stature. His broad shoulders and muscular build were the right balance for Halima's curvier build. His thick hair and full beard made him look a few years her senior, despite being the same age. He kept his hand on his wife as they made their way over to us.

"Sorry we're late!"

Nazir pulled her chair out for her before taking the seat next to her. "Hello. I hope we didn't miss her grand entrance," he laughed.

"She's probably on the roof, ticking off her guest list as people arrive. You know Rani, she'd never want anyone to miss her entrance," Zoya joked.

"Poor Ravi," Nazir remarked.

"How are you feeling?" I asked Halima.

Before she could answer, Yousef said, "Congratulations! I heard your good news."

She offered a smile. "Thank you. I'm feeling okay. Second trimester is a lot better."

Zoya nodded. "You're doing much better than me. I couldn't get out of bed and you managed to not only get dressed, but put in a genuine effort with your makeup."

Halima's eyes flitted to her husband before she lowered her gaze. All she responded was. "Yeah."

Our attention was diverted to the couple of the hour so nobody could question the tension that rose between Halima and Nazir. Everyone cheered and clapped as Rani caught everyone's attention in her mermaid dress. As expected, her hair and makeup were flawless. The champagne-coloured dress enhanced her softly bronzed skin. She laughed and cheered with her guests as they made their way to the head of the table.

Next to her, Ravi was a lot more subdued. He still smiled and waved at his guests, but his energy was much lower that hers. Like Rani, Ravi was tall and slim. His thin facial hair gave him a fresh look, replacing the baby face I always associated with him. Tonight his shoulder-length hair was pulled back into a tight bun, no doubt Rani's idea. She *hated* his long hair and never failed to complain about it. She caught my eye and frantically waved at us. We all waved back, and she blew a kiss our way.

The room was abuzz with chatter, laughter, and the clinking of glasses. The six of us engaged in small talk. Idris never spoke much, but he had always been reserved. It was hard to imagine him being firm with Zoya, as she said, because he was always so quiet. Among the men, Nazir was the most talkative. Yousef was always quietly sociable; never the one to start a conversation, but always engaged when someone reached out. It was nice to be sat with my friends and our partners.

"Zoya, take him," Idris grumbled, handing Nadim to his wife.

Zoya immediately dropped her fork and took her son.

I watched as Idris got comfortable and resumed eating. "Let me take him," I offered. "You finish eating."

She shook her head. "It's fine."

I stood up. "I'm done. Here, just give him to me."

"When you're a mother, you master eating with a child clinging to you. It's no problem."

"Zoya," I warned. "I'd love some time to cuddle him."

Yousef discreetly tugged at my hand. When I looked down at him, he shook his head to say *let it go.* But this was ridiculous; I was just trying to help my friend.

"Are you sure?" she asked.

My only response was to take him in my arms. He stared up at me in wonder. I braced myself for tears, but he accepted the compromise as I rocked back and forth with him.

"You look like a natural with a baby," Halima said wistfully.

"He's just so precious," I cooed.

"Soon you'll have your own," Zoya winked.

I shook my head. "No. Not anytime soon."

Idris surprised me by joining the conversation. "Why not? You're a woman. What are you waiting for?"

My eyes widened in surprise at his abrupt tone. "What is that supposed to mean?"

"He meant nothing by it," Zoya said, alarmed.

I couldn't help but take offence. "I think he did." I plastered on a smile. "We're adults. We can share our opinions."

Rani appeared behind me and stood strong. "I agree. So what if she's a woman?"

Idris would not back down. He shrugged. "You're here to carry children. You get married to carry the next generation. What could be more important than that?"

I wanted to tell him to take his caveman mentality back a few generations because women weren't only seen as a mechanism to make children anymore. We had careers. We had friends. We had lives outside of our marriage.

"Who declared that a woman cannot work *and* be a mother?" I arched my eyebrow.

He laughed in my face. "A woman has no reason to work. That's what us men are here for."

My gaze turned to Zoya, who silently begged me to let it go. Was this how he saw her? Was this life all he expected from her? Was her life to be spent serving her husband and popping out kids whenever he asked? I wanted to voice all this, but Zoya's terrified eyes shut me down. The same couldn't be said for Rani.

"I'm not sorry to say this, but you're wrong. The times have changed, Idris. You live in a first-world country. Women in Pakistan, India, and Bangladesh may be trained to stay home, but not here. We educate our women. We encourage our women. We *empower* our women. It's no longer a man's world." Although she didn't raise her voice, her tone brought a chill down my spine. She was entirely fierce, and she didn't break a sweat. Her trained eyes didn't fear his stony stare. She stared at him as she dared him to argue back.

"There's nothing wrong with having tradition." Yousef's eyes shifted to me. "It's good to have a balance. If the couple can afford to have one parent at home, then what's the harm?"

My chuckle broke out before I could stop it. "One parent?" I asked sarcastically. "By that you mean the woman, right?"

"Well, that makes sense," Nazir answered instead.

Rani scoffed. "Why?"

Nazir looked at her as if she was crazy. "She's the *mother*. The baby's food is literally in her chest."

"Baby formula exists," I pointed out. "So, I assume Halima will stop working when your baby comes?"

He nodded.

"Did you ask her if that's what she wanted?" Rani asked.

He let out a laugh. "Ask her what? She wanted a baby so she can stay home and look after it." His dismissive tone for his child made my heart hurt and Halima flinch.

I looked at my husband. "And what about the men who want a child? Should they stay home instead, Yousef?"

"Honestly? *No*. Women have been homemakers since the beginning of time. Women have a genetically built-in device called mother's instinct; it's there for a reason. I understand wanting to work, but it's not a requirement. The generations before us have been following these ... these..." As he struggled to find the right word, I felt nothing but disappointment.

Rani cut in. "I think the world you're looking for is stereotypes, because it *is* a stereotype. It's a little box us women have been shoved and forcefully moulded into."

Idris tutted. "The problem is you are too modern."

If she wasn't angry before, she was angry now. She scowled at him. "And you like your women to be obedient."

Ravi's smile faded as he slowly approached the storm that was brewing on this side of the room. He scanned our faces. "What's going on here?"

"Your bride-to-be is terrorising her guests." Nazir's attempt at a joke only fuelled her anger.

"Maybe you feel terrorised because you like *your* women to be silent. I haven't heard Halima say a word."

Ravi wrapped his arms around her waist. "Okay. Let's get some fresh air."

But Rani stood her ground. "*No.* Why is a woman vilified for standing up for herself?" She pointed at Idris. "He carelessly offended Sumayyah because it's okay for a man to say whatever he wants. The woman should just shut her mouth and take it. Her husband didn't defend her and instead wanted her to back down because his wife can't be anything short of perfect."

"This conversation had nothing to do with you," Idris butt in. "I wasn't talking to you."

Rani pretended to bow. "Apologies, master. I should have waited for permission to speak. Except it had something to do with me because you were talking about *women* and last I checked, I *am* a woman. If anything, this topic has nothing to do with *you* because men don't get a say in how we live."

Ravi pulled at her. "That's enough. They're your guests."

He could have pulled her away had Nazir not spoken. "We're all entitled to our opinion. If that's how he wants to live, we can't judge him for it. If their arrangement makes them happy, then so be it."

I knew he was right. Everyone was entitled to live their life how they wanted, but I knew Zoya was unhappy. She didn't need to say it.

Rani was thinking along the same lines because she turned to our friend. "Are you happy, Zoya?"

She swallowed hard and forced a smile back onto her face. "Guys, this is ridiculous. Let's all just enjoy ourselves."

"Answer," Idris demanded.

Her glossy eyes scanned all our faces until they landed on a sleeping Nadim. "Yes," she whispered. "I'm happy."

And there it was: the lie women have told themselves for generations. Men openly express unhappiness, while a good woman smiles and pretends all is right.

Happiness.

It's not that we don't feel it. It's that we sacrifice our own happiness to ensure those around us feel it more.

Chapter Fifteen

"I HOPE YOU'RE READY," I scolded as I walked into our bedroom and saw Yousef sat on the bed.

"Yeah." His low tone made me pause with pleating the scarf that came with my kameez.

"What's wrong?"

He shook his head. "Nothing. Let's go." He grabbed his car keys and stood up.

"Yousef," I pleaded as I walked towards him. "Talk to me."

"What is the point? You'll only shoot me down."

I stepped away. I didn't want to argue with him before going to my parent's house. I wanted to be in high spirits as we prepared the thaals, *gift hampers*, for my sister's future husband. This weight on my chest was the last thing I wanted. I finished pleating my scarf and secured it in place. "Let's go," I whispered.

Yousef took in a deep breath. "So we're past arguing about this and now moved onto avoiding it all together. Good to know."

I stepped in front of him as he tried to skim away. "You just said you didn't want to talk about it. And I'm not avoiding it. I just don't want to have a repeat of this discussion right before we enter a house full of happy people."

"I didn't realise you weren't happy."

My stance softened. "I *am* happy, Yousef. You know what I meant. Every time we talk about this, we get upset."

"Talking and *discussion* implies that both sides are heard. From experience, it's usually you shutting me down."

I turned away from him and pretended to clear up the dressing table. I didn't want to face him. I didn't want to know why this came up tonight. "Considering how many times I have to repeat myself, I think it's *you* that has a hearing problem."

Yousef rounded me until he was standing before me. "We've been married for almost three years, Sumayyah. *Three!* My brother has been married less than two and has a beautiful little daughter. I want that, and I'm tired of your excuses." Unlike before, Yousef let his emotions show. Tears threatened to fall as he stared at me. "I love you so much, Sumayyah," he whispered. "There's nothing I wouldn't do for you."

I took his face in my hands and forced him to look at me. "I love you too, Yousef. But this isn't fair."

He stepped away from me. "What you're doing isn't fair."

"Have you asked yourself why you want a baby? Is it because you're ready, or because those you grew up with have taken this step?"

"It can be both! I know what I want."

"But I'm almost there, Yousef! I'm almost at the end of my training. There's only one year left. Why can't you wait a little longer?"

He brushed away the single tear that fell. "I waited my whole life for you, even before I knew you existed. I never looked at another woman because I knew the one for me was out there. I waited to meet you. I waited to marry you. I waited to hold and love you. I've waited long nights while you've been working. I've waited for you to return when you visit your parents. I've waited for you to meet your career goals." He swallowed hard. "I've waited enough, Sumayyah. I've stood back and watched you build this amazing career for yourself. And I am proud of you, but that's exactly what it is; it's for *you*. All I'm asking is that we starting building *our* life. I promised to protect and provide, but I can't do this on my own."

"We had an agreement. I'm not saying never, just not right now."

"Right now is all we have."

"I've worked so hard to get to this point. My dad turned his dream into a reality. Please don't make me choose."

"I won't ask you to choose because I can't bear the thought of you breaking my heart, and it's clear where I rank."

"Abba!" I squealed as I hugged my dad. It had only been two weeks since I'd seen him, but my heart felt empty.

"Amar maya aicheh!" *My love is here.* He shook hands with Yousef and welcomed us into the bustling house.

Music blared from the living room. Aunts, uncles, and grand-children were scattered around the house, laughter on their lips and joy in their hearts as they prepped for Nafisa's wedding. The bride was nowhere to be seen, so I greeted the women in the kitchen.

"Beta aiseh ni?" *Did your husband come?*

"Yeah, he's sitting with the men. Where's Nafisa?"

My mom lowered her tone and leant in closer. "She said they've got something to do."

By *they* she meant Nafisa and her fiancée, Junaid. I wasn't surprised when Nafisa went to our parents almost a year ago and told them about her boyfriend. An uproar ensued, but my Nani, *maternal grandmother*, persuaded my parents to accept the marriage. My dad was disappointed and my mother was ashamed that she was dating someone she met at university. I warned my sister that it would be a difficult feat, but she insisted he was the one for her. After much back and forth, the wedding was set and now we were only a week away.

It was an odd feeling to see my sister prepare for the next stage in her life. She had grown into a beautiful, strong woman right before my eyes. She stepped into my shoes when I got married. While she didn't care to cook or clean, she was filled with love and care. I just worried if it would suffice for her marriage.

Over the years, Yousef's mum and I had our few clashes. She would make indirect comments about me working night shifts. She would complain about the aches and pains of being on her feet all day as she cooked and cleaned. If she caught Yousef making his own breakfast or ironing his own clothes, she would push him aside and announce that she was doing it for him. She failed to appreciate my efforts. Any days I was off work, I would wake up earlier than her and start the cooking; but she would tell me she wanted to cook different curries that day. Guests arrived at all hours, so I stayed in the kitchen to serve them. During the late afternoon, I would offer to make her tea and spend some time chatting with her. I took her and my father-in-law to their appointments. When she needed something from the shops, I would rush out to get it for her. She wasn't a horrible mother-in-law; it's just that I wasn't good enough.

When Younes, my brother-in-law, got married, I thought relief would come. His wife, Amina, was nice. She was reserved, but friendly. She was also a dedicated housewife. I admired her, but she made me feel even more inadequate as a daughter-in-law. She was at the beck and call of my in-laws because she was always home. She didn't leave her husband a few nights a month to go to work. She wasn't too exhausted to wake up and make his breakfast most days. She didn't put off giving them a grandchild.

No. That was just me.

"When will Nafisa be back?"

My mother huffed and walked away without answering.

I left the kitchen and joined my cousins.

"There's my favourite sister-in-law!" Masuma said.

I hugged her. "You are glowing, Bhabi! Not long left."

She rubbed her round belly. "I'm counting down the days. Your niece is a kicker!" She eyed my stomach. "Why is your scarf like that? Have you got something to tell me?"

"No. Definitely not."

She bumped her shoulder with mine. "I'm just joking."

My Nani eyed us suspiciously. "What are you two secretly talking about? Have you got some good news for us?"

I decided then I would never wear that outfit again. It evidently made me look fat. I shook my head. "No!"

She gestured her head towards Masuma. "You're the Bhabi. Tell this one to get a move on. She's been gone for three years and she's not getting any younger."

"Nani! I'm only twenty-eight! I still have time."

She scrunched her face in disgust. "At your age, my eldest was ready to get married. Only twenty-eight," she sarcastically remarked. "It gets harder the old you get. You kids don't understand now, but you will later."

Masuma wrapped her arms around me as if to protect me. "When Allah wills it to be, it will happen. Insha'Allah." *God willing.*

"My time there was none of this tablet nonsense. Allah's will is natural, but you all fill your body with medicine to stop it. At this rate, Nafisa will give me a great grandchild first."

I wanted to let out a long, never-ending scream that echoed across the globe. I needed an escape from this conversation that seemed to follow me everywhere. "Her children will love you the most. Without you, their parents wouldn't have got married," I joked.

My grandmother looked unimpressed. "It's good that she found someone herself. It would have been hard to shop around for her."

My eyebrows furrowed. "Why?"

She leaned in closer. "She's not as pretty as you girls. Her skin is darker," she explained. "Boys would have said no quickly. It doesn't help that she's useless in the kitchen."

Masuma and I stared at each other in shock as my grandmother walked away. We both remained silent, unsure of what to say. When Nafisa returned home, I hugged her tighter than normal and prayed that I'd forget those horrible, untrue words.

"I want a speech, Dhulabhai!" Nafisa cheered. She perched on the arm of the sofa and impatiently waited for Yousef to say something.

His cheeks turned the cutest shade of pink at all the attention. He vehemently shook his head, but Nafisa wasn't someone that took no for an answer. Reluctantly, he stood up. I didn't realise how much I missed seeing him smile. His grey eyes looked alive even through the embarrassment in them. He cleared this throat. "I'm not good with words, so this might be terrible. But Nafisa ... it's been a wonderful three years of knowing you. This house feels empty when you're not here. You bring life to every room you enter. When you laugh, it's hard not to laugh with you. Your happiness is infectious, and I pray that happiness follows you into your marriage. I thought having one sister was enough, but you are one of the best parts of my marriage to your sister."

"Aw! I love you bro!" Nafisa shouted.

He laughed softly. "As you start this new journey in life, I hope you find the best parts of yourself. May your new memories fill you with as much joy as your childhood ones. May your new home be filled with as much love as this one. But most importantly, I pray you and your husband build the life you deserve; one that is fulfilling and everything you have dreamt of. When you marry the one you have been waiting for, the world becomes a beautiful place and you find comfort where you think you'd never find it. Marriage is not easy. It comes with its trials and tribulations. You'll have to learn how to adapt, change, and compromise."

His eyes fell upon me and everything else disappeared. It felt as though there was nothing and no one around us. My heart ached as I watched him, and for the first time, I truly saw how much he was hurting. Then the final blow came and realisation dawned on me *I* was the one that was hurting him.

"Marriage is a choice," he continued. "It's choosing the right person and then choosing them again and again and again, no matter what life throws your way. It's choosing to love them even when it's hard. It's choosing to stand by them, even when it's not what you want. Marriage is hard, but when you've got that person beside you, the one you chose, the one you love so much it hurts, you stand by your decision. You stay even when it hurts. You fight even when you feel defeated. You speak even when you're not heard ... because that's all marriage is; it's two people who want to build something new and something that belongs to you both."

Tears stung as I averted my gaze. His raw honesty and emotions were too hard for me to swallow. Or perhaps it was the bitter pill known as the truth. Yousef's speech was the side I was unwilling to hear, but now his words echoed in my head. They were engraved into my heart and burned onto my skin. I wanted to run up to him and wrap my arms around him.

As he wrapped up his speech on a lighthearted note, all I could wonder was if I was being a selfish wife.

By the time I finished showering, Yousef was already in bed. His bare arms were bent at the elbows and his hands rested behind his head. "How was your shower?"

The car ride was almost silent. We both sat in our thoughts, and neither of us had the courage to share them.

"Good." Sharing my thoughts wasn't enough. I needed to show him I heard him. He needed to know I would always choose him. I opened my bedside draw and held up the box of contraceptive pills.

"What are you doing?"

My lips curled into the softest smile. I walked over to the bin, took a deep breath, and tossed them away. In four slow steps, I made my way back to the bed and settled on my side. My fingers ran through his hair before trailing down his face. Cupping his face, I forced him to look at me. And despite everything I promised my younger self, I promised him only one thing.

I placed a gentle kiss on his lips. "I'm choosing you."

CHAPTER SIXTEEN

"HAPPY ANNIVERSARY." YOUSEF'S WHISPER tickled my ear and broke me from my slumber. His arms wrapped around me in a warm encase.

I snuggled into his embrace and revelled in the comfort it provided. "Happy anniversary," I mumbled back. As he showered kisses over my face, I struggled to keep my eyes open. A long night shift wiped all my energy, and all I wanted was sleep.

"How was work?" he murmured against my skin.

"Tiring."

His beard tickled my skin as he smiled. His voice dripped with a teasing tone. "Are you too tired to try?"

At this, I opened my eyes and gave him a pointed stare. "I'm pretty sure I used body wash in my hair; so yes, I am definitely too tired to try."

The pads of his fingertips trailed down my arms, lulling me back to sleep. "But you're ovulating."

My eyes scrunched shut again. "And I'll still be ovulating tonight."

He sighed. "That article said to try as often as we can."

I was back to staring at him. "I've spent thirteen hours with sick patients and running around a hospital. Unless you want to have sex with a comatose body, I suggest you let this one go."

Gone was my warm embrace as Yousef flopped back onto his pillow. He laid beside me on his back and arms crossed like a petulant child about to throw a tantrum. "That's four nights this month we missed because you worked a night shift. We're supposed to be actively trying."

"And we are," I moaned.

"We've been trying for a year and we've had no luck," he reminded me.

Not that I needed the reminder; my period did that job well. I was reminded with every negative pregnancy test. The thoughts appeared every time I laid in bed with my husband and we were intimate.

"It will happen," I reassured him. I turned around to face him. My head rested on his chest, where his heart beat right into my ears. It was familiar and steady. It was my comfort space.

His arms embraced me again, and I fell asleep while counting his heartbeats.

I rarely wore makeup, but enjoyed dressing up occasionally. My long dress, heels, and makeup were a pleasant change from my scrubs, trainers, and bare face. It also felt good when Yousef would shower me with compliments. I liked the way he eyed me in my dress. Sometimes, I needed that boost of confidence. He looked at me tonight the same way he did on our wedding day four years ago.

"Where have four years gone?" I asked in awe once the waiter took our order.

With wonder in his eyes, Yousef smiled at me. "It's gone in the blink of an eye. It feels like just the other day we were awkwardly changing in front of one another."

I couldn't help but laugh at the memory. "And now you have no shame farting in front of me."

He arched his brow. "You let out a deadly one the other day. It was completely unladylike."

"I'm going to deny that for the rest of my life."

He took my hand from across the table. "I still love you, even though you fart like a man."

I gave his hands a tight squeeze. "I love you too." I shook my head as I let out a nervous laugh. "Every day I think I've reached the maximum of loving you, but I swear the next day my love grows more. How is that possible?"

His grey eyes glistened with gratitude. "I know what you mean. I couldn't imagine loving anyone this much, but then I discover something new about you and love you even more. Thank you for the four amazing years. Life with you has been perfect."

My smile stayed untouched. "Thank you for choosing me."

Yousef opened his mouth, but it wasn't his words that reached my ears.

"Sumayyah Rahman, is that you?"

I turned towards the source of the sound. His hair was shorter and his build broader, but I recognised that face despite five years having passed. "Ibrahim?" I asked in shock. "No way!"

He stopped at our table with a larger-than-life grin. "How are you? It's been *years!*"

"I'm really good. How about you? How has life treated you?"

His head shook as if he couldn't believe he was seeing me. "Alhamdulilah, very well. I'm working as a locum doctor. Where are you based now?"

We stood for a few minutes discussing our careers after university. He was doing well for himself and I couldn't have been happier for him.

"How's your wife?" I asked, having noticed he was still sporting a wedding band.

"She's here, actually!" He turned around and caught the eye of the woman sitting a few tables away from us. He waved her over.

She was exactly what I imagined him to marry: petite, with soft features and an even gentler voice. She broke out into a smile as she waved at me. "Salaam."

"Wa'alaikum salaam."

"This is my wife, Myra." His eyes shone with pride as he looked at her.

I smiled at her, then shifted my gaze to Yousef, who had a disheartened expression. "This is my husband, Yousef. Yousef, this is Ibrahim. We were at university together," I introduced.

As expected, Yousef smiled despite a darker emotion lurking in his eyes. "It's nice to meet you." He offered a handshake, which Ibrahim accepted.

"How long have you been married?" he asked.

With a proud smile, I said, "Today marks four years."

Ibrahim let out a chuckle that warped me back to that day in the coffee shop when he asked if I was interested in marrying him. "Ah! So you definitely weren't ready for marriage back then."

My laugh was one of nerves as Yousef's burning gaze could be felt on my warming cheeks. "Definitely."

Myra rubbed her belly, and it was only then I noticed her growing belly. She caught my stare and smiled. "It's our third."

There was a selfish part of me that envied them. They were getting their third while Yousef and I were struggling to get just one. But my mother taught me to smile and show face even when facing the ugliest emotions. So, I did. "Congratulations! How did you manage that while studying?" I asked Ibrahim.

"It helps that my wife and the mother of my children is also a doctor." He looked at his wife with adoration. "There's a level of understanding when two people are in the same career."

His words felt like a stab to my heart. He said those same words to me that day and perhaps he was right. I wondered if having a baby was her decision or his. She looked content and glowed with pride at the mention of their family. I wondered if they fought about when to start for a baby.

For a second, I was warped back to a few days ago when I officially finished my GP training. Yousef jokingly said I must have been relieved that I got through it without falling pregnant. He then followed that by saying, '*maybe it will happen for us now that you actually want it*'. I said nothing in retaliation, not wanting to dampen my mood by starting an argument, but his comments hurt. Did he really think I was praying for a negative result? Sure, it wasn't what I planned, but that didn't mean I was wishing for failure.

"You're practically superwoman then," I joked. "You should be proud of yourself. I don't think I could have done that. The training was hard enough."

She wrapped her arms around her husband's waist. "It was hard, but we had a lot of support and Ibrahim helped me when I restarted my training. But you're probably much smarter than us by waiting until you were done."

My smile wavered. It wasn't her fault that her statement caused tension to rise between me and Yousef.

I wasn't sure if Ibrahim could see through it or he was genuinely curious because he turned to Yousef. "Are you in the medicine field, too?"

Yousef cleared his throat and sat taller. "No. I'm an engineer. I don't have the stomach for blood and all the other things you see," he laughed. "But I'm proud of my wife. She's a wonderful and hardworking doctor."

"I'm not surprised." He turned back to me. "If you're looking to make more money and pick up shifts, let me know. My locum agency has good rates." He handed me his phone. "Put your number in."

Nothing ever happened between Ibrahim and I. Yes, he talked about marriage, but that line was never crossed. We didn't date and when I said no, he kept his distance from me and we were just friends. That was all fact. So why did it feel so wrong to give him my number? Our spouses were right in front of us. This was only work-related. He was clearly besotted with his wife and their small family. And I loved my husband dearly.

I worked quickly to save my number and hand his phone back to him. "Thank you. I'll let you know if I'm interested. It was good seeing you."

He nodded. "Very much. I'll let you get back to your anniversary dinner. Sorry for intruding."

Like the polite gentleman he was, Yousef shook his head. "It was no interruption."

"Yousef!" His mum shouted as the front door closed behind us. "Is that you?"

"Ji, Maa?" he called back. He walked through the house to find her, while I removed my heels.

Dinner resumed as if we weren't interrupted. Yousef didn't ask questions about Ibrahim. I wasn't surprised when he acted as though nothing happened. I could see that something bothered him, but if he wanted to ask something, he needed to find the courage to say it aloud. I wasn't going to beg him for it. He called my name and I joined them in the dining room. Around the table Amina and my mother-in-law were making samosas. They had a line of operation going on and were about halfway to the finish line.

"Ji?" *Yes?*

Anjuman looked exasperated. In Bangla she said, "Come and help us. We've been sitting here for hours while you've been out. It's late and everyone wants to go to bed."

Her words fuelled the irritation I was already feeling. I worked a shift, slept for four hours and then spent the day trying to make my husband happy by celebrating our anniversary. I just wanted to sleep, but Yousef insisted on having sex and now she wanted me to stay and do this. All the while, I started worked at eight tomorrow morning.

I looked at Yousef to see if he would say no on my behalf, but he stayed quiet. I let out a restrained sigh. Most women would say no and call it a day. But I had spent the four years of my marriage living up to her expectations of a daughter-in-law and failed. I didn't need to give her any more of a reason to hate me.

I smiled. "Okay. Let me get changed." I turned on my heels and made my way to my bedroom. I worked quickly and was back downstairs within ten minutes.

Their conversation was tuned out. My brain disassociated from reality and the actions of making a samosa were automated. I wanted to be in my pyjamas, curled into my bed, but I wore a long maxi dress because my mother-in-law hated people wearing pyjamas outside of the bedroom. My eyes burned from tiredness and my body ached from the lack of rest. But Anjuman didn't call for my attention because she saw that.

"I was just saying, Lena is pregnant. Her mum called with the good news today."

Yousef and I had decided to not tell anyone we were trying. He believed it was a private matter, but I felt embarrassed at the thought of people knowing what we were doing in the confines of our bedroom. We weren't doing anything wrong, yet there was a sense of shame. That was why I couldn't blame anyone when they would bring up the topic of children with me. They didn't know we had no luck, even after an entire year. The fear of being judged consumed me, as if I were defective. Whenever it arose, I would force a smile and go along with the conversation.

"That's good to hear."

She huffed. "About time. They've been married for nearly three years. How much longer was she going to wait?"

"Three years is nothing," I retorted.

"Three years in plenty. This generation of girls are too much."

She wasn't talking about the *generation*. She was talking about *me*. *I* was the daughter-in-law who hadn't given her any grandchildren. *I* was the wife who worked long hours. She would never say it, but I knew she hated that I focused on my career; her indirect comments never failed to reach my ears. I overheard her talking to her husband with clear disdain in her voice as she spoke about me continuing to work despite my husband having a good income and living in this house for free.

But was it free? It was Yousef that paid the bills. It was Yousef that provided the food on the table, and he was *my* husband. I worked so he and I could have something for ourselves because everything that was his was now *theirs*. I didn't care that he wanted to provide for his family. In fact, I respected him *more* for taking care of his parents. He lost some respect when he wouldn't defend me to his mother.

I should have explained that getting pregnant is a sliver of a chance. There were so many external factors that affected one's ability to conceive. There was a small window in the entire month. I should have told her some people struggle to get pregnant. It was no longer a choice for us. It was a fight we were fighting within the private confines of our bedroom. But I didn't want her to think I was a disrespectful daughter-in-law. I kept my mouth shut and tuned out once again.

By the time we finished, it was nearly two in the morning. I dragged myself up the stairs and skipped showering, too exhausted to keep my head upright.

Yousef was still awake in bed. "Finished?"

I flopped onto the bed. "I was done before we got home. My limbs are dead. Can you change my clothes for me?"

His face appeared on top of mine. "I can definitely take them *off* for you." As his lips met mine, I struggled to meet his passion. "Come here."

I groaned. "I'm too tired, Yousef."

He pulled away as if my words were needles that pricked his skin. "Are you kidding me?"

Rolling my eyes, I sat up. "I wouldn't have been tired if I didn't have to sit there for almost two hours making samosas. Maybe you should have said no to your mum."

"How was I supposed to say no?"

Maybe it was the lack of sleep or the frustration that was building inside me; whatever it was brought tears to my eyes. "Of course you couldn't say no. It's your mum, after all. God forbid you do anything to make her upset."

"Sumayyah!" His voice was raised and his tone laced in warning.

I didn't care. I just had to sit there for two hours while she threw one indirect comment after another at me. If I couldn't defend myself, he should at least do it on my behalf. "What, Yousef? Did I say something to upset you?"

"That's my mum you're talking about."

My tears were brushed away. "I'm sorry. I forgot how much she meant to you."

He was out of the bed and stood in front of me. For once, I could see the anger in his eyes. His lips were curled into a scowl, and his chest rose and fell with each deep breath. "You're frustrated, so I'm going to let this go, but show some respect."

My eyebrows shot up. "Respect? What about my respect? What about every single comment she makes at me? Where are you to demand respect from her?"

"And where's mine?" he shouted. "Where was my respect when you had a man come to our table while we were celebrating our wedding anniversary? You completely disregarded me while you were all *friendly* with him. It was like I didn't exist! It was all smiles and laughs and talks about your job! Where was I?"

He was not going to make it out like I was flirting with Ibrahim. As he said, we were talking about work and then our marriages. I did nothing wrong.

"You heard the conversation. Neither one of us brought up our partners until later."

"You mean right before he mentioned you not wanting to get married back then? How would he know that, Sumayyah?"

I never told him about the Ibrahim incident because it was nothing. It was one conversation. There were no feelings involved and when I met Yousef, Ibrahim was long forgotten and had been married for two years.

"He asked me about my thoughts on marriage," I explained. "He wanted to get married young, and I told him I wanted to finish my studies."

His voice was icy and slow. "Did he want to marry you?"

I looked away. "We were just friends."

"Did you have feelings for him?"

I narrowed my eyes. "No, and I don't like what you're suggesting. Me and Ibrahim were university friends and not even that close. He gave his number. Would you like to call and check?"

At the conviction in my voice, he backed off. His shoulders relaxed, and he took a deep breath in. His lip quivered, but he walked away and got back into bed. I stared at him for a few minutes before getting dressed for bed.

"She did it," he whispered.

"Who did what?"

"She studied *and* became a mother."

His words made a home in my heart. Those six words stripped me of all my layers and made me feel worthless. *Was this his realisation he married the wrong woman?*

I tried to keep my voice steady, but even I heard the waver. "I'm sorry I couldn't meet your expectations."

"I didn't mean—"

I cut him off. "Maybe your anger isn't at my distant friendship with a man I hadn't spoken to in years." I turned away from him. "Perhaps it's because you wish you had been the one to marry his wife instead."

"That's not true."

"Isn't it? She would have given you all you wanted. A baby. A family. I'm just the woman who chose her career and now can't even get pregnant."

"Sumayyah..." he pleaded.

I turned away from him so he couldn't see the tears that streamed down my face. "Don't apologise, Yousef. You were only sharing how you felt. Perhaps marrying her would have been better for you." Saying the words felt like someone was squeezing my heart.

"You are the one for me. I *chose* you. I love you. You know that."

I couldn't get anything past my lips except a muted, "Okay."

His torso pressed against my back. His head rested on my shoulder. His arms held me close, as if he knew I was on the verge of falling apart. "I'm sorry," he whispered. "I love you," he begged.

I hadn't thought about Ibrahim in five years. I forgot all about his words that day as he asked for my hand in marriage. But as I laid in bed, with tears soaking my pillow, I recalled everything he said to me. And I wondered, for the first time, how my life would have been different if he were the one beside me.

Chapter Seventeen

My dad placed a kiss on my forehead. "Are you eating?" he asked as he joined me at the table.

"Yes, Abba."

"How long did your *hori,*" *mother-in-law,* "give you for this time?"

"Just the weekend. How about you, Nafisa?"

She hummed at me, too distracted by her thoughts. When I called her name, she looked up. "Oh, same."

My eyebrows furrowed in worry. My sister looked like she was doused in worry. She barely contributed to the conversation as we ate together as a family. I asked nothing in front of my parents, not wanting to worry them.

Once we were alone in her bedroom, I asked what was bothering her.

She hesitated. "I'm pregnant." From her demeanour, it was clear she wasn't expecting the news. If anything, she looked unhappy.

"Congratulations," I said softly. "That's amazing."

Her blank expression warned me of the impending rant I was about to receive. "Are you serious? You've seen the tiny room we're cramped in. Where the hell am I supposed to put a baby in that? His house is already overflowing with people. I *just* moved jobs so I won't get maternity pay. How are we supposed to afford to live? We've got holidays booked for next year! And they're non-refundable." Her face fell into her hands and she rubbed her face.

If I wasn't stunned by her selfish thoughts, I would have laughed. Her biggest worry was losing money on a holiday? She had no idea how blessed she was.

"Okay..." I swallowed hard to stop myself from berating her. "How did this happen, then? Weren't you using anything?"

"We were, but I swapped methods and we were careless during the transition period. What do I do, Afa?"

My blood ran cold. "What do you mean? You're going to have a baby," I deadpanned.

She shook her head like a crazy person. "I can't! We're not ready. We would be shit parents."

I wanted to tell her she was being ungrateful. There were people who would do anything to get pregnant. I would give everything to become pregnant. Another year had passed since we started trying and my worries were well and truly alive. Every month, hope would creep into my heart, but it would shortly be followed by bone-aching disappointment. I'd lost count of how many times I'd cried in the bathroom.

Yousef's sadness matched mine, but he bounced back faster and every failed month pushed him to try harder. We were following all guidance and making sure we were having sex at the highest opportunity of conceiving. We had read and tried every hack and advice out there. Nothing had worked yet.

"Well, maybe you shouldn't have been so reckless." My envy came out as anger.

She arched her eyebrow. "I know that! I don't need you to point out the obvious," she retaliated.

"What do you want me to do?" I should have shown more sympathy, but I couldn't get myself to feel it. She was carelessly handed my dream, and she was ready to throw it away.

With an eye roll, she said, "Let me know what contraception you're on because it seems to work. Five years later and it's kept you from getting pregnant."

I didn't have any right to be angry because she didn't know about our struggle. How could she know that I've sobbed on my prayer mat, begging God to give me just *one* child?

"You don't know what people are going through. Be careful with your words."

She pouted. "Sorry. I'm blaming the hormones."

I took a step out of my green jealousy boots and got comfortable in my worn out big sister ones. I sighed. "A baby is a blessing, Nafisa. Nobody is ever ready to be a mother. It's something you'll learn as you go. I know you're worried about space, but the silver lining to a full house is having all that help. And maybe you guys could look for a small flat. The things you're worried about are trivial. It can easily be resolved. What would you do if you faced something that couldn't be fixed? What if it was reversed, and you were crying because you couldn't have children?" I pulled my lips together, hoping it would stop my emotions from overflowing, but it was too late because while I wasn't talking about me, I finally gave a voice to my biggest fear: infertility.

Nafisa forgot all about herself and instead focused on me. "What's wrong, Afa? What are you not telling me?"

I shook my head. "Nothing."

She looked at me with suspicion. "You promise?"

The lie came out with ease. "I promise."

Rani frowned. "Halima just text me and said she couldn't make it."

We were all sitting in her childhood bedroom like we did when we were schoolgirls. Zoya's boys played on the floor while we kicked back on the bed.

"That's a shame. We could have pretended we were twelve again," Zoya quipped.

"Did she say why?" I asked. We had planned this meet up weeks ago and were all excited for it.

Rani shook her head. "Nope." Her phone started to ring, which made her roll her eyes. "Give me one second." She answered the phone as she left the room.

"Are you okay?" Zoya asked. "You seem a little off."

I looked away from Nadim and Karim. "Yeah, I'm just tired." I nodded towards her children. "They're growing so fast."

She half smiled and half frowned. "I know. Can you believe I have a six and four-year-old? Sometimes I look at them and forget I'm their mother. It feels like I'm babysitting my cousins, until I realise nobody is coming to pick them up," she laughed.

"Would you want anymore?"

"Not really. How about you? When are you ready to build an army of your own?"

My laugh came out strangled. "No army. Just one." *Please God. Just one will be enough.*

"No! You can't do that. Every child needs a sibling. Two is good."

My heart beat rapidly in my chest as I built the courage to ask the question on my mind. I was scared she would figure out the reasoning behind my question, or worse; she wouldn't be able to give me an answer. "Did you do anything to make it easier to get pregnant?"

It was instant; that look of sympathy in her eyes. "Are you and Yousef struggling?"

There was nothing wrong with saying yes, but I couldn't get myself to say it. What if people thought there was something wrong with me? *What if there was something wrong with me?*

"We've only just recently started trying," I lied. "But nothing yet. I've had no issues before. Like my period has always been heavy but mostly regular."

She tutted at me. "Don't worry about it! It's only been a few months. It took me six months to get pregnant with Karim."

Six months? It had been two *years* for me.

"I guess I'm worried about my age. They say it's harder the older you get and I'm already thirty-one."

"It will happen. Don't overthink it. If you stress, it messes with your hormones and makes it harder."

"What makes it harder?" Rani asked as she joined the room.

Zoya looked at me, but I slyly shook my head. I could tell Zoya knew something was up, but she held back her questions. Rani wouldn't do the same. She would ask for the nitty-gritty details, and I didn't want to talk about it anymore.

"Who was that?" Zoya asked instead.

Rani pretended to gag. "My witch mother-in-law. She gave me a lovely lecture because I didn't tell her I was going out." She let out a sarcastic laugh. "Sorry, I mean she lectured me because I didn't *ask* her if I could go out."

"She sounds like Idris's mum."

"I thought she was chill?"

Had Rani rolled her eyes harder, we would have been able to hear it. "She's a backward-minded bitch and one of these days I'm going to let her have it. Stupid cow."

I had never heard someone brazenly cuss out their mother-in-law like that. I had never uttered a word about mine to anyone. Despite her complaints about minor issues, Zoya never cursed at hers.

"Language!" Zoya scolded, pointing at her boys.

She covered her mouth. "Sorry."

"What did she do?" I asked. "You've only been married three years and you hate her that much?"

"She's a conniving little cow and my husband is her lap dog. I cannot wait to get the fuck out of that house."

"Language!" Zoya shouted again. "My behind will get kicked if they go home with those words in their mouth."

"How is house hunting going?"

"It's a..." She backtracked when Zoya gave her a pointed stare. "It's a struggle, to say the least. We've seen about a million houses and he has something to complain about every single time." My friend sighed in frustration. She never wanted to live with her in-laws. It was why she bought a flat beforehand. From what they planned before marriage, they were meant to live there while they searched for their 'forever' home. Rani mentioned Ravi's plan to stay at home briefly after their wedding, but months turned into years.

I wanted to ask what happened to her flat and those plans, but the topic was clearly a sore spot for her and I didn't want to fuel her irritation any more than it was.

"Sounds like he doesn't want to move," Zoya said, voicing my thoughts.

"Oh, he wants to move... right back up his mum's vag—"

"Rani!" Zoya screeched over her.

I was laughing when my phone lit up with Yousef's name. I excused myself and answered the call in the hallway. "Hey."

"Hi," he breathed into the phone. "What are you doing?"

I knew what the call was for. I had received many like this. "Just at Rani's. How about you?"

"Just got back from work. I miss you. When do I get my wife back?"

A ghost smile appeared on my lips. "Tomorrow."

The line fell silent. I counted twelve seconds before he spoke again. "Did it start?"

I lowered my gaze to the floor. "Yeah," I whispered. "I started my period today."

He tried to hide it, but I heard his sad sigh. "Maybe next month."

The crack in my heart got a little deeper. "Yeah, maybe next month," I echoed.

Chapter Eighteen

Sweat trickled down my back from the heat in the kitchen. Bodies buzzed around me as I stared at the bubbling water. I didn't have to think as I pulled the teacups from the cupboards. I was on autopilot mode as I made tea for fifteen people.

"Move quickly! The men are complaining," my mother-in-law rushed as she brushed past me.

"Maa!" Haniya scolded. "What can Bhabi do if the tea hasn't boiled yet? The men can wait a few minutes; they won't die."

"The tea should have been put on ages ago! Everything else is ready. Tell your brother to come and take the tray." This was normal for her. When she was hosting her in-laws, she was rigid and constantly irritated. She had been cooking since yesterday. Amina helped around the kitchen while I cleaned the house from top to bottom. She still found something to complain about.

Haniya bumped her shoulder against mine. "Just ignore her. She gets crazy when Fufu and them come to visit."

I hugged my sister-in-law. "I've been married into this family for almost six years," I reminded her. "I know how it can be. Don't worry, I don't take it personally."

"It doesn't matter. She can speak to me like that because she birthed me. Even then, it makes me so angry. I am sorry. I know she isn't easy to handle."

A warm feeling of love filled me. "It's the life of a woman, Haniya. It's all they know because they were treated the same."

She turned so her back leaned against the counter. She disgustedly observed women rushing to serve men tea and desserts. "That's why it's worse," she muttered. "Life has progressed, but we're stuck in the messed up mindset of older generations. I hope my mother-in-law isn't like that."

My in-laws had started to look for a husband for Haniya. As I looked at her, I prayed that she found the happiness I longed for. Needing to move my thoughts along, I snapped out of my thoughts and poured the tea.

Appearing behind me, Yousef asked, "Are these ready to go?"

"Yeah. The sugar is over there."

"Okay. Did you—"

His mum screeched my name. "Make more tea for the women."

Haniya opened her mouth, but I grabbed her hand and shook my head. She looked at me in despair, but I held her gaze. "I hate this culture," she grumbled. She stared at her brother. "Why are you still standing there? Give the men tea before they explode."

Yousef looked down at me. "What's wrong with her?"

"There's nothing wrong with me. It's this stupid culture. But how would you understand? You are a man, after all."

I couldn't help but smile at her defiance. Haniya had grown into a courageous woman; she reminded me of Nafisa and Rani: unafraid to speak her mind.

"Just go," I whispered to Yousef.

He looked at her in confusion, but took my advice and escaped. Haniya helped me make the next batch of tea. I laughed when she joked about adding salt instead of sugar. She took one tray of tea and I took the other. Before I could sit down, my mother-in-law asked me to dish out the cake Haniya made.

"Where's your other *bou?"* one aunt asked.

"She's putting the baby to sleep." Her narrowed eyes turned to me. "Quickly serve the cake before everyone finishes the tea."

I smiled and nodded.

"You've got lucky with your daughter-in-laws," another aunt praised. "She's been on her feet all day."

But she never told me to relax and enjoy a cup of tea with them.

Anjuman gleamed with happiness. "Amina helped me all day yesterday. They're good. They take turns."

I gripped the knife with too much force. Amina helped her in the kitchen because I was tasked with turning this house into a spotless shrine.

"Bhabi was cleaning *all* day," Haniya defended. "She went to bed after everybody."

My phone buzzed, but I ignored it, preoccupied with cutting the perfect square slices. But when it rang again, I answered and held the phone between my ear and shoulder. "Nafisa, I can't talk right now."

"I think I've gone into labour."

"Have you finished cutting the cake?" Anjuman called from the dining room.

"I'll call you back."

"I'm scared," she rushed out.

"I'm sorry. Get yourself to the hospital." I quickly hung up and finished serving the cake. Needing some space to breathe, I excused myself under the pretense I needed to pray. I took the stairs two at a time until I was leaning against my bedroom door. I closed my eyes and took deep breaths in hopes it would calm my erratic heart.

When Masuma's name lit up my screen, I sighed and answered the call. "Hello?"

"Hey. I was just calling to see if you wanted to go to the hospital with me? Nafisa wants us there."

I sat cross-legged in the middle of my floor. "I can't. We've got Yousef's entire dad's side here."

"Won't your mother-in-law let you go? I'm sure she'll understand."

The idea was so ridiculous I had to laugh. "No, she won't. Please tell Nafisa I'll see her tomorrow."

Masuma paused. "She's quite upset that you hung up on her. She actually called me crying."

I rubbed my temple to get rid of the headache I woke up with me. "What did she say?" I asked, not wanting to hear the truth.

"Just that you've been distant her whole pregnancy and the one time she needed you, you couldn't be bothered to talk. She said she feels like you always pick them over her."

I hated that my sister felt like that, but she should understand. She too was married and knew that your husband's family take priority over your own.

"What am I supposed to do? I can't just rush out of this house. I either be a shit daughter-in-law or a shit sister." My throat felt tight and tears threatened to fall.

"That's not true."

"But it is! No matter what I do, I can't make anyone happy."

Some shuffling occurred on her side. "Nafisa is just scared and emotional. Don't take it to heart. I need to go. I'll be at the hospital with her. If you decide to come, just call me. Okay?" I couldn't speak before she disconnected.

🎀🎀🎀🎀

Yousef tapped my shoulder. "Your phone is ringing," he mumbled in his sleepy state.

I peeped one eye open and saw it was my dad. "Abba?"

He sounded on the verge of tears. "Alhamdulilah! You've become a Khala!" *Maternal aunt.* "Your niece was born ten minutes ago."

My heart bloomed with happiness for my sister and her husband. "How are mother and baby?"

"Junaid said they are okay." My dad began to sob. "I've finally become a nana!" *Maternal grandfather.* "The day is finally here. All my dreams have become my reality. Is Yousef awake?"

I absentmindedly handed him the phone. I stared up at the ceiling as I absorbed his words. It should have been me to make that dream of his come true. I was the daughter that became a doctor. I was the daughter that learned to cook and clean. But it was *she* that got to hear those words. After all I've done for my parents, I never heard them say they were finally happy with me.

But how could they be? My dad always said the dream ended with a good husband and children. I hadn't achieved that yet.

I didn't even notice the tears until Yousef hung up and brushed them away for me. It was selfish of me to be crying for my loss instead of celebrating with my sister. The truth was, I didn't want to celebrate when she got something she never wanted, but I craved. For three years, it was the only thing on my mind. I'd been frozen in life because of this thing. Everyone around me had accomplished this, but it was only me that was stuck.

"Sumayyah?" Yousef whispered.

"It's not fair," I cried. "When will it be my turn?"

"Our turn will come."

I turned to face him. "When? It's been three years of failing. What am I doing wrong?"

"I don't know," he murmured. "I wish I knew what was going wrong."

My hands rested on his chest, above his heart. "What if there's something wrong? What if it doesn't happen for us?"

The distant look in his eyes broke my heart. I wanted him to say it wouldn't matter. I needed him to relieve the burden that weighed on my shoulders. But Yousef went silent and avoided looking at me.

I repeat the same questioned I asked on our honeymoon. "Would you be happy with just the two of us?"

Back then he said he would be happy as long as he had me, but the years of our marriage had taught me it's not enough for him. Every time he saw a baby, family, or stranger alike, his eyes carried longing in them. When he had a baby in his arms, there was a sense of comfort in him. I knew a life without children wouldn't be enough for him.

His answer was one of resignation, not love. He said, "It will have to be enough."

Chapter Nineteen

Aila slept peacefully in my arms. I sniffed the top of her head, enjoying the new baby smell. Her tiny fingers were curled into a fist. Her pink sleep suit was too big for her tiny body and made her look even smaller than she was.

"She looks like a doll," Haniya said, staring down at her.

Yousef's family joined me to visit the baby today. I was yet to pass her to anybody. It was fair to say I was smitten by my niece. When I first saw her, all that envy vanished, and I was truly happy for my sister. She was on bed rest at my parent's house as agreed by her in-laws.

"She's perfect," I whispered. "Isn't that right, Moina?" *Sweetheart.*

"Normal oiseh ni?" my mother-in-law asked.

My mum was the one to answer. "Yeah. She didn't have a C-Section." She said it as if a C-Section was something to be ashamed of.

"How are your stitches?" I asked. "They're not hurting, are they?"

She shook her head. "No. My midwife said they're healing well. I don't think I want to carry on breastfeeding. It's so hard," she sighed.

My mum cut in. "No! The mother's milk is good for the baby."

"But it's so tiring, Amma," she moaned. "Especially at night."

"Why don't you do both?" I suggested. "Maybe try breastfeeding during the day and stick to formula at night."

Anjuman huffed. “The doctor has spoken.”

All eyes were on me. The words were climbing up my throat and getting ready to be blurted out, but my mother’s warning daggers forced me to swallow them back down.

Haniya was the only one brave enough to fight my corner. “What’s that supposed to mean? Bhabi *is* a doctor, and she gave good advice.”

Her mum was unaffected by the irritation directed towards her. “You can study all you want, but you can’t learn to be a mother without actually being a mother. And your Bhabi has decided to never give my son a child or me a grandchild.”

My mum, being the first to run from conflict, let out a nervous laugh. “No, I’m sure she will give us some good news soon.”

Like a two-headed snake, Yousef’s mum smiled. “Maybe you should talk to your daughter. She’s worked enough. Now it’s time to be a real wife.”

My heartbeat pounded in my ears. There was a roar of emotions swirling in me so loud I could barely hear what I said. “What would make me a real wife?”

Still smiling, she said, “These late nights are too much. How can you expect a baby when you’re never home to share a bed with your husband?” She turned to my mum. “Am I wrong? You tell me. Your son-in-law spends more nights alone than he does with his wife. Is this a life?”

Wanting to appease her, my mum nodded. “No, you are right. I’m sure my Sumayyah will work fewer nights. I never liked her working even before she was married.”

“I can’t pick my shifts,” I gritted out.

"Well then, you should have picked a different job or never got married. Work, work and work! I can't even have a cup of tea with my daughter-in-law."

How could she sit there and talk about me like that in front of my mum? *How could my mother not defend me?*

"And my dad never gets a call from his son-in-law," I fired back. "Maybe you should have a word with him."

"That's different. When a woman gets married, her life changes. She has new responsibilities."

I wasn't going to back down. Today I was not going to keep my mouth shut. "Have I not fulfilled my duties?"

"Here and there."

"Where have I failed?"

She ignored my question and asked one of her own. "Don't you feel even a little embarrassed that those younger than you have had children? You should at least try before it's too late."

My fingers clenched. I wanted to belittle her to the same size she was making me feel. I wanted to hurt her the way she had hurt me. I wanted to watch as shame and dread filled her face. "We've been trying for three years, but we're still waiting for a blessing. But yeah, it's me working a few night shifts that have made me fail as a wife. What happens between me and my husband in our bedroom is nobody's business! Don't you feel disgusted talking about your son's private life so openly?"

Movement in the doorway captured my attention. Yousef stared at me in disbelief as disappointment poured out of him. My chest rose and fell as adrenaline coursed through me, but I wasn't going to break our stare. He should have defended me. He should have stood by my side and fought this battle with me, instead of letting me feel alone in this.

He looked at his mum and I looked at the eyes on me. "What? Nobody has anything to say? Does anybody else want to tell me how selfish I am?" My laboured breathing was the only sound in the room. I looked at my husband. "How about you? Don't you want to tell your mum how unhappy you are because I can't get pregnant? Why don't you tell her how hard I've tried?" My voice cracked, and the dam broke.

"Bhabi..." Haniya whispered. "It's okay."

I shook my head. "No, it's not. It's an embarrassment that my younger sister had a baby before me. She achieved so much in half the time I've been married."

"Afa," she murmured. "That's not true. You've accomplished *so* much. This isn't something you can control."

I stood up and passed Aila back to my sister. I wiped away my tears and stood tall. The two older women remained mute and watched as I silently left the room. I didn't know where to go, but I had to escape that suffocating room. I climbed the stairs until I was back in my old childhood bedroom. The room mirrored my emptiness. I knew telling her would be useless. She wouldn't have any sympathy for me. If anything, it just proved her point that I failed as a wife and woman.

My quiet was broken quicker than I wanted. Yousef came in and closed the door. Not even my husband held any sympathy for me. "Mum left."

Was I supposed to comment on that? I didn't care. She dragged my name in front of my family. I didn't care that she was gone. If anything, I was glad.

"The way you spoke was wrong, Sumayyah."

A small part of me had hoped that he would come and hold me. The naïve part of me believed he would, for once, fight for me. I should have known it was a stupid dream to have.

"She started it. You didn't hear what she was saying about me."

"Still. You shouldn't have shouted at her like that. She's your elder. She is your mother."

I stared at him. "She'll be my mother the day she treats me like her daughter."

His teeth ground together. "What has got into you? So what if she was talking about grandchildren?"

Anger like never before swam with my blood. I felt it *everywhere,* and I wanted to scream or hit something. I settled on standing toe-to-toe with Yousef. "*Talking* about grandchildren?" I asked sarcastically. "She said I failed you as a wife. She said I was a terrible daughter-in-law. She said I was an embarrassment because my youngers had children before me. She said I was stopping you from becoming a father because I prioritised work. She said our life was wrong because you spent a few nights without me. So unless you agree with her, I suggest you have a word with your mum and, for once, defend me!"

He looked at me as if he couldn't recognise me. Maybe he was right. The Sumayyah he met was slowly torn apart. She tried so hard to make everyone else happy that all she was left with was anger and bitterness. I hated the side of me that just came out, but I couldn't take it anymore.

Everywhere I went, I was hounded by old women about children. Why did nobody stop to think that it was none of their business?

"What am I supposed to defend? The way you spoke was *wrong*. You could have explained our situation calmly. She didn't speak to you aggressively. What was the need to retaliate like that?"

"Because!" I screamed.

"Because *what*, Sumayyah? What reason did you have to raise your voice at my mum? Why would you disrespect her like that? How could you dishonour like that, in front of your family, of all people?"

"Who gave her the right to humiliate *me* in front of my family?" I screamed back. "She makes comments every day! I take it and take it and today I had enough! I retaliated like that because I can't take it anymore! Six years, Yousef! Six years of taking her bullshit and I never opened my mouth. I kept my head down and kept my mouth shut because that's what a good woman does!" I hated that my tears betrayed me. My voice dropped. "But a good man stands by his wife. A good man protects her. Where have you been?"

Sympathy finally made an appearance. "You don't know what happens when you're not there. Do you think I haven't said anything to her? I just respect her enough to avoid doing it publicly."

"What about your respect from me?" My voice matched my icy emotions. "You lose respect for me every time you let her speak to me like that."

His tone matched mine. "What do you want me to do?"

I smiled at him. "You don't need to do anything. You just carry on living your life, Yousef. As a man, you aren't expected to get your hands dirty. It's my job to clean your mess; and make no mistake because this is *your* mess. You should have set a boundary with your mother so she wouldn't ever have the audacity to suggest I don't have enough sex with her son. Why is it she never speaks to Amina like that? It's because the one time she tried, Younes shut her down."

I took a deep breath to calm my erratic breathing. I was depleted, both physically and mentally. It was beginning to feel impossible to maintain everything. Instead of spinning my plates, they were falling to the floor and smashing. I didn't know what to do anymore.

Yousef was yet to show any understanding. "It has nothing to do with Younes. It's because she has a proper relationship with Amina."

My chest rose and fell. "What's that supposed to mean?"

He shrugged. "She spends all day with Amina. They cook together. Amina is home to help around the house and eat with her. How often does she see you? You're either working or in our bedroom."

Despite covering my mouth, the laugh slipped out. "Are you serious? You're blaming me for the way she behaves?"

"I didn't blame you," he snapped. Everything else he said faded into a muffle.

Yousef had been wanting one thing since the beginning. I could argue that I never knew it because he never said it outright, but part of me always knew. *He didn't want me to work.* He wanted the wife that stayed home and catered to him and his family. He needed the wife his mother loved and praised. And in his head, the barrier to that was my job. He didn't defend me to his mum, because he agreed with her. He was just too much of a coward to say it out loud.

I didn't study and train this much to give it up, but I also needed my marriage to work. I tried it my way, and it wasn't working. So, I decided to give Yousef what he wanted, in hopes we could complete our dream.

My eyes latched onto his stormy ones. When I spoke, I was filled with conviction. "I'll give you everything you want. Tomorrow I'll hand in my notice. If it's okay with your mum, I'll go locum and work only day shifts a few days a month just so I have something of my own because it's clear I have nothing else."

"That's not true. You know you have me."

I shook my head. "No, I don't, and today made that *very* clear. You have and always will belong to your family. And that's okay. At least I know that now. I'll be home to cook and clean. Every night I'll be in bed with you. Will that be enough?"

"Sumayyah," he pleaded. "I never said I wanted any of that."

"But you did when you said nothing at all. Silence is so much louder than a scream."

He grabbed my arm as I tried to walk past him. "What will you achieve by doing this? You'll end up unhappy and resenting me."

I looked up at him. I still saw the ghost of Yousef that I met on the first day. The one that asked me all those silly questions. The one that made me feel seen in a world where I was overlooked for everything except my achievements. But he was only a ghost that came to haunt me when I desperately wanted to run and never stop running.

I didn't answer him.

I didn't need to.

My silence said it all.

Chapter Twenty

The cheese sandwich from the vending machine was as disgusting as I expected it to be. Normally I'd make my lunch, but after yesterday's events, I quietly slipped out the house. When I returned home, his mum was nowhere to be seen. I didn't seek her out. I readied myself for bed and drifted off to sleep, disregarding Yousef's pleading stare.

I threw the bread back into its packet and slumped onto the table. I closed my eyes and tried to shut my mind off.

"Are you okay?"

I lifted my head at the soft voice. My eyes squinted as I tried to place the familiar face. But she got there first.

She grinned. "Sumayyah, right? It's Myra – Ibrahim's wife. We met two years ago."

Reflexively, I ran my hands over my hijab to make sure my exterior didn't match the mess on my interior. "Hi! Sorry, I'm so out of it today."

She grabbed her lunch from the fridge and joined me at the round table. "It's fine! Do you work here?"

"I did." My smile felt pathetic. "I handed in my notice today."

She mixed her pasta around with her fork and my stomach grumbled at the aromatic food. "Why are you leaving?"

To make my husband happy.

"The hours are a bit too long for me now."

"Yeah, I get that. Working and kids is a hard balance to find."

My heart sunk. "No, I don't have any children."

She stopped chewing. "Sorry, I didn't mean..." She sighed. "Let's just pretend I didn't put my foot in my mouth."

I waved off the awkwardness. "It's fine." I had no reason to lie to her, but it slipped out as a habit. "We've only just started properly trying."

Myra's smile radiated warmth. "I pray it happens for you soon. I should warn you that after children, work feels like a holiday," she laughed.

"How old are your little ones?"

"Eldest is eight, second is five, and my youngest is just under two."

"Wow," I chuckled. "That must be a handful."

"One house. One woman. Four boys and my husband is the biggest baby of them all."

Reflecting on my training, I tried to envision being a mother as well. Juggling the roles of wife and daughter-in-law while working must have been tough for her. "I honestly admire you. I didn't even want to get married at that age, let alone start a family."

She pushed her food away and sighed. "I love my life, but yeah, it was hard. I don't regret getting married young or getting pregnant, but if I could go back in time, I'd probably wait."

I felt foolish for finding reassurance in her honesty. It wasn't just me, and I was tempted to call Yousef and ask her to repeat herself just to make a point.

"If you don't mind me asking, why didn't you wait?"

"Our culture. The day after my wedding, one of his aunts asked when I was going to have a baby. I was barely twenty," she deadpanned. "As unfortunate as it is, it's how things are. I just tired of the questions and thought I might as well."

Frustration built in me. "Why don't the men get questioned? Why is it always us?"

Her laugh was accompanied by an eye roll. "When has a man ever been asked to justify his actions? It doesn't matter what they do, it's always excused." She resumed eating. "I might be overstepping here, so feel free to tell me to be quiet but, maybe a break from the home would be good for you. I know it is for me. If I was stuck at home every day with my kids, I'd go crazy. Why don't you do locum work?"

I nodded. "Yeah, I need to look for an agency."

She took out her phone. "Do you still have Ibrahim's number? He's friends with the manager of an agency. Give him a call."

My thoughts went back to that night when Yousef expressed his distaste for my friendship with Ibrahim. He questioned if there had been more there than I shared. He was wrong, but I didn't want to add any fuel to his suspicions.

For a moment, my heart clenched, and I remembered crying myself to sleep that night. He compared me to the woman sat across from me. He didn't give any thought to my feelings when he spoke. I had spent the last six years constantly catering to him and what he wanted. I'd given enough. It was time to prioritise myself, regardless of his feelings.

I nodded. "I think I will."

ꕤꕤꕤꕤ

I held my finger up to silence Yousef when he entered our bedroom.

"You have enough experience to join his agency. He'll just need a reference," Ibrahim said.

My cheeks ached from my wide grin. "Thank you so much! I don't know what I would have done without you."

Ibrahim chuckled. "You would have easily found an agency to join. This way you make *me* look good for bringing you in."

"I owe you." Yousef pressed a kiss against my temple. "I need to go. I'll be in touch soon with my references."

A wail screeched through the phone. "That's my cue to go as well. Thanks for calling. It was good to catch up."

"Same here. Thank you again for pushing this through so fast. Just this morning I was worried, and you just saved me."

"No problem. Take care of yourself. Speak soon."

I said my goodbyes and hung up. A breath of relief passed over my lips. I didn't expect Ibrahim to jump into action so fast, but within an hour of calling him, the agency manager had been in contact. I felt relieved, one stress lessening from my shoulders.

"What was that about?" Yousef asking, getting undressed.

"Just work. How was your day?"

"Fine." He dumped his dirty shirt into the hamper. "What about work?"

I kept my tone neutral, hoping he wouldn't see through my nerves. "I handed in my notice today and Ibrahim helped me get registered with a locum agency."

Yousef froze. "Why would you do that without speaking to me?"

My eyebrows furrowed as I stared at him. Did he hit his head and forget about yesterday? "I told you about it yesterday."

"That was a stupid argument. You said those things in anger."

My eye twitched in anger. "Nothing about yesterday was stupid and don't tell me whether I meant something. I meant it all, Yousef. All you've done is moan and complain about my work shifts, so I fixed the problem. Why are you not happy?"

The gulp said it all. The flicker to my phone said it even louder.

I couldn't help but laugh. "Are you serious? It's because he helped me?"

"Do you blame me for feeling that way?"

I blame you for making me quit my job.

"Do you really think I'd cheat on you?"

He pulled his t-shirt on with more force than necessary. "It's not you I'm worried about."

"He's *married* with children." I shook my head, "And anyway, I won't even be working with him."

"I don't like it. You don't need to work."

If looks could kill, Yousef would've been on the floor.

"Come again?"

He sighed. "I didn't mean it like that."

"You seem to say a lot of things you don't mean," I grumbled.

"What is wrong with you?" he snapped. "I get you're upset, but this isn't how this marriage is going to work. You don't get to make decisions without discussing with me first. You don't call your old friends and take jobs without talking to me first. I am still your husband; even when you're angry with me." He stepped closer. "Even when you can't stand to be in the same room as me. You don't get to stop loving me!"

His scream made me flinch. His words made me cower away.

"You think I don't love you?" I whispered.

"Do you? You have been so distant, Sumayyah, and I don't know what to do. I want my wife back."

"Your wife has been here the whole time. You just haven't seen how much she's hurting. I love you so much Yousef. My love is the only thing that has kept me here."

"Then show me that. Show me how much you love me," he begged.

After all I've sacrificed, how could he say something like that? *How much more was I supposed to give him?*

"What else would you like to take, Yousef? I left my family, and I have lived with yours. I gave up my dream job! What more do you want?"

The room fell silent as we finally faced all the unsaid truths between us. The room's tension was palpable. He wanted a baby and until he had one in his arms, he would never be happy.

"I want you to apologise to my mum," he stated. "And then we draw the line under this and move on."

"Have you asked her to apologise to me?"

"She's the elder," he argued.

"Respect isn't given, it's earned. The same goes for forgiveness."

He cupped my face. His thumb brushed the top of my cheeks. "Please don't make me choose. You live under the same roof. How long will this continue?"

I repeated the words he once said to me. "I'd never ask you to choose because I can't bear the thought of you breaking my heart." I stepped out of his embrace before continuing. "And I know where I rank."

CHAPTER TWENTY-ONE

THE RING OF THE doorbell could be heard from outside. I could already hear the voices of my friends as I waited for someone to let me in. When the door pulled open to reveal Halima, I gave her a tight squeeze with one arm while balancing the gifts in the other.

"Come in!" she said, leading me through her short hallway to the open living room.

The space was elegantly decorated, aside from the corner piled with toys. The fuchsia pink Barbie clothes and stuffed animals didn't match the neutral aesthetic Halima was going for, but it added a warmth that was missing. The owner of said toys ran past me in a whirlwind and tipped her toys over.

"Jannah!" her mum scolded. "Mummy just tidied up! We have people here. Only take out one toy."

I waved Halima off. "Leave her! Let her have her fun."

Rani spun around the room. "You did a marvellous job with this flat," she complimented. "It looks so fancy."

She brought a tray of refreshments over to the table. "Thanks. It's hard work when you have a four-year-old."

Zoya scoffed. "It's going to be even harder to clean." Her head jerked towards to sofa. "Nadim! Stop jumping on the sofa!" She winced at Halima. "I'm sorry."

"I guess our peaceful evenings are officially over," Rani quietly muttered to me. "Maybe we should start doing these meet ups, just me and you."

Zoya tossed popcorn at her, but missed, and it landed on the table in front of her. "Keep dreaming."

Rani popped the fallen snack into her mouth. "I'm only joking." She winked at me. "Not," she whispered.

I laughed at her. "Where is Nazir?" I asked Halima.

"I kicked him out for the evening so we could have some girl time." Nadim let out a scream. "*With* Nadim, of course. Can I get you ladies anything else?"

Zoya patted the seat next to her at the table. "Sit down! It's only us; you don't need to get all fancy *schmancy* with us."

With all of us sat around the table, talking and laughing, I finally felt normal. I felt a sense of peace my life had been missing. Things with Yousef were strained, and it was only worse with my mother-in-law. A week had passed since the argument and the silent treatment continued. Yousef wouldn't budge on me apologising, and it seemed my parents agreed with him. Her being older didn't convince me. My mum lectured me about being insolent and disrespectful. My dad reminded me that wasn't how I was raised. I knew I wasn't in the right, but neither was she. *Why was it just me who had to say sorry?*

"Do you know what this room is missing?" Rani asked to the room, but answered before we could. "A coffee table. That beautiful couch and rug need something to tie it together."

"She ordered one. Has your coffee table not come?" Zoya shouted to Halima, who was in the kitchen plating dinner for Jannah and Nadim. "I was on the phone with her when she placed the order," she explained to us.

Halima entered the room with two plastic plates. She sat cross-legged on the floor next to the child-sized table.

Jannah came running to her mum and her eyes lit up at the sight of her dinner. "Noodles!" she exclaimed.

Halima smiled at her and helped to get her seated. As Jannah struggled to spoon her food, Halima ran her fingers through Jannah's curly hair. She was a mini version of her mother from her curly hair, round cheeks, and chocolate coloured eyes. My heart felt that all-familiar pull as she whispered something to her daughter that made a sweet giggle resound in the room. Jannah offered her mum a bite of her food, which Halima accepted. The love in their eyes and silent bond brought tears to my eyes.

"When's your coffee table coming?" Zoya repeated.

Halima looked away from her daughter as if our presence caught her by surprise. "It came, but we accidentally broke it."

Rani smirked at her. "Couldn't carry both of your weights?"

That earned her a blank stare. "No. Nazir accidentally dropped a hammer on it and it shattered. We're avoiding a glass table now," she joked.

As she and Rani discussed interior decor, my eyes couldn't move off the children. When Zoya scolded Nadim for the third time, I wanted to beg her to stop. If I had a child, there wasn't anything I wouldn't give them. I would've gladly let them jump on the upholstery. I wouldn't care that they dropped food on their clothes or floor. The sound of their screams and tantrums wouldn't have driven me crazy. The evidence of your child's presence lies in all those things. Every jump would leave an imprint of their existence. Every spill would be a stain of their growth. Every scream would've filled the silence I heard and felt.

"How's your sister?" Halima asked, snapping me out of my thoughts.

I forced my lips into a smile. "Good. Aila is such a good baby. I told Nafisa I'd be happy to keep her overnight while she's this quiet."

"It would be good practice for you because nights are the worst," Zoya groaned.

Halima nodded. "Agreed."

My gaze lowered. A lump of emotions formed in my throat. My gulp was loud enough to gather the attention of all the girls. When I looked at them, I saw the concern they held for me, and it made my eyes sting with emotion. I had told no one about our struggle because I felt embarrassed. But the worry on their faces had me forcing the words out. "I don't know if that will happen for us. We've been trying for a long time now and we haven't been able to get pregnant."

Rani rubbed my shoulder. "I'm sorry to hear that."

"Same," Zoya consoled. "Have you got pregnant at all?"

I shook my head. "No. Not even once."

"How long have you been trying?" Halima asked. She quickly added, "Only if you want to share. I completely understand if you don't."

I squeezed Zoya's hand when she held mine. "Three years." Hearing it out loud hurt just as much as thinking about it. "At first I thought it was just the aftereffects of the pill wearing off, but it's just..." I trailed off, not knowing what to say.

How could my friends understand? One of them had two beautiful children. Another was content with the one perfect child she had. And the last never yearned to have a child.

"Have you spoken to a doctor?" Zoya asked.

Rani gave her a pointed stare. "She *is* a doctor."

She rolled her eyes. "I meant a gynecologist. There could be something medically wrong that's stopping you from getting pregnant. It might not even be a major thing. Maybe you just need a boost of hormones."

Both Haniya and Nafisa asked me the same question, and I lied and told them I was on a waiting list because the truth was much harder to face. Facing the truth, my three lifelong friends were the only ones I wanted by my side.

"I haven't been," I admitted. "If I don't go, then I still have some hope, you know? I can blame it on missing my ovulation or stress." My heart was racing. My vision blurred as tears formed in my eyes. "But if I go to a doctor ... if I do those tests..." I used all my strength to try to get the words out my mouth, but nothing came except the fall of my tears.

"If you go, then you'll have to accept that there is something wrong," Halima finished for me. She had abandoned the floor and joined us back at the table.

"What if they say it's impossible and I'm infertile? How do I go on from that? How do I break Yousef's heart by telling him I can't give him the family that he so badly wants? What do I do if they tell me my body is broken? What do I say if they tell me my body is incapable of doing the one thing a woman *should* be able to do?"

"Aw, sweetie," Rani pouted. "You are not broken. This isn't something you did wrong. It's just biology."

I shook my head, refusing to belittle it to something so trivial. "It's my marriage," I cried.

"Yousef loves you so much. It's clear as day. I'm always moaning at Idris to be more like Yousef," she humoured. "He wouldn't leave you over this."

I swept away my tears and, for the first time in six years, I shared some ugly truths about my marriage with my friends. I didn't tell them everything because the urge to protect Yousef and his family from their harsh judgement was too strong. But I let out some of the small heartbreaks I hadn't shared with anyone and the one that had left the biggest crack: the argument with his mum. At the end of my unloading, my friends took some time to process it all. I waited for some advice and opinions, confident they would be honest.

Rani went first. "First of all, his mum was out of line. She had no right to speak to you like that, let alone in front of other people. Ravi's mum tried that once. I had a much bigger reaction than you, so Yousef needs to chill."

Zoya clicked her tongue. "I don't know. I agree she was out of line, but I understand where Yousef is coming from. He wasn't hurt by *what* you said, more the *way* it was said. If I spoke to Idris's mum like that, my tongue would have been cut by her and my head chopped by him. Every family is different but that wouldn't go in my house. It's just a respect thing." She shot me a pleading look. "I'm not saying you were wrong for snapping. I think it was a long time coming, but maybe you should apologise."

"Hell no!" Rani jumped in. "Don't you dare apologise to her. You're just letting her know she can get away with it and she'll do it again."

Zoya shook her head. "But this isn't about her mother-in-law. This is about Yousef." She looked at me. "He's upset, and he's asked you to apologise. It's just a word."

Halima chuckled. "That's true. An apology is just a word. People say it all the time and never mean it. Even if you wait for her to apologise, what's to say she won't just do it again?"

"The point is, she'll say it," Rani deadpanned.

"Okay. And then what?" Halima retaliated. "She'll do it again. And then what will you do?"

I shrugged. "I don't know."

She sat taller. "I'll tell you. You'll wait for another apology and she'll apologise for a second time. And then there will be a third incident. You *might* get another apology if you're lucky. But after the fourth or fifth time there will be no asking of forgiveness." She looked past me at the wall behind me as if she was lost in a thought, but she snapped out of it just as quick. "An apology means nothing. It's just a word, so why let it come between your marriage? Why upset Yousef when ultimately you'll end up forgiving him?"

"You mean her," Zoya interjected.

She flinched. "Yeah, sorry. That's what I meant."

Zoya took a softer approach than Halima. "I get why you don't want to give in first. *Believe me*, I do. You think there aren't times I want to scream at my in-laws and Idris? Sometimes I've been on my feet all day and then someone turns up and I have to make them tea. In those moments, I want to tell everyone to fuck off." Her eyes widened. Checking if Nadim heard, she relaxed as he was absorbed in the TV. "But I don't because that's just the way life is sometimes. I just hold it in and do whatever they ask because it's easier."

Rani looked taken aback and then, slowly, her shoulders relaxed. "I hate that you're right," she moaned. "I do the same. When Ravi complains about my clothes being too revealing or tells me to get back earlier than I would like, I just do it because it's not worth the hassle. His mum will nag his ear off, which means he'll moan at me."

Jannah climbed onto her mum's lap, rubbing her eyes. Halima snuggled her daughter against her chest. "Is this worth having a crack in your marriage?"

"Can you find it in you to let it go?" Rani asked.

"You and Yousef are already going through so much. Do you really want to add more to your plate?" Zoya added.

I sighed and looked at my friends. *Were they right?* I sought their advice and, ultimately, they all agreed.

Halima sighed. "I know it's harsh, but this might just have to be a reality that you accept because what other choice do you have?"

Divorce wasn't on the table. It wasn't something I wanted. I loved my husband. I wanted to make this work with every fibre of my being.

"What if I'm never happy?"

Silence descended on the table. We all stared at one another.

Finally Zoya said, "We have to find a way to be happy because if unhappiness was a good enough reason to get divorced, more women would be the ones that asked for it."

The laughter that the evening started with had vanished. Around the table were four women who hid behind pretty smiles and the reflection of their wedding rings. We hoped that if we spoke of the happiness we created for ourselves, it would be enough to fool the world. But as I sat with my friends, I realised that perhaps their marriages were just as hard as mine.

I thought Halima was enjoying the freedom of moving into her own flat with her small family. But the pained look in her eyes made me wonder what Nazir had done that warranted an apology she never got.

I thought Rani was enjoying the fancy dinner dates and her busy social life. But the defiant scowl on her face made me wonder how much Ravi wanted to change about her.

I thought Zoya was enjoying building the safe and loving home for her children that she wanted for herself as a child. But her downcast gaze made me wonder if Idris was any different from her controlling father.

As I drove home, I thought about the life I had imagined for myself; one that had a loving husband, caring in-laws, and the warmth of children. The heartbreak I carried made me wonder if it would ever come.

I entered the house with a heavier heart than I left with. Yousef caught my gaze as I walked past the living room, straight to the kitchen. I thought about my dream one last time. Halima was right; a life without caring in-laws and children may be a reality I have to face.

But divorce was never an option.

Having a loving husband would just have to be enough.

I stepped into the kitchen and offered an apology to the woman who never offered one back. She told me that God will bless us. She told me she was praying for me.

"Have you told anyone?" she asked before I could escape.

On instinct, I shook my head. She would never know I told my friends. "Just my family."

She eyed me from head to toe. "Good. Keep it that way." *She was ashamed.* "People already have so much to say. If they hear about this, they'll laugh behind my back." She turned away from me as she continued to ramble to herself. "The doctor *bou* that can't even fix herself. What a shame."

I held back my tears as I climbed the stairs to my bedroom.

That night, Yousef held me for the first time in a whole week. He kissed, caressed and loved my body. Right before he fell asleep, he whispered, "I love you, Sumayyah."

As my eyes closed, one thought emerged.

It's just words.

Chapter Twenty-Two

No matter how hard I willed myself back to sleep, slumber was fading quickly. I reached out to Yousef's side of the bed, only for cold sheets to greet me. On Saturdays, he typically slept in much later than I did. It was nice waking up to his body warmth for the last two weeks. Things were back to normal. I used my remaining annual leave to complete my notice period, which meant I had been jobless for three days already. I was itching to get out of the house, but I needed to prove to him that this was enough for me. I didn't *need* work. I needed him and my marriage.

I sat up and stretched. I thought about ways to make today go by faster. It would be better today because Yousef was home. Maybe we could run errands and have some time alone outside of the house. I nodded to myself. That was a good idea.

I furrowed my eyebrows when I heard my mother-in-law hiss Yousef's name. His heavier footsteps were followed by hers as they climbed the stairs to our floor. Their hushed whispers became clearer as I crept towards the door. I pressed my ear against it and tried to listen in.

"I've never seen you like this before. Look at the state of you," she said. I imagined her scanning his face with the look of pain she only reserved for her sons.

"Maa," he quietly groaned. "I'm fine."

She tutted. "If this is you fine, then just kill me. My son was never this upset before. Look at what this girl is putting you through."

This girl? I was his wife. I was her daughter-in-law; not some random woman off the street. I had spent six years in this house with them. I had cared and loved for them and that was the title she gave me.

Yousef didn't correct her. Instead, he said, "This has nothing to do with her."

"It's everything to do with her," she hissed. "She didn't want children because she was too educated. What did that education get her? Did it give her happiness? Did it give her children? All that studying and it's *her* body that is ruined. Now she's older and it won't happen for you."

I didn't realise I was biting down on my lip until the metallic taste of blood laced my tongue. Tears pricked at my eyes. Goosebumps rose on my skin. My heart pounded in anger and anticipation. He said he defended me in private. This was my chance to see if that was only words.

"You don't know that."

My heart stopped beating altogether. Was that supposed to be my defence? Disappointment filled me once again. *No.* This was bigger than disappointment. His silence left me heartbroken. Why couldn't he protect me the way he protected her?

When she spoke, she sounded genuinely pained. "I'm your mum. I know everything. I know you're not happy anymore."

Tell her you are. Tell her we went through a rough patch, but we've made progress the last two months. Tell her you love me even when it's been hard. Tell her you won't let anyone speak about your wife like that. Please Yousef, prove to me it's not just words.

"She's going to wake up. I don't want her to hear what you're saying."

My hand covered my mouth to hold my sobs in. Afraid of a few spilling out, I moved away from the door. But even with the short distance I heard what she said next.

"Islamically, you have your right to leave a wife that cannot bear children."

My eyes closed in hopes it would stop me from hearing the rest of the conversation. But it didn't.

Yousef sounded appalled. "What are you saying?"

"This life isn't enough for you. She won't be able to make you happy. Leave. You can start over. It's easy for a divorced man to find a wife."

I couldn't take anymore. I didn't want to hear what he said because what if he agreed? Every time we looked at one another, spoke or touched, I would always wonder if he wished I were someone else. That thought already crossed my mind when I would catch him staring at me, but hearing him validate that would break me.

Climbing back into bed, I threw the covers over my head and forced my tears away. I wanted to confront him, but what would that get me? He would justify her words and I'd be made into the villain again. I would not apologise to her again. I didn't want to argue, but I knew being with him all day would lead to it. *I needed to get out of here.*

Grabbing my phone, I scrolled through my contacts and wondered who to call. My friends were all occupied with their own families and I needed a distraction, not a place to talk about all this. I sent a text to the locum agency manager asking if he had any shifts available and that I was willing to travel out. When he texted back minutes later with the details, I immediately accepted and jumped out of bed.

By the time Yousef entered, his mum was no longer on the staircase. "When did you get up?" he asked. But I knew he really wanted to know if I overheard his conversation.

My tone and pitch remained neutral. "Only a few minutes ago. Dr Lloyd asked me to pick up a shift today. Is that okay?" I ruffled through my draws because one look at him and he would know how much I was hurting.

"It's the first weekend we've both been off in ages," he moaned.

I offered a disheartened look. "I know, but he's really desperate and I don't want him to think I'd flake or else he'll drop me. I'll be home in the evening. Maybe we can do something then?"

He had the audacity to look annoyed. "You couldn't even last a week without needing to go back to work." He had no right to speak to me like that after the conversation he just had. If he hadn't been so weak in front of his mum, I would have stayed home.

But I couldn't say that.

I pulled my scrubs on. "He knows I'm off and was begging me. I couldn't really say no. You have me all day tomorrow," I promised.

"Will *he* be there?"

From the bitter tone, I assumed he meant Ibrahim. His misplaced jealousy had irritation burning in me, but I ignored it because I wanted to rush out of there. "How would I know that? I didn't ask."

His grey eyes turned dark. "I don't want you working with him."

The irony almost made me laugh. He was worried about me running off with another man, while his own mother was propositioning a divorce and a new start for him. I didn't recall this level of anger when she bad-mouthed me.

"I can't control that. Even if we were at the same hospital, we wouldn't be working together. You've got to let this Ibrahim thing go," I snapped.

"I don't have to do anything of the sort. I don't want another man sniffing around my wife."

"And I don't want my husband to look at other women!" I shouted.

He looked startled. "When have I ever looked at another woman?"

You're not yet, but you will.

I cleared my throat. "I meant at work. Aren't there women at your workplace?"

For a second, he looked caught off guard and stared at me. His teeth ground together as his jaw clenched. "None that wanted to marry me," he argued.

"These days people don't care about being married. Sometimes they have a good spouse at home, but it isn't enough." I grabbed my bag and headed for the door. "I'm leaving."

He grabbed my arm and studied my face. "What's that supposed to mean?" The panic was alive in his eyes. He was trying to figure out if I had heard this pathetic attempt to bat his mother away. If he loved or respected me and our marriage, even the smallest amount, he would have commanded her to never mention divorce again.

I shook his hold off me. "Nothing," I muttered. Turning on my heels, I exited the bedroom.

"Tell Maa before you go."

Without turning around, I said, "Of course. I wouldn't want to disrespect her."

"Have you just delivered bad news or about to?"

I smiled at Ibrahim. "What are you doing here?"

He gestured to his scrubs. "Well, I'm not a patient." He took a seat on the couch opposite me. "Locum shift?"

I nodded. "My very first. It's weird not knowing all the staff. It's like the first day of school in the middle of the year when everyone has their friendship circles."

He waited until he finished chewing the large bite of his apple before speaking. "I like it. You can choose to be whoever you want to be." Ibrahim was always the tolerable confident type. But over the years, he had become self-assured. He radiated kindness and gave an aura of being content, no matter what life threw at him.

"Who are you today?"

"Ibrahim: doctor by day, but my real dream is to be a musician. How about you?"

I gave it some thought. Who would I want to be for a day? "Sumayyah, doctor by day, astronaut by night."

He let out a laugh. "That's a good time to be an astronaut because the stars are much more visible." He leaned back in his seat and crossed his ankles. "Tell me, Sumayyah, what made you become an astronaut?"

The scene made me feel like a child again; roleplaying with my friends. I sat taller and pretended I was on a live TV interview. "Who wouldn't want to become an astronaut? The freedom that comes with floating in space. Nothing weighing you down. No responsibilities except staying alive. The anticipation of something new around the corner. It's just you floating around with no expectations placed on you. It's just wonderful."

A tender gaze filled Ibrahim's eyes as he smiled at me. "That does sound pretty perfect."

I sighed and fell back against my seat. "I'm learning perfection doesn't exist."

"That depends on who you ask and what you're talking about."

"What do you mean?"

"From the outside, everything looks perfect. Just look at our jobs; a patient will look perfectly healthy and then you do an MRI and see that cancer has spread across the entire body. You look at your family and friends, and their lives look so perfect you wish it for yourself. But then you speak to them and realise it's not as good as it seems. What may be a problem for them may be the perfect solution for you. Perfection isn't a science. It's subjective."

I shook my head. "Not for some people. For some people, it's a checklist." And I have marked my perfection against the checklist everyone else has written for me.

"Those people are mistaken," he said sadly. "There is no right way to live this life we are given. Those who order life by a checklist will spend it so busy trying to tick the boxes that one day, when it's too late, they'll realise they've forgotten to live. Their lives would have passed them by and all they will have left to hold is a list that remains incomplete because though perfection is subjective, it's also unattainable a *person* to be it. You can't make everyone happy." He paused. "So settle for yourself."

Chapter Twenty-Three

The tassels hanging on my sari chimed when I walked and served as a warning that I was approaching. That was why Yousef turned and smiled at me as I approached him. I loved when he wore a crisp white shirt with a grey suit that matched his eyes. I couldn't stop myself from trying to fix his lopsided bowtie, but even after tweaking it, it remained uneven.

The family friend who we called an aunt gushed at the interaction. While she came across as sweet, she was obnoxious and felt entitled because she had a career. It was impressive that she held the position of a senior inspector in hospitals, particularly since her generation mostly comprised housewives. But that didn't give her permission to shamelessly brag every chance she got. I kept conversation with her limited, and thankfully I rarely saw her. But that evening, she was also invited to another fellow family friend's son's wedding.

Her forced posh accent added to my headache. "You tell aunty when you're pregnant because so many hospitals have poor maternity wards." She shook her head in disbelief.

My smile wavered. Yousef's didn't. He wrapped his arms around me. "Of course, aunty."

Her husband placed his hand on Yousef's shoulder. "Is that a hint?" he laughed.

Yousef laughed with him. "No. Soon, Insha'Allah."

"Don't wait too long, darling," his wife intercepted. "I've seen it all when I was a nurse. The older women take much longer to recover."

I was used to it. Everywhere we went, the conversation of babies came up. I knew I had to swallow the lump in my throat and change the subject. "How is Maria?" I asked. "Has she graduated?"

The couple shared a look of pride before bragging about their daughter securing a place on a prestigious PhD course. I had mastered the act of feigning interest. I knew precisely when to smile, nod, and gasp, all the while ignoring the breaking of my incomplete heart.

I escaped the conversation and was pulled into conversation with women my age. Nevertheless, my patience wore thin as they incessantly bragged about their children's milestones and who reached them first. Forget winning; I couldn't even enter the game.

Haniya chuckled as I sighed and took a seat next to her. "Had enough?"

"I think people turn up to these things so they can gloat about all the things they've achieved since we last saw them. Saira wouldn't stop telling us how much her house extension cost."

She scanned the room and rolled her eyes. "It's a sad life." She shuffled closer and lowered her voice. "Did mum tell you about the family coming to see me next weekend?"

I matched her low tone. "Yeah. They seem to really like him. I think Younes knows him or something like that?"

She nodded. "It's Suto Bhaiya's friend's brother."

"What do you think of him?"

She shrugged. "He's alright looking. Good job. Small family."

I sensed the hesitation. "What's wrong with that?"

"That's just information on a paper. It doesn't really tell me anything about him."

"That's why you meet him before you agree," I laughed. "You'll get the chance to speak to him and ask him about the things you don't see on paper."

Her unimpressed glare reminded me of Nafisa. "And I'll have all of thirty minutes to do that. Lucky me!" she retorted sarcastically.

It was evident she felt nervous about the next weekend. This being the first man to pass the initial test, she was scared. Her parents were nitpicking through the number of potential suitors. Nobody had been good enough to meet their daughter. Until now.

"If he or his family were terrible people, Younes would have said no from the get-go. You don't have to decide on that day. You can ask for some more time to speak with him. My cousin asked for the families met *again* before they both agreed."

Her panic was seeping through her words. "What if that isn't enough? What if I don't ask all the right questions? What if I don't really know him by the time the wedding day comes?"

Without realising, my eyes found Yousef, who was weaving through the crowd. My heart ached as I watched him. There were times it felt like we were the two strangers who met for the first time. We would ask questions about the smallest things, wanting to learn every part of one another. But then there were times it felt like I was looking at someone I didn't recognise. The old Yousef wouldn't smile and talk to the young woman his mum was introducing him to.

I turned back to Haniya. "The truth is, you don't know someone until you are married and living with them. And even then, the person you marry won't stay the same. They change because life forces them to. It's about growing with that person."

She followed my line of attention to her brother. "Are you are Bhaiya growing together?"

I absentmindedly nodded. But the truth was, we were growing apart.

"Who is that?" I asked, unable to stop staring at the woman in question.

"Aunty Habiba's daughter."

"I've never seen her before."

Haniya scoffed. "That's because she never goes anywhere, but..." The smirk on her face and mischievous tone warned of some gossip coming. "She goes everywhere now because her parents are desperate to get her married. She's close to thirty and they're struggling to get her hitched."

"Why?" I found that hard to believe. She was tall, slim and beautiful. She was fluent in Bangla from the little bits I could hear. My mother-in-law seemed very interested in whatever she was saying.

"Apparently, she gets rejected because of her age."

While I didn't like the excitement on her face while speaking to my husband, I felt bad for her. There was nothing wrong with getting married later in life. Once I turned twenty-three, people starting asking my parents if they were looking to get me married. I was lucky that my dad wanted me to finish my studies first. It felt like I was missing out because two of my friends were already married and many of my peers were settling down too. Now I'm grateful because I could not have survived marriage that young. Even at almost thirty-two, I didn't know how to navigate this responsibility.

"Hopefully she finds someone." *Just not my husband,* my subconscious added.

"I thought it was you. What a small world!" Myra gushed as she joined us. "What are you doing here?" Without waiting for an invitation, she took a seat.

Haniya looked at her in bewilderment. She looked at me; mentally asking if I knew her. My smile offered her some reassurance.

"I'm here with my in-laws." I introduced Haniya.

"Are you related to the bride or groom?"

"Neither," Haniya joked.

"Family friends," I clarified. "How about you?"

"The bride is some niece five-times-removed from my mother-in-law," she laughed. "You know how these weddings are. You invite everybody you ever crossed paths with. I don't usually come to these, but my sister-in-law couldn't make it, so Ibrahim's mum forced me and the kids along."

"Where are they? I'd love to meet them."

She stood up and scanned the room for her children. She excitedly waved at someone and sat back down. "Here they come."

Two sulky boys walked ahead of Ibrahim. The third was propped in his arms. When Ibrahim saw me, his eyes widened before he smiled. "First at work, now here! Are you stalking me?" he joked.

"I was at both places first, which would mean you were stalking me," I retaliated. "Your boys are adorable!" I gushed.

He pinched the youngest's cheek. "Take after their Abbu." His eyes landed on Haniya. "Is this your sister? She's grown so much!"

We both laughed at the same time. Her arms wrapped around my shoulders. "I'm the sister she chose."

Realisation dawned on him. "Yousef's sister?"

I nodded. "The one and only."

"We don't run into each other for five years and now we can't seem to escape one another. Is Yousef around?"

Not wanting to draw attention to the conversation he was clearly invested in, I pretended I didn't know where he was. "Yeah, he should be around here somewhere. He's the social butterfly."

"Bhaiya is the people pleaser. He puts us siblings to shame," Haniya remarked. "Honestly, he should have been a girl."

Myra laughed. "At least he's doing it for you! Saves you the hassle."

"And what about you?" Ibrahim asked, looking at me. "Who are you today?"

My laugh came out as a breathless sigh. I smiled as a nod towards our conversation a few days ago. "Today I'm a bear who wishes to hibernate. How about you?"

"I'll follow the animal theme and say I'm a kangaroo lugging my children around." At that, his second son clung to his leg.

Myra playfully slapped her husband. "Is this a new game you came up with?" She shook her head.

My heart clenched. "What's that?" I asked.

"When he knows I'm sad, he makes up a silly game to make me smile again."

Was my sadness that apparent? Could everyone see it on my face? Did it weigh down on my shoulders for the world to bear witness to? If that was true, why couldn't Yousef see it as well? Why wouldn't he offer to carry some of the burden with me? Why would he leave me alone to face it?

Myra excused herself when someone waved at her, and two of her children followed her. Haniya looked between me and Ibrahim. She cleared her throat and also left us alone. Ibrahim saw it as an invitation to take her seat. His son shied away and used Ibrahim's neck to hide his face.

"What's his name?"

"Adam."

"You have a beautiful family. Three boys must be a handful."

Subconsciously, he held his son tighter. "Work is peaceful compared to home," he mused. "Dr Lloyd is looking for shift cover the day after next if you're free."

My gaze instinctively fixed on Yousef, who was still in conversation with Habiba's daughter. He didn't like me working with Ibrahim, but I also didn't like him talking to another woman for so long. He hadn't even told me about the conversation he had with his mum yet. I doubted he would ever tell me.

"I'm pretty sure I'm free. I'll call him."

"What are you doing sitting here in a corner? You didn't dress up to hide away."

My eyebrow arched. "Firstly, I didn't *want* to dress up at all. I hate wearing a sari, but I'm a married woman, so I must dress like one. Secondly, I'm not hiding away. I did all my socialising before you got here. This is a quick break to recharge."

Ibrahim chuckled. "Myra hates these as well. I give it an hour before I get the daggers to leave."

"Can you tell her to give my husband the same because mine never works on him?"

"Sometimes it's easier to *say* it. I never know why Myra looks like she wants to kill me. We can't read your mind."

His statement had an undercurrent to it. I wondered if he knew there were deeper issues between me and Yousef. He was right; things wouldn't be so terse if I shared my worries and heartache with Yousef. But silence had become part of our marriage. We didn't discuss our struggles with having a baby anymore. We wordlessly undressed one another and completed the motions with no whispers of passion and love.

My head lowered. "It feels pointless to speak when you know you won't be heard."

I jumped when Sahil, my father-in-law, called my name. I stopped in the living room's doorway room. Despite wearing a floor-length nightgown and a scarf draped across my chest, I felt inappropriately dressed. "Ji?"

He pointed to the beige sofa opposite him. "Come and sit."

Nerves creeped into my skin and formed a lodge in my throat. I did as he asked. "Is everything okay?"

Sahil had a face of feeling at home. His kind eyes and gentle smile never failed to put me at ease. I had never heard him raise his voice. Yousef often said his dad was softer as he entered his old age. He was a passive man; never getting involved in the family politics unless there needed to be a final ruling of silence.

"You've heard about the boy coming to see my Haniya. What do you think of him?"

I wasn't expecting that. I never spoke in these matters. I was just the daughter-in-law. My opinion didn't matter, so it meant a lot that he asked me. I offered a reassuring smile. "He has a lot going for him. He's educated. He can provide for her. She'll be okay."

"What does she want?"

The trust between me and Haniya rested on my answer. She didn't say our conversation was private, but I also didn't know how much she wanted to tell her father. But she needed someone to say the things she was afraid to, and that was my job as her Bhabi.

"She's scared. She wants some time to get to know him. I explained that they can speak before, but she's young. It's scary for us women to get married."

He hummed quietly under his breath. He leaned back and his shoulders slumped. I sat still, waiting for him to say something more. I didn't know if I should leave or stay. The wrinkles around his eyes deepened as his eyes screwed shut. When he opened them, I was surprised at the tears that welled in his eyes.

"Baba?" I called.

When he spoke, his fear was clear. "Children build pieces of your heart. When I had a daughter, I was so sad. Not because she was worth less than my sons, but because she was worth much more. I knew that one day I would have to give part of my heart away. There would come a day when she would belong to someone else and I would have to continue living." He looked at me. "How am I supposed to do that?"

Before me was pure, unconditional father's love. It was wrong of me to smile, but it brought me joy for Haniya that she was loved so dearly.

"That's the way of life," I said. "She's in your home temporarily, but her love will never leave. She will always belong in your heart."

He took in a deep breath. "When I looked for a *bou*, I looked at her education and exterior. That was enough. But this time this isn't enough. How will I know if another man will love my daughter like I do? How do I know he will make her laugh? She will pack everything I built for her and live with strangers. Who cares about education and height? Those things won't build a home for her."

When his tears fell, I cautiously walked until I was sitting on the floor at his feet. "You've raised a strong daughter. She will know if he can make her happy."

His pained eyes were difficult to face as he glanced down at me. "Did you know that about my Yousef?"

My answer was honest. "I thought he would make me happy."

"Are you happy?"

The word 'yes' couldn't get past my lips. I tried so hard to force it out, but it wouldn't come. Perhaps it was because his raw honesty left me in a chokehold.

"I'm trying."

My father-in-law rarely ever touched me aside from a hug on Eid or my birthday. He gently placed his hand on top of my head. His tears fell as we stayed locked in this moment. "You are a daughter. Maybe I didn't truly understand that before, but I do now. You are a daughter," he repeated, his voice broken.

My head fell as I cried. For the first time in six years, I felt like somebody could see me as a person and I never thought that person would be Sahil.

"Your father trusted us with you. He put half his heart in our hands. What have we done?"

As his question resounded in my head, my head collapsed onto his knee. I let out the cry that had been building in me like a wave. Sahil stroked the top of my head as we cried in the middle of the night as quietly as we could. He was a father crying for one daughter he was being forced to let go and another who he had let down.

Once my tears had run their course, I lifted my head and wiped them away. This conversation wasn't about me. He needed to know that his child would be fine. "Haniya will be okay."

His fingers rested under my chin. "What about you? Will you be okay?"

I cleared my throat. "I have to be."

He nodded. "I love my son very much. He has always fulfilled his duties as a son. I have never felt ashamed to call him my son until now. If my Haniya cried like this in front of her father-in-law, I hope he would tell her to do whatever it took to stop those tears. I pray he would understand her pain and make her happiness come back."

"I pray for that too," I whispered. I cleared my throat and stood up. The sudden burst of emotion had rendered me speechless. While part of me felt embarrassed, another part of me felt lighter. Yet I asked myself the question that popped into my head earlier: *if everyone could see my pain, why couldn't Yousef?*

"What will it take?" he asked before I could leave the room.

"For what?"

"To bring your happiness back."

Without hesitation, I answered honestly. "My husband."

He slowly nodded his head. "Forgive me, Sumayyah. It took me losing my daughter to understand your hardship."

"Please don't apologise."

"Asking for forgiveness is easy. It's harder to be the one who has to forgive."

Chapter Twenty-Four

Music filled the quiet that sat between Yousef and me in the car. His eyes were trained on the road ahead and mine gazed at the trees that blurred past us. I was equally excited and nervous about a weekend alone. Reconnecting was exactly what we needed. We were so busy with other parts of our life that we neglected one another. We were co-existing with one another. We crossed paths in the house without acknowledging one another. I'd plate his food and hand it to him without sparing him a glance. Yousef would shuffle to his side of the bed once I had climbed in.

The talk I had with his dad three weeks ago was my wake-up call that it needed to stop. Our path to happiness started with a weekend getaway. No work. No family. No phones.

"Let's stop and get some groceries. Maybe we can have a nice romantic dinner," I suggested.

"That sounds nice."

I tried to think of something else to say to keep the conversation going, but my brain fell short. I had to do better, or the weekend would drag. How did it get to this? Where did it go wrong? Before we got married, we never wanted to hang up. In the early days of our marriage, it felt like there weren't enough hours in the day. We would lie in bed, talking about everything and nothing. And there I was, struggling to find something to say to my own husband.

"Haniya quite liked Ali," I eventually said.

"That's good."

"She said she wanted to speak to him a bit more, though."

"Is it?"

I realised the problem wasn't just me. Yousef was hardly trying himself.

Come on, Yousef. Give me more.

I kept trying. "Yeah. Mum wasn't happy, but dad agreed."

His eyebrows lifted in surprise. "Why?"

"He wants to make sure she's happy before things progress."

He shrugged his shoulders. I slumped back and spent the rest of the ride in silence.

After buying enough food to last a whole week, we eventually arrived at the cabin. It was larger than I expected, but not big enough to avoid one another. That was a good thing. An earthy scent hit us when we opened the door. Yousef carried our bags in and left me to wonder around. The small fireplace let me dream about spending the cold evening wrapped under a blanket in front of the fire. We would roar with laughter before he pulled me into his arms and promised to love me until the end of time. We would reminisce about the good times in our marriage instead of letting the bad times build a wedge between us.

When Yousef called my name, I snapped out of my reverie. Before I joined him in the kitchen, I promised myself that dream would come true. "Yeah?"

"Do you want to cook now or later?"

I shrugged. "Later. Why don't we go for a walk?"

"I'm tired from driving. How about later?"

My disappointment was concealed with a smile. "Okay."

He rounded to my side of the kitchen. His arms wrapped around me in a tight vise. "It's the first time we've been alone in a *long* time," he whispered. Kisses were layered on my face, starting from my temple down to my jaw.

Anticipation tingled on my skin. "Oh, yeah?" I giggled.

He hummed. My hijab was unpinned and removed. "I love your hair." He inhaled in the scent of my coconut shampoo. "You don't need to hide it away here."

My fingers ran through his soft locks. "How do you like it styled?"

His devilish smile rekindled a sleeping part of me. "Splayed across my pillow." A kiss on my neck. "What do you say to that, my wife?"

I almost cried at the title. It had been so long since he called me that playfully. I pecked his lips. "I think that's my favourite too."

With my hand in his, we left the groceries unattended. We sped up the stairs to the main bedroom. It had the same wooden furnishing as the lower ground. Yousef didn't stop to take in his surroundings, already getting undressed. The moment felt like resuscitation. Our intimate life had become mundane. It was something that we did because it was part of the package. But *this* was passion. We desired it. When I caught his gaze, I could see lust for *me*. He wanted to love me.

"Come here," he begged.

I slowly padded over to him and stood in his embrace. His toned chest was falling and rising with excitement.

"You're beautiful," he whispered. "*So* beautiful." His voice crackled with emotion.

"Make me feel beautiful," I pleaded.

I needed him to make love to me. Sex had become about getting pregnant. I needed more than that. I needed him to touch my body because he craved it.

He started to undress me gently. His lips followed where his fingers travelled, kissing every inch of my skin. He treated my body with love and care. As he placed me on the bed, I prepared to finally be with my husband. Every brush of our skin was an act of love. Yousef's eyes never left mine, as he loved every part of me. My arms enveloped his neck, craving his closeness as we were emotionally. His whispers of love, propelled by his sexual desire, did more for me than his physical movements. I held onto my husband like my life depended on it.

But then Yousef pulled the trigger and killed the part of me that had just found a reason to live again.

His head fell into the crook of my neck. "Please, Sumayyah," he begged. "Give me a baby."

My arms fell to my side. My eyes opened, and I stared up at the ceiling. My body became limp. A single tear fell onto the pillow.

He paused. "What's wrong?"

My chest felt like it had caved in. "Nothing. My leg cramped."

After that, every brush of our skin, every whisper, every kiss felt as empty as me. When he spilled his hope into me, a kiss was placed on my stomach and then he was gone.

A frustrated sigh left my lips as I struggled to style my hair with the limited tools I had. Dinner was cooked and ready to be plated. I showered and wore makeup. While cooking, I had an epiphany; we needed to fall in love with each other again. Both of us were clinging onto the people we married, but they had changed. I longed for the old Yousef while neglecting to fall in love with the new version.

I settled on letting my hair down, only pinning the front back. I didn't pack any fancy dresses, so my only option was a plain maxi dress. The water was still running in the bathroom when I plated our food and set the table. Rummaging through the cupboards, I hoped to find candles but came up empty. The lights couldn't be dimmed either, so the bright lights ruined the romantic feel I was going for.

"Something smells amazing," he complimented as he climbed down the stairs.

"I hope you're hungry."

He kissed my temple. "I wasn't talking about the food," he winked.

I lightly slapped his arm. "Behave yourself."

He looked around the room. "There's nobody here, and that sofa looks comfortable."

Playful Yousef was my favourite. I rarely saw him anymore and if earlier didn't hurt so much, I would have given in. "If you eat all your dinner, you might get dessert."

My attempt to match his light mood worked. He chuckled as he took a seat. "I've always loved dessert."

"Liar," I accused. "You've always hated dessert."

"When I said that, you weren't on the menu."

My cheeks warmed. "Eat your food."

"Thank you for cooking. It's a nice change from normal life."

I ignored the irritation I felt at his statement. It insinuated that I never cooked for him, despite me being in the kitchen with his mum most days. But he was right: it was nice to have dinner where his mum wasn't fussing over him like a toddler. There was nobody who needed to have their glass refilled. We could talk about anything. We could tease each other. It was only us, and I never realised how much I wanted that.

"How are you?" I asked. When he looked at me, confused, I elaborated. "I can't remember the last time I asked you if you were okay."

His forked twirled around his plate. "I'm okay. Work is getting busy—"

"I'm not talking about work, Yousef. I'm talking about *you*."

He looked at me. "I'm fine."

I tilted my head. "Is that the truth?"

When his phone pinged, he hesitated before picking it up and checking the notification. It only stole his attention for a few seconds, but it added to the hurt I was already carrying. He shoved another mouthful of spaghetti in his mouth. "How are you?"

Ibrahim's advice about voicing my thoughts resounded in my head. "I'm tired and not just physically. I am mentally exhausted."

Yousef wasn't expecting my honesty. He looked like a deer caught in headlights. "Why do you feel like that?"

I laughed as I put my fork down. "Isn't it obvious?"

"No. It isn't Sumayyah," he said as he shook his head. "I can't tell anything about you anymore. You shut down when you're around me. It's like living with a ghost sometimes."

My defences built up. He was the one who offered a few words. Even then, he only said two words to me. I was trying to see how he was feeling and he chose to read his texts. *And he accused me of shutting down?*

"That's because you're so wrapped up in your own world. Have you stopped to wonder why I've become like this?"

He resumed eating. As a matter-of-fact he said, "It's because you resent me."

I wanted to yank the fork out of his hands so he would devote all his attention to the conversation. "Why would I resent you?"

"You quit the job you love because you thought it was what I wanted."

"It was what you wanted," I pointed out.

"No, it wasn't." He let out a groan. "Can we talk about something else? I don't want to argue with you."

I had more to say. But I let it go because this was supposed to remind us why we chose to get married. "Okay."

Nothing else came. We chewed our food in silence. We cleared up in silence. We sat in front of the fire in silence.

"What time is your appointment on Monday?"

I had my first gynaecology appointment for a routine check. While part of me was nervous, another part was ready to know if I should give up. "Ten."

"Do you want me to come with you?"

I shook my head. "You'll just be sitting around." It was silly that I felt disheartened that he didn't insist on coming with me. I just wanted Yousef to show that he cared about me.

We were sitting on the floor, watching the flames flicker. Yousef had his back against the sofa and I sat between his legs, resting my head on his chest. Our intertwined fingers rested in my lap. Every few minutes he placed a kiss in my hair. Despite being physically close, it felt like we were millions of miles apart.

"Do you remember when we went to Dubai?" he suddenly asked.

"It was our second wedding anniversary."

"Our second night there, we went for a walk along the beach. It was so hot and clammy. We were sweating." He sounded lost in a trance as he recalled the minor details. "We had the meat sweats after the steaks we had for dinner."

A sad smile crossed my lips at memory I hadn't thought about in a long time. "They overcooked your steak."

It was as if Yousef had never heard me. "You wanted to get a cab back to the hotel, but I said we should walk it off. Your dress was white and I remember thinking there was no way you could be human because you looked like an angel. You loved me so much I kept trying to match it."

I angled myself to see his face. "You did love me."

"Not enough." His teeth bit down on his lower lip. "I held your hand the entire time, so scared that if I let go, I would lose you."

I cupped his face with one hand. "I'm here."

He finally looked at me. "Do you still love me?"

"Of course I do! Why are you talking like this?"

His lip quivered, and the first tear fell. "Because I let go."

"What did you do, Yousef?" My heart hammered in my chest as I prepared for a big betrayal. Had he fallen in love with someone else? Did he lay in bed with another woman? *Did he tell his mother he wanted a divorce?*

"I stopped being the man you married."

I shuffled around until I was kneeling before him. Taking his face in both hands, I forced him to look at me. "We *both* stopped being who we were. That doesn't mean we give up. Marriage is hard work, but we *will* make this work."

"But you're tired." He thought that meant I was throwing in the towel, but he was wrong.

My forehead rested against his. "I won't let go," I promised. "I need you, Yousef." My tears mixed with his as we held each other and cried.

"I need a family," he begged. "I want a baby. I want to love your growing bump. I want you to break my hand while in labour. I want late night feeds and nappy changes."

It was time to ask the question we had avoided. I asked it six years ago on our honeymoon, but this time I needed a real answer.

"And what happens if I can't give you that?"

Yousef squeezed my hip tight. "I don't know."

"Say it," I pleaded.

"Don't make me choose."

I pulled away from him. I moved backwards until we faced one another. "You already did."

The heat from the flames wasn't anywhere near as strong as his stare. He reached out for me, but I skimmed away. "Sumayyah..."

I took a deep breath, even though I felt like I couldn't breathe. With a confidence I didn't feel, I said, "I need to hear it."

Yousef shook his head. "This is killing us. *Both* of us. This isn't a life we deserve to live."

I was fighting for our marriage, while he was fighting for himself.

"Say it."

"I want more for you."

"Say it, Yousef!"

He stared at me long and hard. And then, for the second time in one day, he pulled the trigger. "I'll let go."

Chapter Twenty-Five

The splash of cold water made me feel more alert. I looked at my reflection and hated how emotionless I looked. I resembled a corpse because I appeared utterly lifeless. I pinched my cheeks, hoping it would bring a flush to them, but it brought nothing but pain. I gave myself one last look before making my way back to the office.

"Hey!" Ibrahim called.

I slumped onto the seat next to him and spun around to face him. "Hey. Are you on the late tonight?"

"Yeah. Myra has gone to her parent's house, so I thought I might as well or else I'll be up all night missing them. If I'm here, I can make some money while missing them."

"That's what I call a smart decision. It's been quiet since I got in, so you might be moping in the office."

He jokingly shook his head. "Just my luck. How's Yousef?"

Yousef was back to being fine. The rest of our weekend went without discussing his bombshell. I allowed myself one night to cry and spent the second night coming up with a plan because divorce was not an option. It was hard enough being the infertile woman. My life would be over if I was the infertile *divorcee*. Even if I had no children, I still had Yousef to fill part of the void. In my culture, a divorced woman was already used goods. A divorced infertile woman was destined to be alone because she wasn't any good to a man if she couldn't bear children; she was just *used*. I couldn't have that. My marriage would have to work. Yousef just needed to remember why he chose me.

My smile was back. "He's doing well." The itch on my arm was too hard to ignore and caught Ibrahim's attention.

"What's that?" he asked, nodding to the lump.

"I had some bloods done today. The medical plaster is irritating my skin."

He frowned. "I hope everything is okay." He wasn't prying for information. He was sincere in his words, but the words rushed out of me.

"We'll find out soon enough. It's to check my hormone levels. We're struggling to conceive."

The look of sympathy I was used to appeared. "I'm sorry to hear that. What have they said so far?"

"I've had a quick check of my cervix and she said it seems normal. We just have to wait on the bloods to see if it is hormones. If it's not, then they'll run further tests and scans."

Ibrahim nodded. "Well, you're in the right place. It could be nothing."

Speaking to Ibrahim felt refreshing. Perhaps it was because he was also a doctor. Or maybe it was because he always offered an alternative perspective. "How hard would you judge me if I said I hope they find something wrong?"

"I wouldn't judge you at all."

"Really? Because sometimes I do." I hesitated. "If they find something wrong, then they can offer a solution. Medication or surgery ... whatever it is, it gives hope that we can have a baby. If they don't find anything, then it just means we're going to keep trying and feeling disappointed. I don't know how much more of that we can take."

When he looked at me, I saw sincerity and understanding in his eyes. "I can't imagine how hard this has been on you and Yousef as individuals and on your marriage."

My scoff turned into a forced chuckle. "You have no idea."

"You need to stick together. Whatever happens, it's only the two of you who understand your pain. If you turn on each other, then what hope do you have?"

I stared down at my empty finger where my wedding rings usually rested. Years of wearing them had left an indent on my finger. It was a reminder that Yousef was part of me. He was embedded into my skin. He was a permanent part of me.

"Not being able to give him the child he wants has made him stop loving me," I admitted.

There was a sharp intake of breath and then silence. My honesty had rendered him mute. I didn't want him to think poorly of Yousef, but perhaps he could offer me some advice. I had no other man to confide in for advice on winning my husband back.

"What if the roles were reversed?"

I looked at him in confusion. "What do you mean?"

Ibrahim looked at me as if I was missing something obvious. "You've put all this pressure on yourself, Sumayyah. You're putting yourself through all these tests and scans. You think you're losing your husband because *you* have something wrong with you. Stop for *just* a moment and think like a doctor. What have you missed?"

I tried to follow his train of thought, but I was coming up blank. "We've tried to do it naturally. We've read every article and book on fertility. This is the only way."

He looked at me, appalled. "How much do you love your husband?"

I felt flustered at the question. "A lot."

"Would anything change that?"

I shook my head. "Like what?"

He sighed. "Like *him* being the one who cannot have children?"

I flinched at the question because he was right; I hadn't considered that. Everyone immediately assumed I was the one who had the issues. Hell, even *I* blamed myself. But it takes *two* to make a baby. This burden wasn't just on me.

My silence propelled Ibrahim to speak. "I think he should get tested. Men can be infertile too."

I bid my mum goodbye and hung up as Yousef entered the room. I took several deep breaths to calm my nerves. The conversation with Ibrahim wouldn't leave my mind. I felt stupid for not considering Yousef may also have a problem.

"Can we talk?"

He abruptly stopped getting undressed. "That doesn't sound good."

I tried to give a reassuring smile. "It's not bad. Just a suggestion, really."

"Make it quick because I need to take mum shopping." His dismissive tone and indifference to what I wanted made anger swirl in my veins.

"I'm sorry," I retorted sarcastically. "I didn't realise I had to book an appointment to have a conversation with my husband."

He rubbed his hands over his face. "I've had a long day, Sumayyah. I don't have time to argue with you."

These moments made me question why I was fighting for this marriage when he had clearly given up. "I wasn't trying to argue with you. You're the one that came in with an attitude."

His eyes closed, and he took a deep breath. When he looked at me again, he was a fraction calmer. "Okay. What is it?"

The speech I had practiced was thrown away. My plan was to delicately suggest it to him, but I wasn't about to spare his feelings when he clearly had no regard for mine. "I think you should undergo fertility tests too."

He looked at me in disbelief. "Why would I do that?"

"Because," I gritted out, "There's a chance you might be the one with the issues."

He pulled a t-shirt over his head. "No."

My fingers gripped the bedsheets to hide some of my rage. "Why not? The fertility specialist said we should *both* run tests." *That was a lie.* The gynaecologist wasn't a fertility specialist, but I didn't want to mention Ibrahim's name and definitely turn this into an argument.

"Let's get your results back first."

"But that wouldn't tell us if you have problems too."

He pulled his attention off his phone before shoving it into his pocket. "I need to go."

I stood and blocked the doorway. "We're not done talking."

"Move," he demanded. "Mum is waiting."

My arms folded across my chest. "We're not done. You aren't going anywhere until we have reached a decision."

"I told you I'm not doing it!"

"Why not?" I shouted back.

"Because it's degrading! To pleasure myself and provide a sample is disgusting."

My laugh ripped out of me. "And it's not degrading for me to spread my legs and have fingers and medical equipment stuffed *inside* me? To have the most intimate parts of me examined? This is the sacrifice for the baby you want so badly!"

"Lower your voice," he hissed. "There is a house full of people."

I didn't back down from his stare. "How can you stand there and refuse to do this for me? For our future? For our marriage?"

He checked his watch as his jaw clenched. "Let me out of this room."

How many times were we to have this conversation? How many more of my tears was he going to watch fall and do nothing to stop it?

I moved to the side. "Go. I can't even have two minutes with you. Somebody always needs you more."

Yousef shook his head. "That isn't fair. I told you now wasn't a good time."

"It's never a good time!" I screamed. "I was stupid to think you would do anything for me when you can't even give me more than five seconds of your attention."

"I would do anything for you."

The irony wasn't lost on me. "Except this."

"I said to wait for your results first." The determination turned his eyes to steel.

He wasn't going to change his mind, no matter how hard I pleaded. I expected to be consumed by sadness, but to my surprise, anger took over. Our entire marriage had been me meeting his demands and my requests going unheard. I was silent in my marriage, but only had myself to blame. Had I ever stood up for myself before? When had I ever been firm with him as he was with me? *That was about to change.* I wanted to demand the thing that would hurt him the most.

I brushed my tears away. "Okay. But on *one* condition." My throat tightened. "We move out of this house."

He stepped away from me. Betrayal shone in his eyes, followed by anger. "This is my home. It's my duty to look after my parents."

"It's your duty to look after your wife," I spat. "I want to move out. That's final." My knees felt like they had turned to jelly. It took all my focus to stay upright.

"Why? What's so bad about living here?"

"I'm done sharing my husband. Somebody always needs something and *I'm* the one that faces the consequences. I sit in this house all day, waiting for you to come home only for your mother to steal you away. We are never alone! There's always somebody in our marriage and I'm tired of it!"

Not even a trace of understanding was present in him. As expected, his shoulders tensed in defence for his mother. "It's *one* day. How often does she ask me to take her shopping? I'm her son. If she can't ask me, who is she supposed to ask?"

"She has another son! Today it's shopping, tomorrow it will be something else and the next day another thing! It's always *her* before me. You are her son, but you are also my *husband*."

He stepped towards me. "What do you want me to do, Sumayyah?"

"Stand up to her! Tell her no the same way you do to me! Be a man!" I screamed so loud, I couldn't recognise my voice. It felt like someone else had taken over my body and was saying all the things I felt.

Something in Yousef snapped. His lips turned to a scowl. His grey eyes turned to a thunderous storm. His voice was unnervingly calm, but cold. "*You* are the only one that strips me of my masculinity. The big-shot doctor," he drawled. "The wife who sits with another man at a wedding and laughs with him."

"And *you're* the husband who, at that same wedding, spent much longer with a woman who's looking to get married."

"I'm not done talking!" he bellowed. "Why would I feel like a man? My wife doesn't desire me. I have to beg her to have sex with me and even then, she lays there like a corpse."

I matched his stature. "*You* are the reason I'm like that," I said slowly, hoping each word penetrated through to him.

"Then go." He dared me to call his bluff. "Go and find a *real* man. Find a man that will move out and get into bed with him. See if he is man enough to get you pregnant."

Bile rose in my throat at his crude, disgusting words. This couldn't be my husband stood before me. My husband, *my Yousef*, would never say something so vile. He would never suggest me laying in bed with another man. There was no love in his eyes; only repulsion. My resolve broke and my chest crumpled under the weight of heartbreak. My eyes couldn't tear away from his face, but my mouth produced no words.

I waited until I heard the front door slam shut before I fell to the floor and cried. I tightly pursed my lips, fighting back desperate sobs. My hands rested on my chest as if they could stop my heart from falling apart. But every gasp brought a fresh wave of pain and that pain solidified inside me until I was nothing but a perfect example of what broken dreams are.

At least I was finally perfect at something.

Chapter Twenty-Six

My bag felt light compared to the weight on my heart. I slowly climbed down the stairs with the few things I packed in a rush. I was taking the coward's way out and leaving before Yousef returned with his mother. I could only imagine the thoughts and ideas she was filling his head with. I had to leave before seeing either of them.

No matter how badly I wanted to leave without saying a word, I knew it would turn this into an even bigger scandal. I stepped into the living room. "Baba?"

His eyes landed on the weekend bag hanging off my shoulder before resting on my blotchy face. "Are you going home?" From the look on his face, I knew he had heard the argument upstairs and was asking if I was leaving for good.

I had no reason to protect Yousef after his vile behaviour, but a good wife wouldn't come between a son and his parents. I also didn't want them to call my parents or come looking for me, so I shook my head and fed a believable lie, despite him knowing the truth. "I've been asked to cover a night shift. Is that okay?"

A frown etched itself into his face. "I think it's good you offered to help. You are a good person."

With a nod, I thanked him, but never told him the gratitude was for playing along. I gave him my salaam and headed for the front door. Before I could make a quick escape, Haniya called for me.

"Where are you going?"

It wouldn't be fair to put her in that position. Yousef was her brother and no amount of cruel words towards me would change that.

I forced a smile onto my face. "I have a night shift."

She didn't believe me. She latched onto my hand before softly asking, "Bhabi ... what happened up there?"

"I don't know," I said honestly. I was done trying to make sense of who those two people were because it wasn't the Sumayyah and Yousef I knew. They were vicious, and I didn't want to stick around and see what else may come.

"I'm going to fucking kick his ass."

I squeezed her hand. "No," I begged. "He's still your older brother. You still have to respect him."

Her solidarity with me almost resumed my tears. "That man was not my brother. When will you be back?"

For the second time, I said, "I don't know." I gave her a hug and rushed out of the house. They had been gone for about two hours and were expected to return soon. With my bag in the backseat, I sat taller and pressed down on the pedal. Just as I had done throughout my marriage, I did as Yousef asked: I left.

I drove around aimlessly. I had nowhere to go. I couldn't go back to my parents because that would mean telling them the truth and I couldn't put them through that. My dad's heart would break. My mum would make me apologise. They'd eventually find out, but that was a problem for later. I went to the only remaining place.

My hands trembled as I pressed the doorbell. I shifted my weight from one foot to another as I waited to be let in. The breath I didn't realise I'd been holding was exhaled when the door was pulled open.

Masuma grinned wide until she saw the bag and tears that had already begun. She stepped to the side. "Come in."

I stepped over the threshold and left my bag at the foot of the stairs. "I'm sorry for coming unannounced, but I didn't know where else to go." I barely sat on the sofa before I curled forward and cried into my hands.

She sat cross-legged on the other side of the sofa. "You don't need to apologise. Our door is always open to you. Your brother has just run out to the shops and Khadijah is asleep. Talk to me, Sumayyah. What's happened?"

For the first time, I told someone the whole truth. She patiently sat back and listened, only asking a few questions here and there. It felt like a load off my chest as the words flew out of my mouth. She let me say my piece at my pace and didn't get annoyed every time I started crying again.

The sound of a car rendered us silent. Panic rose in my chest at the thought of Yousef turning up and causing a scene. It was stupid to believe he would fight for me. He already told me he wanted a divorce.

"I think that's your brother. Do you want him to know?"

I frantically shook my head. "Can we keep this between us?"

"Of course. Let's talk tomorrow when he's at work. Why don't you take your bag upstairs and freshen up?"

I thanked her once again and rushed up the stairs. Their voices were muffled as I paced around the bathroom. I started to worry that leaving was an overreaction, but then I reminded myself of the horrid things we said to one another. We needed the space to help us calm down.

Just as I stood firm in my decision, my phone rang. *It was Yousef.* I debated if I should answer the call, but everything still felt too raw. I silenced the call and left the bathroom. My screen lit up again with a call from him. Putting my phone on silent, I left my phone on the bed and joined Abdul and Masuma.

"Hey," I greeted. "Hope you don't mind me intruding."

Abdul's face displayed an enormous grin. "You could never intrude. Have you eaten?"

I had no appetite, even though it had been hours since my last meal. "Yeah," I lied. "But you guys eat."

Masuma had her stern maternal voice on. "I don't think so. Sit. I'm bringing food for you. It's nothing much."

Food was the cultural way of showing love and care. It was practically the Bangladeshi love language. Abdul and I sat at the table and made small talk. I waited for a question about Yousef, but it never came. Maybe his wife had told him, or maybe it was the sad aura following me. But most likely it was because normal people didn't turn up with a weekend bag unless they were running from something.

"How are you enjoying locum work?" he asked once we had finished eating.

"It's going okay. The hourly rate is so much better."

Masuma let out a wide yawn. "I'm heading to bed. Your niece wakes up as soon as sunlight appears." She gave me a hug before she disappeared into her bedroom, leaving me and Abdul alone.

"You don't have to tell me," he started. He pursed his lips and slightly nodded his head. "I won't ever ask, but I'm always here if you need me."

My teeth clamped down onto my bottom lip as emotions swept over me. "I know."

"Does he know where you are?"

I shook my head. "I just needed some space to *breathe*, Bhaiya. It's like everywhere..." My words fell away as I gave into my cries.

Abdul let out a sigh. "Listen, marriage is hard work. Nobody said it was easy, but they never tell you how trying it really is. Give yourself some space and try to sleep. You know you are welcome here anytime."

"Thank you."

That evasive conversation was enough for me to know I wasn't alone. We both stood and tucked our chairs in before slipping into our own bedrooms. When my door clicked shut, I let out a heavy sigh. I couldn't believe that my shift with Ibrahim was only hours ago, when so much had happened. I needed to turn off the replay that was on my mind. Even knowing that, I checked my phone to see if he had called again.

36 missed called. 27 messages. 12 voicemails. All from Yousef.

Running wasn't a healthy decision, but I needed some time to decide where I went from there. I swiped away the notifications and climbed into bed. I resented the part of me that missed my bed. I judged the part that wanted Yousef next to me. But that part of me was naïve. She was the part that was still holding on. I stared up at the ceiling, sleep unwilling to befriend me tonight.

When my phone lit up again, I was expecting to see Yousef's name but it was Nafisa. "Hello?" I said.

"Where are you?" she hissed.

"Home. Why?"

The accusation was clear in her voice. "Why did Yousef call me asking where you are, then?"

I groaned. "It's fine. We just got into an argument and I needed a break. Please don't worry."

"Are you with a *friend*?" Her tone was off. Her emphasis on the word 'friend' made my eyebrows pull together.

"What?"

Nafisa was rarely ever serious. She was the laid-back one out of the two of us. So when she asked again, I felt betrayed by the suggestive tone. "Are you with a *friend?* "

She thought I was cheating on him?

"What the hell are you trying to say?"

"I don't know, Afa!" she yelled. "Your husband is calling me in the middle of the night, asking where you are and if I have Ibrahim's number."

I didn't think it was possible, but my heart sunk even further. My heart was broken, but this was a complete evisceration. How could he think I'd sleep with someone else? How little did he trust me? Did he really think I loved him so little?

My tears swam into my ears. "I need to go."

"Afa—"

I hung up. My chest heaved. My dinner was begging to come back up. I covered my mouth, so I didn't wake the house with a wail. My phone kept ringing, but I was angry at Nafisa too. She was my sister. She knew me better than anyone else and should have defended me.

She should have told him I was not immoral. Maybe I wasn't a perfect wife, but I definitely wasn't an adulterous one.

I answered the call, ready to give her a piece of my mind.

"Bhabi?" The soft voice belonged to Haniya. "Are you okay?"

"I'm..." My mouth clamped shut when his deep voice travelled through the phone all the way to my shattered heart.

"Sumayyah," he breathed in relief. "Where are you? I've been calling for hours."

Every word I knew ceased to exist. Even if I wanted to answer, my brain had shut down. Hearing his voice was more painful that I could have imagined because this Yousef wasn't the one that hurled those comments at me. This was a Yousef who sounded like he was in pain.

"Come home," he begged. "I'll come and get you. Where are you?"

He didn't care. He just wanted to know if I was with Ibrahim.

"Sumayyah, *please* talk to me."

You didn't want to talk before.

"I know you're there. I know you can hear me. *Please.* This is killing me."

Good. Now you know how it feels to be killed by the one you once trusted with your life.

Chapter Twenty-Seven

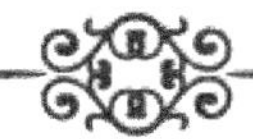

"What are you going to do?" Masuma asked while nibbling on her biscuit.

I rubbed my temples. Sleep evaded me last night; my brain was too overactive, replaying every moment and accepting that there would be consequences of leaving. Every time my phone rang, I thought it was my parents demanding to know why I dishonoured them by walking out. But it never came. That could only mean Anjuman never called to notify them. Was that her decision or forced upon her?

"Realistically, what are my options?"

"Technically, you can do whatever you want."

I sensed a 'but' coming and I was right.

"But it would be foolish to leave your marriage over one argument." She held her hands up when I opened my mouth. "Let me finish. I *know* it wasn't just this one thing, but ultimately it led you to come here. As crap as it is, this is part of marriage. Sometimes me and your brother have screamed at one another. We take our space and then sort it out. That's just marriage."

I twisted my rings around. "He didn't even say sorry last night," I whispered. "Because he's not sorry. In his view, he did nothing wrong.

He was just defending his mum as a good son should. Why should I have to accept that reasoning?"

She shrugged. "You don't. What do you want the most? You won't get everything you want from him, so decide what means the most to you?"

"Why should I have to do that? He's getting *everything* he wants. Why should *I* be the only one who has to choose?"

Sitting in Masuma's living room, I was warped back to my bridal shower in Rani's apartment. I zipped through the memories of walking in, eating cake and opening presents. For a moment, I was back in the moment when Halima warned me that this was my future.

It's a man's world and you'll do anything to keep him happy and satisfied.

My friend wasn't wrong. That was exactly what my life had become: making Yousef happy, and I had no more to give. I needed something back.

Moving out with him wouldn't give me what I wanted. I would be left with an unhappy husband and no children to warm the ice that would centre my home. If I couldn't have the loving husband, I would do anything to have the warmth of a child.

Haniya did a double-take when she saw me. She ran towards me and hugged me tight. "Thank God!" she whispered. "I missed you."

I let out a soft laugh, despite my blue mood. "It was only one night."

She scanned over me as if my scars were physical. "Are you okay?"

I cupped her face. "I will be." I excused myself and let my mother-in-law know I was home.

She surprised me by asking about my work, even going as far as asking if the ward was busy. I played along with her sweet antics, knowing she knew exactly why I left. Wanting to get this conversation over with, I feigned tiredness and took the stairs as slowly as I could.

Yousef must have heard me coming because he opened the door to our bedroom before I could. "You're home."

I didn't glance at him. I walked past him and began unpacking my clothes. I felt his presence more than ever. Every breath he took shook my core. When his ardent gaze landed on me, I wanted to melt into his arms. But that was the problem. I gave in to him every single time. I started trying for a baby before I was ready. I quit my job. I stopped working night shifts. I'd let him walk all over me. *No more.*

"We need to talk about what happened."

I placed my toiletries back where they belonged.

"You're giving me the silent treatment?"

I folded my towel away. "No, I'm just not talking to you unless I have to. We only speak when there are people around. When it's just the two of us, we sit in silence."

"That's ridiculous."

My gaze finally fell on him. Last night I conjured up an image of a broken Yousef; one that had purple hues under his eyes and pain written over him. But he looked exactly the same.

"I'm not wasting my breath on speaking when it isn't heard."

He stopped before me. "I'm listening. I was out of line. What I said ... it was wrong. I know that, but it came out in anger."

My head shook in disappointment. "Anger should never supersede love. I would *never* say something so haram to you."

With an annoyed expression, he said, "I didn't mean it like that."

My lip quivered in anger. "You told me to *fuck* another man."

"Don't use such foul language!" he snapped.

"I'm only repeating what you said."

He reached out to touch me, but I stepped away. "That isn't what I said."

"Yes. It. Was," I gritted out. "Maybe not those *exact* words, but that was what you meant. You told me to let another man touch me."

"Stop it."

Speaking over him, I continued to press every button to make him hurt. "Caress me."

"Sumayyah—"

"Kiss me."

His hands balled into fists. "Stop it!"

"*Fuck* me."

"Shut up! Stop saying those words!"

I almost smiled when he looked as disgusted as I felt. "Let those words burn you from the inside out. Every time you close your eyes, I hope you hear me saying it because I will *never* forget my husband saying that to me."

With pleading eyes, he caved. "What do you want me to do? What will it take to make this right?"

I backed away from him and threw his own words back at him. "Give me a baby, Yousef." With that, I left the room and headed to the bathroom.

Turning the tap on, I sat on the edge of the tub and let out my shaky breaths. I couldn't tell if my tears were anger, hurt, or nerves. I swallowed a large gulp of air and readied myself to get back out there. From the storage room next to ours, I took out two spare blankets and pillows we kept for when guests stayed over. On the floor of our bedroom, I laid one out.

"What are you doing?" he asked.

I ignored him and turned the lights off. My makeshift bed was uncomfortable, to say the least, but I couldn't lie next to him. It wasn't just what he said to me, but the fact he asked Nafisa for Ibrahim's number.

The lamp flicked on. "You've made your point. You don't need to sleep on the floor."

I positioned myself with my back turned towards him. "It's not a point."

"Of course it is!"

"No," I snapped back. "I don't want you anywhere near me."

His blanket was thrown off his body, and he sat up. "Get into our bed, Sumayyah! My wife is not sleeping on the floor when our bed is perfectly fine."

I turned with narrowed eyes. "The bed isn't my problem. Now turn the light off. I'm tired."

"Why are you acting like this? We had an argument and now you're behaving like a child!"

"Lower your voice," I said calmly. "There is a house full of people." I bit back my smile as the words pressed the buttons I wanted.

When he spoke again, it was at a lower level. "I said sorry."

I stared him dead in the eyes. "No, you didn't." My plan of not speaking to him was quickly falling apart. I had to find the strength to ignore his comments. I retook my sleeping position.

He turned the light off. "I *am* sorry."

"That means nothing to me. *It's just words.*"

CHAPTER TWENTY-EIGHT

MY EYES BURNED FROM the lack of sleep. I could hardly keep up with the conversation between the girls. My eyelids felt heavy, but a shrill laugh from Rani stopped me from dozing off on Halima's sofa. Meeting my friends straight from a night shift wasn't my smartest idea. I had forgotten we scheduled this weeks ago, before I picked up every night shift this past week.

It had been two weeks since I returned home and I'd been successful in my plan. When we were surrounded by friends and family, I was the loving wife. Once people were gone, my act disappeared.

I'd also slept on the floor every night we'd both been home. He made the same arguments on the second night as he did on the first. On the third night, he rehashed the argument about moving out. He said he knew I was doing this to force him to move. I reassured him it had nothing to do with that. His response was praise because he would never leave his parents. On night four, he told me I was an obstacle in the morning. I offered to sleep in a different room. He shut that down before I could even finish speaking. On night five, he said nothing. He thought giving me the silent treatment would guilt me, but it was a futile attempt. It was night six when he offered to exchange places. I politely declined. Night seven, I worked my first night shift. When I returned home, I slept peacefully in the bed. Before he returned home, I made the bed. On the eighth night, he hugged my pillow and inhaled my lingering scent. He scowled at me on night nine because I changed the sheets and I had done that every day since. I work during the nights and change the sheets after I wake in the afternoon.

Despite all that, Yousef was yet to give me what I wanted. I hated being that way with him, but I needed him to know I was being serious. I would not give in.

"Earth to Sumayyah! Did you hear that?" Rani asked.

My friends looked at me like I was an alien.

"Sorry, I was daydreaming. What did you say?"

Zoya sighed. "I'm pregnant."

My first genuine smile broke out for my friend. I pulled her in for a hug. "Alhamdulilah! That's amazing news."

"Yeah," Halima dragged the word out. "She missed the entire conversation."

I put my hands up in surrender. "Sorry! Sorry! I just came off a thirteen-hour shift. I'm totally present now. I'm all ears!"

"I was just saying I'm not ready for another one. I don't want to do the whole newborn-mother thing again. It feels like I've *just* got some of my life back. The boys are old enough for me to leave with extended family. I can finally poop in peace! There are no more nappies and potty training. They're *finally* in school!" she whined.

"Sounds like they're old enough to raise the baby for you," Rani joked, earning chuckles from us.

Halima rubbed her shoulder. "It might be easier thing time *because* the boys are both older. With Nadim, you still had a small toddler."

"And you've got tons of experience," I added. "You'll see that this baby is a blessing."

Zoya slapped her forehead. "Oh, God! I'm such an insensitive bitch. I'm so sorry Sumayyah."

No part of me felt anything but happiness for my friend. I didn't feel bad for myself until she said that. I didn't let her know, though. With a smile, I said, "Don't be silly. Just because I'm having struggles, doesn't mean you can't feel the way you do." When the tension never went away, I added, "Seriously, guys. I'm okay. I took no offence."

She shot me a pleading look. "Accept my apology anyway?"

"If you insist."

Rani perked up. "Hey! If you're looking to give your baby away, I've got a great idea. My mother-in-law won't stop nagging me about giving her a grandchild. Let me take yours and plop it on her lap. She said she wanted *a* grandchild. She didn't specify that it had to be biologically hers."

Laughter burst out of us all.

"Would you ever consider having one?" Halima asked her.

"Hell no! I'm perfectly content with the life, body, job, and money I have."

"You don't ever just wonder what it would be like to carry a baby?" I asked curiously. "Have you never craved a little creation of you and Ravi?"

She shrugged her shoulders like we were talking about the colour of the walls. "Not really. Why is that so hard for people to understand?"

"I didn't mean—"

She waved me off. "Not you, but generally. The day after I got married, at least three people asked me when I would want to try because

I was getting old." She added quotation marks with the last word. "You should have seen their reaction when I told them I didn't want children. You'd think I told them I murdered their father and framed their mother for it. Some people just aren't meant to be mothers."

🎀🎀🎀🎀

"How are your friends?" Yousef asked.

We were already in our new sleeping arrangements. I ignored his question.

"No night shift tonight?"

I closed my eyes and tried to sleep. After being tired the whole day, sleep slipped away. I knew I was on full alert because I was seeing my husband after more than twenty-four hours.

Just as I was drifting into slumber, Yousef began shuffling around on the bed. "Please, just come back to our bed. I won't behave like that again. I've learnt my lesson. I miss having my wife in bed with me. I miss *you*. Please, just come back to me. I will spend the rest of my life making it up to you." He paused for a moment. "I love you, Sumayyah. I have waited my whole life for you and I am sorry I fucked it up. But I promise to be better because I love you so much it hurts when you're not next to me."

His raw emotions took a knock on my strength. I clutched my blanket tightly, as if it embodied the sheer determination I needed to hold on, because a mere declaration of love wasn't enough. He had to prove it by getting his fertility tests started.

"I've had a long day. Stop talking."

"I'll talk until sunrise if it annoys you back in our bed."

"It'll just annoy me to another room."

"Sumayyah." My name itself was the plea. His desperation was clear, and it only pushed me to keep going until he gave me what I wanted. "I've had enough of this. I will pick you up and drag you here."

A migraine was oncoming. "Touch me and I will scream until the entire street hears me," I threatened. "I've been nice and hidden our problem from everyone, including *your* family. It's the only reason I came back and I'm sleeping in this room."

His smile of hope could be heard. "That means you haven't given up on me."

Dammit. Why did I have to say that? Time to do some damage control.

"It's only because I can't put my parents through the pain of knowing the husband they chose for me has hurt me. It would break their heart." My harsh words finally brought me the silence that I wanted. I pulled the blanket around my body tighter and prayed that I could escape reality for a short few hours.

That never came.

Before I knew it, Yousef was on the ground next to me. He pulled me towards him so my back pressed against him. His arms locked me in place and his head rested in my neck.

I tried to shuffle out of his hold, but he was too strong. "Get off me," I snapped. "I'm not having sex with you."

His hot breath fanned my skin. "I don't want sex. I just want to hold my wife. *Please.*" His voice came out weak and desperate. "Let me hold you."

When I failed to elbow him, I said, "Don't make me say it again."

He didn't lift his head. He stayed in that position and held me tighter. "They didn't choose me. You did. Tell me you chose me." His racing heartbreak could be felt on my back. "Please. Say it. Tell me you chose me. It wasn't them. It was you. Sumayyah. You chose me. Tell me you chose me." His voice cracked and when his cry followed, my resolve broke.

My face turned into my pillow, hoping it would catch all my tears. That didn't stop me from feeling his tears dampen my skin. "Stop," I begged.

"I need to hear you say it."

My cry hiccupped. "I can't because this isn't what I chose. This isn't the life I wanted. You aren't the husband I dreamed. You broke my heart with just a few words. All I wanted was something from you. I *needed* you to share this weight with me and you walked out instead."

His body shuddered. "I'm sorry." He lifted his face, only to rest his cheek against mine. "I'm so sorry. Forgive me. I'm begging you."

"It's not enough."

He sat up and pulled me up with him. With ease, he turned me around and held my face. "What will be enough? I'll do anything."

I kneeled before him. "I want a baby."

His forehead rested on mine. "Then come back to me. I want my wife back."

"And I've needed my husband."

"I'm here," he promised. "I'm not going anywhere."

"Your silence broke one part of me. Your words broke the other. Neither of those will mend me."

When he looked at me, it was with determination. "What will?"

According to Masuma, I had to select what mattered the most. Maybe this one thing could grant all my wishes. Maybe, just maybe, I'd be the perfection my father dreamed of me. I would have the dream job, husband, and children.

I matched his determination. "Get your fertility tests done. Take ownership of your half of this failure."

Chapter Twenty-Nine

I HELD BACK ANNOUNCING my arrival to my parent's house because it was eerily silent. Normally, my mum would be running around with some form of housework and my dad would be speaking to someone in Bangladesh loudly over the phone. There was nothing but silence. The front door clicked shut behind me and I wandered into the house looking for either of them. When downstairs was empty, I climbed the stairs up to their bedroom.

"Kitha oiseh?" I asked.

My mum was tucking my sleeping father into bed. She hissed at me to be quiet and pointed for me to leave the room. When she joined me a few minutes later, she couldn't hide her worry. "Your dad hurt his back somehow. He hasn't been able to walk the past few days."

I followed her down the stairs. "Has he been to the doctors?"

"Who's going to take him? He can't drive in this state."

I snatched the laundry out of her hands. "You could have called me or Nafisa. One of us would have taken him."

She waved off my concerns as though we were talking about the weather. "You guys are busy. He'll be fine with some paracetamol and rest."

"Amma! I'm a doctor and I am telling you he needs to be checked out. It could be so many things."

Her lips turned to a mocking smile. "Go then, Mrs Doctor. Examine your dad."

My hand rested on my hip. "He needs to have a scan."

She strutted away with her basket of laundry, muttering on about how my generation thought we knew everything. I came to relax, not to hear her lecture. Thankfully, Nafisa's yell travelled through the house. I rushed to the door in excitement to see my niece. She was growing all too quickly. I was letting too many weeks pass between my visits, but it was hard to find the time to make arrangements.

"How's my Moina?" I asked, already unbuckling her out of her car seat and pulling her into my arms. She stared up at me in wonder, having no idea who I was. "She's getting so big!" I gushed to Nafisa.

She was still in her jacket as she unpacked Aila's stuff. "I know right! The days are flying by. Gone are the days of sleeping twenty-two hours. Your niece is a right attention seeker."

I playfully poked her cheek. "Just like her mummy," I joked. "Do you need a hand with that?"

"She's overdue a feed, so get ready to hear her screams."

Nafisa was not wrong. Aila was loud enough to garner the attention of the entire street. Her eyes screwed shut and her mouth opened to let out the loudest cry of hunger. I couldn't believe that such a sound could come out of a tiny body. I bounced her as I walked. I tried baby talk. I turned and twisted her. But nothing calmed her until she was sucking of the teat of her bottle and warm milk eased the hunger in her stomach.

"Amar nanu aicheh!" My mum smiled brighter than ever at the sight of her granddaughter. "Why was she crying?"

Nafisa answered with one word. "Hungry."

My mum tutted. "No good. No crying," she said in her broken English. "Do you want to eat?"

Her eyes came alive at the question. "Yes! She never let me eat the whole day. She was crying non-stop."

"Aicha." *Okay.* "Let me make the curries hot."

I took a seat on the sofa next to my sister. "Why has she been crying?"

Nafisa rolled her eyes. "Just one of those days and her dad has been sleeping all morning because he worked the night shift yesterday. My in-laws have gone back home and all his siblings were out. So it was just me with a screaming baby."

"You should have told me. I would've picked you up."

Her sigh was one of tiredness. "It's fine. This is life now that I'm a mother." She looked out the window onto the street. "Where's Abba? His car is there."

I pointed up to the ceiling. "He's upstairs in bed. Apparently he's hurt his back. How do you not know?"

She shot me a look of annoyance. "When did you find out?"

"Today but—"

"But what? Why are you acting like it was a crime that I didn't know?"

Her attitude caught me off guard. "I didn't *say* anything."

"Your tone said it all."

I didn't want to argue with her. I missed my family and wanted a nice evening with them all. I evened my tone in hopes of killing the building tension. "I just assumed you would know because you live just around the corner. I thought you spoke to mum every day. That's all."

Another eye roll was directed at me. "Yeah, well, I have a baby. What's your excuse?" The irritation in her voice attacked less than her insinuation.

"What's that supposed to mean?"

She turned slightly away from me and looked down at her daughter. With a shrug, she said, "You're not working. You don't spend your days running around like a headless chicken after a baby. Why don't you have the time to call mum and see how they're doing?"

I sat taller. "You think because I don't have a child, I've got all this free time?"

"Don't put words into my mouth, Afa. That isn't what I meant and you know it. I was simply asking you the same question you asked me. You basically judged me because I hadn't called mum and found out about dad. I was simply asking what was your excuse because if you think *I* have the time to call when I've got a baby, then that means so should you."

It was hard to admit that she upset me. Did she think she was entitled to live her life because she had a family and I didn't? She assumed I was sitting at home watching the paint dry. It felt like she thought my life had no purpose or meaning.

"Just because I don't have a baby doesn't mean my life is easy," I retaliated.

Nafisa put the bottle down on the coffee table and began burping Aila. "Okay. I never said it was."

"But you did," I pointed out. "You just said that."

"Oh, for fuck's sake!" she snapped. "Why are you making this into such a big deal? Neither one of us knew. Okay. Get over it. I don't understand why you're turning it into an argument."

"I'm not arguing with you!"

"Yes, you are! Just get out of my face."

I stood up and stared at her. "What is wrong with you today?"

She looked up at me with anger. "I'm sleep deprived. My body is aching. My baby hasn't slept properly and keeps crying. I came here to relax, not have you act like a miserable cow."

"You don't need to take it out on me," I grumbled as I walked past her. I helped my mum bring the curries to the table. When she set out only one plate, I asked, "What about me?"

"I thought you already ate. Just get another plate out."

Why hadn't she thought I would be hungry? Like Nafisa, did she believe I had no obligations before arriving here?

When Nafisa joined us, she handed Aila to our mum and took a seat at the table. "How long has Abba been unwell?" she asked.

"Only a few days," she answered. "If he doesn't get better, I'll tell Mahmood to take him to the doctors when he's free."

I stopped plating my food. "One of us can take him."

"I hope you're talking about yourself because I'm on my own with Aila for the next few days."

My irritation was taken out on the saucepan lid by slamming it down a little hard. "You can leave her here with mum, or take her with you."

Her eyes narrowed. "Do you know how hard it is to get out with a baby?"

A repeated mantra of *no* came out of my mum. "Don't bring her out unless you need to. The GP is full of sick people and you don't want her to catch anything. Sumayyah can take us if needed."

And there it was again: the assumption that my life had no purpose because there wasn't a child for me to take care of.

"What if I'm busy?"

"Eh? Busy with that? What work do you have?" My mum sounded baffled at the idea of me having something to get on with.

I raised my eyebrow at them both. "I might not have a baby to look after, but what about my in-laws and husband? My hori would never shut up about me leaving the house without getting the housework done."

"So take him when you're done."

Her attitude made me snap. "Or maybe you can finally step up and do something for your parents."

Nafisa stopped eating. Her gaze burned with disbelief and anger. "I stepped up when you were married and it was just me here. How often did you come unless it was for a break? You stopped doing your part the second you got a new family."

"That's not true! I did as much as I could."

She looked at my mum as if she knew her side would be taken. When my mum gave her a look to drop it, it was ignored. "You did nothing. It was all about your husband and his little family. I still did my part after I was married. I popped in to see them. I called mum every day and asked about dad. I still completed their forms and offered to take mum places. You did nothing and nobody ever complained. But now you want to sit there and say that *I* need to step up?" She scoffed. "I grew up. I did my part, but my life has changed and I have a new priority. You don't."

There was resentment in my sister towards me I had never noticed, or perhaps she was right; maybe I just never cared. I knew she tried to fill my shoes once I was married. But I had done it for twenty-six years while she skated by. I had to become everything they wanted because they knew she would never try to fulfil their dreams.

"You think just because you have a baby, you can give up your family?"

"If you can give it up for your husband, why can I do the same for my child?"

I pushed my plate away. "I didn't do that."

"Yes, you did," she gritted out. "The night I went into labour, I called you, but you were too busy playing wifey."

"You know how my mother-in-law is."

"Maybe you need to grow a backbone then! For God's sake, Afa! It's pathetic how hard you try to please them."

Tears brimmed in my eyes. "You have no idea how hard my life is!"

Her chair scraped across the floor as she stood up. "No! *You* have no idea how hard my life is because you don't have a child! The constant fear that I'm doing it wrong. The sleepless nights and dragging days. I don't have a minute to myself! It's hard being a mother and until you do it, you have no right to judge me."

Because you don't have a child.

My heart ached at the way she threw those words at me so carelessly. It wasn't a lifestyle choice. It was a burden that I had to carry and she knew how heavy it was.

"How dare you throw that in my face?" My voice shook with a blend of disbelief and hurt.

There was no remorse in her face. She held a look of confidence as she stood by her harsh words. "Here we go again. You can't use that as an excuse to win every argument. You don't win brownie points or have every one of your faults excused because you are struggling to have children. That isn't how life works. You win some and you lose some. Find a way to live with it."

I couldn't believe that this was my sister speaking because the woman before me wasn't the sister I had nurtured since she was born. The person sat opposite me had forgotten how many times I had comforted her when people spoke ill of her skin colour or when she would get yelled at for being terrible at housework.

How could my own sister not understand my pain?

"That's easy for you to say when you've carried a baby. Just imagine your life if Aila never existed. If there was no nighttime cuddles or the sound of her babbles to fill the silence in your home. What would you do if you yearned for something that wasn't destined for you?"

The ice in her expression thawed a little. "You've spent your whole life thinking you were *destined* for happiness. Happiness isn't granted. You build your happiness based on what you have around you. But nothing has ever been enough for you. No matter how much you achieved, you craved more because you have an obsession with being the most perfect person ever."

I stood tall, no matter how small I felt. "There's nothing wrong with having big dreams."

"Maybe if you stopped for just one moment and looked around you, you'd see there's plenty for you to be happy about. Not all dreams are meant to become reality. Perhaps this is all a test for you to learn to be grateful for everything you have."

My mum finally stepped in. "That's enough. Both of you be quiet and eat."

I sucked in my sobs and silently ate the food on my plate. When my dad came downstairs, I kept my head bowed as he played with his grandchild. Nafisa said less than two words to me for the rest of the day. I said nothing to her at all. I kept my composure until I got into my car. I drove away from the home that was once filled with proud parents and a loving sister.

At that moment, I wanted nothing more than to be held close, so I didn't feel so alone. There was nobody that understood me. So, I parked on a quiet street and cried by myself in the middle of the night. I wrapped my arms around myself and reassured myself it would get better. I wept until there was nothing left. And when I went home to Yousef, I put on a smile, let him undress me and strived for my dream once again.

CHAPTER THIRTY

MY HEART POUNDED AS I waited for the doctor to give me the bad news. I knew it was bad news because if she hadn't found anything, then I wouldn't have been asked to make an appointment to discuss the results of my blood test.

"Overall your bloods came back normal," she started. "Your oestrogen levels were a little too high."

I nodded. *Okay, this was easily fixed.* "How do I combat that?"

"A few lifestyle changes such as lowering your stress levels and maintaining a healthy diet. A low-fat high-fibre diet will help your liver process the oestrogen."

Her advice didn't ease the anxiety I felt. My stress came from this issue, and my diet wasn't particularly unhealthy. "What about medication?"

She rummaged through her draws before presenting a contraception leaflet on the table. "Many of my patients have found that the combined pill, IUS or implant help relieve the symptoms and control the bleeding."

I pushed the pamphlet away. "This won't work for me because I'm trying to get pregnant."

That captured her interest. "How long have you been trying?"

"About three years?"

She turned to her computer and tapped at her keyboard. She skimmed through my notes before turning back to me. "Have you fallen pregnant at all?"

I shook my head. "No."

The cogs were turning in her head as she hummed to herself. "Tell me more about your methods of trying to conceive."

"We've been tracking my cycle and actively trying during my ovulation period. I've been monitoring my basal temperature to try during the optimal window. We try our hardest to do this every month and I'd say we've upheld it ninety-five percent of the time."

The loud clicking of the keyboard added to the oncoming headache. "What is your period like? Are they regular? Is it a heavy flow?"

I shrugged. "They're fairly regular. I've always had a heavy flow, but nothing too abnormal. I get period pains, but it's never been unbearable." As a doctor, I knew when a patient presented pieces of the puzzle we're trying to put together. I saw that on her face. *She knew something wasn't right.* I continued, hoping she would understand how desperately hard I'd tried. "We've read all the books on trying to conceive. We've tried every method, position ... everything. I don't know what we're doing wrong."

She directed an understanding smile at me. "Dr Rahman, you have done all that you can. I'm going to refer you for an ultrasound scan just to make sure that everything is okay."

"And if it isn't? Or worse, what if it is?"

"If we find something, we will look at the best course of treatment. If the result comes back normal, then we will run further tests."

As I looked at her with despair, I wanted her to tell me I would be fine and there was nothing wrong with me. "Is there a chance I could be infertile?"

She looked away. "Let's not jump ahead too soon. Let's start with the ultrasound."

🎀🎀🎀🎀

When Yousef asked me what happened at my appointment, I recapped everything and waited for him to say something.

"At least she's doing something about it. That's good, right?"

I was standing between his legs as he sat on the bed. My fingers brushed through his hair before resting on his neck. "I guess. I just want to know what it is so we can do something about it."

He reached up and took my hands in his. My heart warmed when he kissed my row of knuckles. "We'll know soon."

We both sighed into our empty bedroom. I allowed myself one moment to close my eyes and envisage a future where we both held our baby and looked back at this time, knowing that it was all worth it.

"I guess I took a day off work for no reason," he mused, breaking the silence.

"What do you mean?"

"I can cancel my appointment now."

My body stilled. "You still need to go to your appointment."

"Why?" he asked, confused. "We know it's a hormone problem."

I took a step back. "If that was the sole problem, she wouldn't be sending me for further tests. That isn't the reason we can't have a baby. There might still be a problem with you."

He shrugged. "Well, let's just wait and see what happens with you."

A scream of frustration begged to be released. I settled on pulling at my hair. "And what if my tests come back normal? Are we really going to wait *another* month for your appointment? Then wait weeks for your results? We need to be on top of this Yousef! We've wasted three years just hoping and praying. It isn't enough anymore. We need science and medicine!"

He looked at me, unimpressed. "I'm hardly shooting blanks."

I could have screamed. We could have argued. Medical jargon could have been thrown at him, but I knew it was futile. After the promise he had made to me, he was turning on his word and I wasn't going to beg him again. With that in mind, I shook my head and told him I was heading downstairs to help get dinner ready.

I was tired of feeling like helpless and invisible. How much more could I beg him to do this one thing for me? I never asked for anything. I was ready for every crevice of my body to be examined, but his pride was too big for one appointment.

The waft of spices attacked me as I reached the ground floor. I followed the trail to see my mother-in-law rushing to get dinner on the table.

"Tell Yousef to close the windows."

Had I waited until I was calmer, I would have kept my snarky comment to myself. But in my rush to get away from my husband, I forgot about his family. I scoffed at her. "Do you think I can get your son to do anything? You tell him. He worships you."

"What did you say to me?" Her voice shook with disbelief.

"You tell him."

Her furious stare stayed trained on my back as I carried plates to the table. She waited until I was back in the kitchen to respond. "How dare you speak to me like that?"

All I could hear was Nafisa telling me to stand up for myself. "Did I say anything wrong? You say run, and he goes like a mindless idiot. I ask him to go to his appointment and he throws a tantrum."

In an overdramatic fashion, her hand flew up to her mouth to swallow her gasp. "How could you call my son an idiot? Don't you have any shame that you're saying such things about your husband to his mother?"

"He's your son, not my husband."

"Astaghfirullah," she whispered. The arabic word expressed shock and disapproval. "With such a loud voice, you said he's not your husband. Have you lost your mind? Do you understand what you have declared?"

I wanted to remind her she was the one that told him to divorce me and find himself a sparkly new bride, but that would mean admitting I was eavesdropping. Instead, I said, "What part of being a husband has your son fulfilled? In my entire marriage, my husband has never been mine. He has done nothing for me. Even now, when it is to help us have a baby, he won't do as I asked and go to the doctors!"

She waved the spoon in her hand at me. "Why should he go to the doctors when you've got the problem?"

I slammed the glasses down on the countertop, forcing the cold water to spill over and create a mess. "Maybe because your son isn't as perfect as you think!"

Footsteps came rushing towards us as our shouts resounded in the house.

"What happened?" Younes asked.

At the same time, Haniya asked, "What has mum done now?" Her glare was directed at her mother.

In a blur of words, she answered, "She came down and started giving me attitude. She started saying that Yousef isn't her husband. This is what her family has taught her." She spat at the floor. "She's been sleeping with a man that isn't her husband, apparently."

"I'm sure that isn't what she said," Younes said, trying to calm the situation.

With my back turned to her, I faced Yousef's siblings. "Tell her," I pointed at their mum, "To stop talking shit on my family."

"Sumayyah!" She screamed. "Lower your finger! Do you think being a doctor makes you a big woman to point a finger at your elder?"

I turned on my heel and laughed at her. "When I first married into this family, it was your pride and joy to have a doctor as a daughter-in-law, and today it's the thing you hate the most. Why?"

She looked at me in disgust. "Even a man doesn't work as much as you, and you are a woman. A woman who failed in her duties as a wife and daughter-in-law. What have you ever done for us? First, you showed all this fake love by taking me shopping and to one or two appointments. Now, you can't even make me a cup of tea." She scoffed. "You've done nothing but make my son miserable."

I stopped going out of my way to help her because it was never appreciated. She always found something to complain about, and I just didn't want to hear it anymore. The truth was something she was never ready to admit: the only power she had was in this house and she would never risk losing it. But I never wanted to replace her or take away her role in her son's life. I just wanted to be part of it. I bled and all for what? It was only me that was dying because I was the only one cut. I'd spent so much time stitching their wounds, I hadn't realised it was me that was bleeding out.

"I've done everything I can to make him happy!" I screamed. "There isn't anything left for me to give to you people!"

This time she laughed. "Except give a baby."

Haniya pulled on my arm. "Bhabi, let's go."

I yanked my arm out of hers. "Do you think I haven't tried? Every time I close my eyes, I pray for the chance to be a mother. Every day is a reminder of what I don't have. I don't need you or anyone to remind me of something I can't have. As a woman, how can you not understand my pain? As a woman, how can you come between my marriage?"

"Bhaiya, take her from here," Younes said.

Yousef's hand wrapped around my arm. "Come."

I struggled against him. "All I have done is try to be what you want me to be. What more do you want?" I stared at her, wanting an answer.

Her lips curled into a snarl. "Get her out of my house."

I pushed Yousef off me. "This isn't your house. It's my husband's house."

"Sumayyah!" Yousef roared. His fingers painfully dug into my arm. "Be quiet!"

She smirked at me as his eyes burned holes into the side of my head. "Just a few minutes ago you said he wasn't your husband, and now I mentioned this house and you've changed your mind?"

If I hadn't taken the Hippocratic Oath, in that moment, I would have lunged for her. Instead, I used my words to inflict the same volume of pain. "Do you think a woman like me needs to freeload of a man? My father raised me to be better than that. I have never, not even once, taken a penny from your beloved son, even though it is my *right.*" I looked around the room in an overdramatic fashion. "Have your precious house, because it is all you will ever have."

Yousef yanked me. "Shut your mouth, Sumayyah!"

"*This* is the wife you chose," she chided him. "Behsharam." *Shameless.* "No respect. No honour. Just an education."

I stepped to her. "And what do you have?"

Her eyes shifted from disgust to mockery. "It's a good thing Allah never blessed you with children. Maybe there's a reason."

She intentionally chose the one statement that would weaken me. I would not cry in front of her. She would not know how deep her words cut me.

"Mum!" Haniya screamed.

"What's all this shouting?" Sahil asked as he made an appearance.

I looked at my father-in-law and repeated the words he once said to me. "I am a daughter, but not to this family. Here I am shameless and disrespectful." I put both my hands up in a begging motion. "Forgive me."

He walked behind me as I left the kitchen. "Sumayyah," he pleaded. "Stop."

When I looked at him, I couldn't stop a few tears from escaping. "You asked what it would take to bring my happiness back, and I said my husband. It turns out I never had him in the first place. He was only ever meant to be a son. A man that isn't ready to fulfil the duties of a husband will never be ready to fulfil the ones of a father."

Chapter Thirty-One

I NEVER IMAGINED MY marriage to look like this. I expected arguments and disagreements, but I never thought I would pack my bags to escape the hell I was living in. My knees felt weak as I rummaged through my drawers and wardrobe to fill a bag with my stuff. I knew it was unfair to turn up to Masuma's house again, but I feared what would come if I stayed here.

The bedroom door slammed shut. "What the hell was that about?" Yousef shouted.

I brushed my tears away and ignored him. It was pointless to talk to him, as he would never see things from my point of view.

He threw my bag to the floor before screaming, "Sumayyah!"

Picking up my bag, I avoided looking at him. "Let me go," I begged. "Just ask me for a divorce."

His firm hands came down on my shoulders and shook me. "Talk to me! What happened down there?"

I stepped out of his hold. "Ask her because I'm done Yousef. I can't do this with you anymore. Every day is a battle and I can't keep up anymore."

His voice was cold. "You raised your voice. You showed no respect. You said some despicable things. All she asked you to do was relay a message, and you completely blew up on her."

"Everything is always my fault. Fine. Whatever. Blame me. I don't care."

I didn't want to argue with him. There was nothing left for me to say, but Yousef wasn't ready to let this go until he nailed my coffin shut. "This was your fault. You were upset with me and took it out on her. She reacted the way she did because of the way you spoke first. You may run your household, but you do not run mine. In this house we listen when an elder speaks. We don't point fingers and raise our voices."

I zipped my bag shut and slung it over my shoulder. He could speak until he turned blue; I had no interest in hearing his excuses for her bullying.

"You belittled me in front of my own mum. You stood tall and declared I was not your husband. How does that make me look? How do you think that makes me feel?"

Blindly, I turned on my heels and shot him deadly daggers. "What about how I feel? Or does that not matter because I'm just the woman? My life is *not* about making you happy. I've been doing that and where has it got me?"

He gestured to the bag on my shoulder. "Your solution is to run away at every minor hurdle."

I looked at him in disbelief. "If you think this is a small hurdle, then perhaps that is the problem. You heard what she said to me. Did you ask her to explain herself or is she excused because she's the woman that gave you life?"

"How would you feel if your son turned his back on you?"

"If I deserved it, then I would live with it. But as your beloved mother said, maybe there's a reason I haven't been made a mother. I'm starting to believe it's because my son would let me down the way my husband has. You do whatever you have to do to make your mother happy. Just leave me out of it."

Yousef stared at me with a mixture of anger and disappointment. "You walk out of here, and there won't be a place for you to come back to."

Maybe it was the exhaustion of this life that made it so easy to pull my weddings rings off my fingers. His facade wavered as I called his bluff. I tried to ignore the way his fingers trembled and his chest caved. His mouth opened, but nothing came out as I placed my rings on the bedside draw.

I stood tall and nodded at him. I took one last look at him and memorised this version of him in my head because it was this memory I needed to keep myself away from him. "That night when you begged me to say that it was me who chose you, I wondered why it meant so much to you. I think I finally understand. My parents convinced me you were a good match. That wasn't the case for you. Your mum never liked me." It was liberating to say it out loud. "You begged her to approve of the marriage. It's why she never liked me, because her perfect son had found someone else to love. You fought for me then and it made you less of a son to her. It's why you've spent our whole marriage making it up to her."

He swallowed hard. "That's not true."

"Yes, it is. She's your mother. I never wanted to take you away from her. I just wanted a piece of your love for myself. But your love will only ever be hers. You weren't fighting for *me*. You were fighting for a wife; a woman to lie in your bed who will cook and clean for you. I was unlucky enough to tick those boxes. Forgive me, Yousef. I can't stay confined in your boxes anymore."

"I'm the only one fighting for our marriage," he pointed out. "If I didn't love you, I wouldn't be trying to fix this."

"You're trying to fix *me*. You want to change everything about me to make her happy, but I won't do it because nothing will ever be enough. Not me, not any woman. Marry a woman of her choosing and you'll see that I'm right. She's already offered to find someone else for you." I didn't stay long enough to see the realisation dawn on his face that I overheard that conversation.

When I left the house, nobody came to stop me. I got into my car and drove to Masuma's house with tears blurring my vision. I was so lost in my thoughts; I didn't stop to notice the familiar cars parked outside her house. Had I done, I would have prepared myself for the house full of guests. With one look at my face, Masuma sent me straight upstairs.

The heavy sets of footsteps made it clear it wasn't her climbing the stairs. The doors swung open and Abdul and Mahmood entered. My cousins looked at me with concern and shut the door behind them.

"Masuma is keeping the guests entertained," Abdul explained.

Mahmood leaned against the wall opposite me. "Tell us what happened."

Growing up with only a sister, people often asked if I wished I had brothers and I always answered no because these two cousins never let me feel the loss of a brother's love. My childhood was filled with memories of laughing together. That laughter carried on throughout our lives and only turned into roars as we played games, ate food, and spent our evenings talking. If I needed something, they never turned their back on me. That is why I shared my heartbreak with them, because I knew they wouldn't turn me away. They wouldn't hold me and offer false promises, but these brothers would understand my wounds and offer honesty. Exhausted from shouting and not being heard, I longed for someone who would listen.

When Mahmood returned with tissues for my tears, we sat in silence until I pulled myself together.

"You shouldn't have spoken to her in that way," Mahmood said first. "You have to understand why Yousef was angry at that. You should have just done as she asked because at that moment, she wasn't saying anything wrong."

I covered my face with my hands. "I know, but I was just so fed up of being told what to do. That is all my marriage has been."

Abdul nodded. "You will need to apologise for reacting that way."

"But will she apologise to me for *all* the stuff she's done?"

Mahmood shrugged. "When have you ever got an apology from your parents?" The question went unanswered. "That generation doesn't know how to apologise, even when they are in the wrong. You have to accept that's the way they are."

"Why? Why should we have to accept the lack of respect? Just because they're elder, it doesn't mean they can treat us how they like."

"They don't know any different. Nobody is saying that it's right," Abdul tried explaining.

"Then it's our job to teach them when they're wrong. Who said parents can't learn anything from their children? Time is moving forward, yet this culture is stuck in the past."

"We can't change them. We can only be better for our children. We learn from their mistakes and do better."

Mahmood sighed. "You said they don't treat you like their own daughter. Do you treat them like your own parents?"

I scoffed, but before I could list off all my examples, he put his hand up and stopped me.

He continued. "I've never heard Sasa and Sasi apologise to you. Did you demand an apology for them or did you take it because that's just how they are? When you felt hopeless, did you pack your bags and leave, or did you stay because it was your home?" His rhetorical questions went unanswered. "If you can't see them as your parents, then how can you expect them to see you as their daughter? Our parents hurt us more than anyone else, but they are also the ones that love us the most. Even if we can't see it, we have to believe it."

My head bowed, and I stared down at the ground. "I tried at the start. I did everything they expected of me and I did it because I loved my husband and wanted my marriage to last."

Abdul sighed. "When I've snapped at your Bhabi, she could've easily retaliated the same way. If she shouted back, then something small would turn into a mountain. You can't bag your bags and leave whenever things get hard. You stay and work through it."

Before I could speak, my phone rang. I thought it was Yousef or Haniya, but I was surprised to see it was my mum. *It wasn't a coincidence.* Someone must have called them. I slid my finger across the screen and braced myself for her anger.

"Where are you?" she asked as the line connected.

"Bhabi's house."

"Get here now." She hung up.

CHAPTER THIRTY-TWO

I AWOKE WITH A headache. Last night's event came rushing back at full force: the argument at Yousef's house, Masuma's house and the hour-long lecture I got from my parents when I arrived here. My mum kept muttering about the shame I bought on them while my dad went on a rampage about my behaviour. He was ready to send me back on my way had it not been so late. I curled up into my childhood bed and prayed for better days to come before sleep finally took me away from my cold reality.

My dad was back on his feet after overdosing on painkillers. I could hear him groaning as he climbed the stairs. He knocked on my door. "Come down."

My dad was a calm man. He rarely raised his voice, but when he did, you knew he was not messing about. Most of my memories included a father who had a smile on his face and hope in his eyes. He had neither yesterday. He looked at me with disappointment. I didn't want him to look at me like that. I remembered the day I got my place at university to study medicine. He was aglow with pride. That only got brighter when I graduated. He pulled me into his arms and wept because the immigrant's daughter had made a name for herself. On my wedding day, before I left the house, my dad held me back and reminded me I was just one step away from the life he dreamed for his daughter.

Overwhelming relief flooded me at that moment. It made all the stress and tears worth it because I had lived up to his expectation. I turned his dream into reality for the sake of his happiness. But when I descended the stairs and joined him and my parent-in-laws in the living room, I realised how I had shattered that. He was at an age where he should've been relaxing and enjoying time with his grandchildren. He had done his part and got his daughters married. We shouldn't have been a concern for him anymore. But there I was, bringing my troubles to his door.

I lingered in the doorway with my gaze lowered. I returned the salaam my father-in-law offered.

My mum brushed past me with a tray of tea and biscuits. She practically forced it into my mother-in-law's hands. "Do you need anything else?" she asked.

Sahil looked at me with sadness. "My daughter-in-law back."

My dad sat taller in his seat. "We aren't holding her back from you."

I couldn't bear to look at anyone as they discussed me as though I wasn't there. Their words were loud and quiet at the same time. Yousef's mum started her dramatics and started crying as she recapped yesterday's events. As she yapped on about how hurt she was, I met Sahil's gaze. He looked genuinely upset and desperate.

He lifted his hand and cut his wife off. "A lot of things were said yesterday on both sides. Let everyone ask for forgiveness and move on. Relationships go through this. Mothers and daughters fight like this."

My eyes finally rested on Anjuman. She didn't look the slightest bit apologetic. She waited patiently for me to go first, but I already apologised to her once and got nothing in return. It was her turn.

She wouldn't have gone first had her husband not given her a pointed stare. "Maaf khoro." *Forgive me.*

I smiled at her. "Of course, but that isn't the end of my problems in that house."

Sahil gestured to the empty seat next to my mum. "Tell me what you want and I will try my hardest."

Disregarding glares, I sat down. This was my final attempt, and I needed someone to witness the promises made to me. If these weren't honoured, then it was going to be my excuse to get out. It was no longer a negotiation. These were my demands because I was done being the one to give. I was exhausted trying to be perfect.

I started out strong with the thing that started all of this. "Yousef goes to the doctors and gets himself checked."

Sahil nodded. "That's why he isn't here. He went to his appointment today. Our agreement was for him to go and in return, I'll bring you home by the time he returns."

My heart wavered. When I walked in, I wondered why he wasn't here. I thought it was because he didn't care to fight for me, but the reason behind his absence proved he was still willing to try. This gave me hope to put in my second demand.

I stared directly at Anjuman. "I want to move out with my husband."

"Why?" she hissed.

With a blank expression, I said, "My marriage is going through a hard time and it's made even harder by living with people. We need time for ourselves to sort things out. We can't do that when there's so many people in our marriage." I hoped she knew I was talking about her.

She couldn't get a word in as her husband nodded. "Okay. Nobody will stop you from moving out."

"I don't want to hear any comments about having a baby."

My mum, trying to sweeten the woman opposite us, softly added, "These don't come from a bad place. We all just want a grandchild to love."

"You might have to accept that it might not happen for us." I hated how cold I had become when talking about having a baby, but it was easier to be like this than accept how heartbroken I was.

"Insha'Allah it will," my dad said. "Make duaa and Allah will give you a baby."

Anjuman huffed. "Allah is bigger than science and medicine. If He wants to give you a baby, no doctor can stop it."

Sahil waved his hands to stop the debate. "Nobody can predict the future." When he spoke again, the words were just for me, like a warning signal. "If you and Yousef are apart like this, then your future is already written. *Try*," he pleaded. "People make mistakes. Find it in you to forgive, because none of us are perfect."

When I spoke, the strength I had sat down with was gone. I wore my heart on my sleeve. "You're saying that to someone who has strived for perfection her whole life because number two was never good enough. I never wanted perfection, but I still tried Baba. I still tried, but where I was successful in one area, I failed elsewhere. Tell me what I can do to pass this test."

It was only he who showed me any compassion. Despite my parents sat a mere few steps away, he was the one who stood and offered his hand of solitude and unity. "Come home."

True to his word, Sahil brought me home before Yousef returned home from his appointment. When he saw me sat in the living room with Haniya and Amina, he looked like he couldn't believe his eyes. The room grew quiet, and our eyes met. As I made my way here, I contemplated all the things I needed to unload. I knew we needed to speak, so I reluctantly excused myself and followed him up the stairs. I reminded myself that he went to the appointment to prove he wanted this to work.

"Thank you," I said when I shut the door. "For going to the appointment. It means a lot to me."

He tossed his jacket onto the bed. "The results of my sample should be ready in a few weeks."

I crept over and sat on the bed. "That's good." My breath came out shaky. "I have something to say."

The bed creaked as he took a seat on the other side. "Go on."

"I shouldn't have spoken to your mum that way and for that I apologise. I'm not trying to excuse my behaviour, but yesterday was the straw that broke the camel's back. It was a buildup of small moments and I just lost it. It doesn't make it okay and I can't promise it won't happen again if her behaviour continues. As my husband, it's your duty to tell me when I'm wrong and hold me accountable for my actions. You also have that duty as a son. I'm not asking you to choose between me and her. I'm asking you to stand by my side when I deserve your support."

"You don't give me that chance when you run out of here."

"I run because it feels like it's the only time you realise I'm being serious. It's like you don't hear me when I'm standing before you." I shuffled closer to him. "Why does it take me being gone for you to realise how hurt I am before you do something? You're my husband. You should be able to read me like a book, but it feels like we're in completely different stories."

"You feel distant from me."

"Because I am," I admitted. "You've pushed me out of your life. Sharing a bed doesn't make that distance go away. We lay in bed and it's like you have nothing to say to me."

He closed his eyes and let out a frustrated sigh. "I don't know what to say anymore, Sumayyah. I've run out of ways to beg you to show me some love and compassion."

I predicted this would be his sticking point, as it always boiled down to this. "Sex isn't the only way to show love," I deadpanned.

"It's a big part," he retaliated. "It's not wrong for a husband to want his wife to show some sexual interest in him. I won't be shamed for wanting to have sex with my wife. It's like you avoid it. If I touch you, you skim away. If I kiss you, you turn the other way. If I touch you, you pull the blanket around you tighter. How many nights have I slept alone? How many times have I waited only for you to shut the light off?"

I tried not to scoff, but my eyes narrowed. "You're acting like I'm a prude and we haven't had sex in months."

"It's not enough, Sumayyah!" he snapped. "Physical intimacy is an important part of this marriage to me."

Of all the problems we had, this was the one that bothered him the most?

"So, what Yousef? You're horny?"

Frustrated, he ran his hands up and down his face. "No! You're not even trying to understand."

I crossed my arms. "All you have said is that I don't have enough sex with you."

"It's not about frequency!" His eyes closed, and he took calming breaths. "I just want you to be present when we're together. I want you to want me. It wouldn't hurt if you instigated it from time to time. Make me feel like you want me, like there's some love between us. It wasn't always like this. And now you sigh when I touch you. Your hands lay by your side when before they would explore every part of me. You stare up at the ceiling when you used to look at me with so much love I felt like I would combust. You used to giggle when I would tease you. Now you lay there silently."

The desperation in his voice broke through me. I knew I had stopped trying in our intimate life. I dreaded it because after every embrace, there was always a small part of me that had hoped that maybe we finally did it; we finally made a baby. But I never told him that. I never explained that a large part of me knew disappointment was coming. I never needed to say it though because I hadn't realised how mechanical it had all become. *Was I really that lifeless when we were intimate?*

"It's hard to enjoy it when I know the end goal is to get pregnant."

Yousef closed the distance and cupped my face. "Who said that?"

"You."

His thumb brushed over my lip. "I'm sorry. I can't lie and tell you I don't want that because it's true. But I also want you to be present. I want you to love me the way you did the first time we shared our bodies. I need more from you."

Everyone had made that statement to me at some point. My dad needed better grades. My mum needed more help around the house. My sister needed more support. Anjuman needed more respect. Sahil needed more forgiveness.

"Is that what you need to fix our marriage?"

His lips pressed against mine. "It's a start."

My forehead rested against his. "Okay."

My fingers thread through his hair before I pulled back. Like the dutiful wife, I undressed my husband and gave him the love he craved. Our eyes met just as our bodies did. Just as he wanted, I looked at my husband with all the emotion I could muster.

I just hoped he didn't realise it was mostly disappointment for both him and myself. My disappointment towards him was because of what he had reduced our marriage to. He didn't take accountability for his wrongs, nor did he apologise for them. The disappointment I felt in myself was much stronger because I didn't ask him to. I simply accepted my faults and did everything to be the perfect wife he needed.

After when we laid naked in bed, a soft silence filling the room, I understood why; I had accepted Yousef couldn't accept me with flaws, so I would have to do everything to be perfect because too much hung on this marriage: my dad's dream, and Yousef's proof that he married right.

When that small voice in me asked *what about you*, I ignored her because this wasn't about my future. It wasn't even my life anymore. I was just doing what was expected of me, even though it was soul-crushing and impossible.

Chapter Thirty-Three

We had got through four weeks of no hiccups. Things between my mother-in-law and myself were civil. We both knew where we stood and we stayed clear of one another unless we had to. We had guests over and nobody suspected a thing. Yousef and I were doing better. Our long-lost harmony was finally restored. We had gone away for the weekend and it was a delightful break. I laughed with him and it reminded me of the early days of our marriage. We cooked together. We went on long walks. We relaxed in front of the TV. We made love.

I did everything in my power to ensure Yousef enjoyed the weekend because it was proof that we would be much happier if we moved out. He hesitated about moving out, but knew I wouldn't change my mind. He insisted we buy another property as he refused to rent, saying it 'was a waste of money'. Instead of arguing with him, I listened to his argument and said I would consider it.

"Jannah is so precious!" Rani gushed as she joined us in the kitchen.

Halima had invited us girls and our husbands to her flat. It was a rare occasion we all got together, but it felt wholesome. It was a *nice* perk of being a grown-up as opposed to the difficult side we faced daily.

The men were in the living room, heavily debating about football teams. I rolled my eyes at how cliched that was.

"She's a sweet girl," her mum said proudly. "Shall we break up the football talk?"

We all followed her in a line, each carrying a pre-dinner snack she made. We placed it on the table and took a seat on the floor.

Ravi stood up. "Zoya, come and sit here. You're pregnant."

She shook her head. "No. It's okay. I'm alright here."

"Don't be ridiculous. You can't sit on the floor. I insist."

Zoya looked at her husband before shaking her head. "The stench of you men would make me gag. I'd rather stay on this side of the room," she joked.

Ravi retook his seat. "Fair enough. How are you doing? How long do you have left?"

She rubbed her growing belly. "We're okay. We've got just over four months to go."

"Do you know what you're having?" Halima asked.

Zoya shrugged. "Not yet. We find out next week."

Yousef's face expressed longing. "What are you hoping for? You've got two boys, so hopefully it's a girl."

Zoya frowned. "I'd be happy with another boy."

Halima gasped. "No! You want a girl because it's the best having a little version of you to play dress up with."

"O-M-G! Right?" Rani said. "Boys are so boring."

Ravi scoffed. "You don't want either."

So much for having a nice evening.

Rani skipped right over his comment. "What do you want, Idris?"

"A father never wants a daughter because she's only ours for a short time. Before you know it, you give her away to someone else."

Nazir shook his head. "Not me. No man is ever touching my little girl."

Halima looked at him in surprised. Their eyes met, and she had a sad, faraway look in her eyes.

"I had this discussion with a colleague of mine," Yousef said. "She said she wants four children – all boys because she'll have the best of worlds once they get married. She'll get to keep her sons with her, but she'll also get four daughters without going through the struggle of raising moody teenagers."

Everyone else chuckled except me. All I could focus on was who this mystery female colleague was. In six years, I had never heard Yousef mention a woman at work. Being an engineer, he was usually surrounded by men. Even if there were women around, he wasn't the type to speak to them. I reminded myself I had plenty of male colleagues that I spoke to, so it probably didn't mean much. My eyes landed on his wedding band. She knew he was married. *He knew he was married.* I had nothing to be worried about.

Zoya shook her head. "Not me. Once my boys are married, I'm forcing them out of the house. Let them go and live their new lives. They don't need to be running around after me."

Rani lifted her palm for a high-five, which Zoya met. "Preach sister! Our culture is the only one that forces the woman to live with her in-laws. The normal thing is to get your own space."

It was clear to us girls that was an aim shot at Ravi. She had been trying to get him to move out since they were married, but he made no move. From the look Yousef shot at me, it was clear he thought I had told Rani about our situation and she was making an indirect at him.

That's why when he spoke it was with an edge. "Our culture reinforces an environment of family. It's hard to cultivate that when you hardly see them. There's nothing wrong with living with your husband's family."

"Easy to say when you're a man," I retaliated. "At the end of the day, it's *your* family. For the woman, it's different."

"How's that?" Ravi asked.

"It never feels like your own home. It's our husband's home. Having one room in an entire house doesn't equal having your own space and privacy."

Idris laughed. "What do you need privacy for?"

I hated how he laughed at me like I was a fool. I wanted to make him feel the same way. "Did you get your wife pregnant in front of your parents?"

Yousef's eyes widened.

Idris's darkened. "I got her pregnant without moving out. That invalidates your argument."

Since the day of her engagement party, it was clear Rani didn't like Idris. She played nice for the sake of our friend, but she didn't turn down an opportunity to ridicule him. "No, it just means you can't make your woman scream."

I choked on the air as others gasped and some snorted.

Nazir intercepted. "Okay. Let's move this along before there's bloodshed in my apartment."

"These are delicious," Zoya choked out, pointing at the mini quiches.

"I found the recipe on this website..." Halima never got to finish her sentence because Idris cut her off.

He turned to Ravi. "You wife owes me an apology for speaking so crudely."

Rani snapped her fingers. "If you want to ask for an apology, then ask me. My husband doesn't answer for me."

His eyes narrowed in her direction. "Your husband should put you on a leash."

"If he ever wants one, I'm sure he'll ask you because you're a pro at that."

"Rani," Zoya pleaded. She looked hurt at our friend. "Stop."

"He just called me a dog."

"And then you referred to me as one," she argued.

"That isn't what I meant. I was trying to say he's always trying to control you."

Ravi stood up. "Okay. Maybe we should just leave."

Halima pouted. "Come on, guys. I've spent all morning cooking us a nice meal. Let's all apologise and forget about it."

We all looked at one another and like children, we muttered a meaningless *sorry*.

"What happened?" I asked Yousef as he got back into the car.

He rolled his eyes. "She gave me another appointment for Monday next week."

Irritated was an understatement. After waiting four weeks for his results and hearing nothing back, I finally pushed Yousef to chase the clinic. It turned out they lost his sample and hadn't realised.

"They should have given you an appointment for today," I snapped.

He took my hand in his and kissed it. "It's a human error. She said they'll put a rush on it."

"They better," I muttered. "I've had my ultrasound and started hormone therapy and you haven't even got your initial test results back."

He squeezed my hand tight. "Stop stressing about it. A few more weeks won't make a difference."

This was a different side of Yousef. Perhaps it was his way of trying to take the stress off me. I appreciated it, but we were still nowhere. My ultrasound came back normal, but my doctor still had some concerns. She had requested a CA-125 test, which could confirm her suspicions of endometriosis. Only a laparoscopy could confirm and assess the damage. The label hung over me like a gloomy cloud because I knew the repercussions of such a diagnosis. Conceiving would be a one-in-a-million chance.

I sighed. "I guess."

Sleeplessness gave me a headache. Uneasiness lingered as sleep eluded me. The remaining part of dinner at Halima's went as well as it could. Tensions were high, even between Rani and Zoya. We kept the conversation light and called it an early night, most of us feigning tiredness.

"Are you okay?" Yousef asked, reading the fatigue on my face.

"Can you run into the pharmacy and get me some painkillers?"

He kissed my temple and left the car. I rested my head against the window, hoping the cool glass would alleviate some of the pain. Yousef's phone buzzed a few times in a row, which I ignored. I picked his phone up to silence it, but when it buzzed again as a call came through, the name caught my attention.

Maisha.

Was this the female colleague he spoke of yesterday?

My stomach turned and twisted. What reason did she have to text him? Why would she text unless she thought Yousef would return the same attention?

Glancing up to see if he was coming, I quickly typed in his passcode to reassure myself that nothing untoward was happening right before me. I was thrown off when his password didn't work. I tried again, thinking I mistyped in a rush. But when it was rejected again, I understood loud and clear.

Yousef changed his password because there was something he didn't want me to see.

My headache turned into a migraine as one thought played on a loop.

My husband is having an affair.

Chapter Thirty-Four

I STARED AT THE clock, watching the seconds pass by. I was alone this evening. My in-laws had gone to a dawat and my excuse to stay home was my early shift tomorrow morning. Anjuman reluctantly agreed to let me out of this one. Yousef was out with his friends Jameel and Daniyal. I had only met his friends a handful of times because Yousef said he felt uncomfortable having his male friends mix with me. He said none of his friends bought their wives along and I didn't question it because it felt normal. Tonight I wondered if it was because he was worried they might expose him.

It was just after midnight when I heard the front door close. The silent entry ruled out the possibility of it being anyone but him. His footsteps matched the beat of my heart. I dropped my head to my pillow and pulled the blanket up, not wanting him to know I was up waiting for him.

My doubts faded when he slowly lent down and placed a kiss in my hair. "Goodnight, wife," he whispered.

I pretended to stir and slowly opened my eyes. Forcing a crack in my voice, I asked, "Did you just get in?"

"Yeah. Sorry for waking you. Go back to sleep."

Knowing that I had an opportunity to poke holes in his story, I sat up. "You got in later than usual. What were you boys up to?"

"Jameel wanted to try this new steakhouse, and it was packed." His playful smile tugged at my heart. "Did you miss me?"

I smiled back. "Very much."

He made his way to me and pecked my lips. "Now you know how I feel when you leave me to go to your parents and friends. Let me shower and I'll join you."

I grabbed his hand. "You can shower tomorrow. Come to bed."

He took a whiff of his top. "I smell like meat. I'll be ten minutes."

"Yousef," I pleaded. "Please?"

"Why don't you join me in the shower?"

The idea of intimacy with him, knowing he might have been with her, disgusted me. I instantly released him. "I'm tired and have work tomorrow. Plus, your family will be home any moment now." I gave him a pointed stare. "Another reason to find our own place quickly."

He saluted. "Done," he said, followed by a laugh. "Get some sleep. I love you."

"I love you too," I sighed once he left the room.

Myra dropped her lunch on the table. "I haven't seen you in a while!"

She wasn't wrong. I had barely seen her or her husband in weeks. Ibrahim and I worked together more than she and I did, but I had barely worked any locum shifts recently.

"What's on the menu for today?" I asked. My stomach growled at the aromatic scent wafting from her lunch.

"Pasta with the Bangladeshi twist."

"That definitely beats the salad I had. How are you?"

She let out a fake shudder. "Glad to be out of the house. It's been chaotic recently. How about you?"

The smile my mother made me perfect was slapped onto my face. "Good. It's about to get busy because my sister-in-law is getting married in a few months!"

After speaking over the last two months, Haniya finally said yes. I wasn't surprised when I heard she agreed, because she would smile whenever a text message came through. I heard her hushed whispers late night when she was on the phone with him. She reminded me of a younger me when I was getting to know Yousef.

"That's exciting! Good luck with the wedding shopping. It never seems to end."

I shook my head. "Haniya is really simple. She complains when she has to wear a kameez."

Myra waved her fork at me. "It's never about what the bride wants. It's all about her and the groom's parents."

I laughed with her, remembering the tiresome journey of planning my wedding with my parents. Everything required their final approval – down to my wedding favours. Shopping for my wedding dress was hell because in this culture the bride's outfit was gifted by her in-laws. That meant my mother-in-law had to love the dress. I quickly learnt that we didn't have the same taste. While I loved my dress in the end, it wasn't my first choice, but my parents grew tired of me rejecting every dress she picked out.

"The times have changed, Myra. These young ones are a lot more assertive than we were."

She chuckled. "Time may change, but our culture doesn't." She huffed when her phone rang. "Sorry. It's my four children."

I waved off her concerns with a laugh at her calling Ibrahim her child.

"Hello!" she answered gleefully.

"Ammu! Look at my drawing."

Her eyes widened in awe. "Wow baba! That's such a nice drawing. Did you do it all by yourself?"

Before her second child could answer, her eldest took the phone. "Mum, can you get some batteries for my car?"

"Okay baby. Anything else?"

I caught a glimpse of him shaking his head. The phone was passed along again and this time it was Ibrahim who appeared, looking more exhausted than I'd ever seen him.

"How's work? Is it quiet?" he asked.

"A little. How are you? You look like you've been to war and back."

He smiled at his wife. "Don't worry about us lads. We're okay."

I was happy for my new friend. She was fortunate to find a good man among the few. He clearly was having a tough time managing the children, but he didn't want his wife to worry. My guess was that she needed some time away from the home. I tried not to listen to their conversation, but after a few minutes I sat taller.

"Guess who I bumped into," she said. She turned the phone, so it was me on the camera.

"Hi."

He looked genuinely happy to see me. "Look who's risen from the dead! How are you?"

I let out a laugh. "I'm good. I've been busy. How are your little ones?"

Ibrahim let out an exasperated sigh. "Energetic. Who are you today?"

This little game was a staple in our routine when we saw one another. I gave it some thought. "Doctor by day. Assassin by night."

There was a nod of approval. "Save lives by day. Take lives at night. I like it. Who's on your hit list?"

Maisha.

I was startled by my train of thought. Since when was I the person who had violent thoughts towards others? I'd always believed in killing with kindness. I'd been taught to be the bigger person. I had always been the understanding one. This was a new side to me and I didn't like it. When did I become someone who argued with my husband in public? At what point did I become someone who had the nerve to walk out of my house? *What was wrong with me?*

"The person who stopped making the BBQ flavoured *Walkers.* Who does that?"

Ibrahim wrinkled his nose. "Someone of sane mind."

After a few more minutes of small talk, Myra begged her husband to hang up so she could go back to having a normal adult conversation. When the line was cut, she apologised to me once more.

"It's no worry. It's sweet they want to talk to you."

Her shoulders deflated as she let out a sigh. "When I'm away from them, I miss them so much. But sometimes..." She shook her head, almost scared to say how she really felt. "Sometimes I just feel like screaming and running out of there. It's so overwhelming when it's just me and the kids all day, every day. Ibrahim works most days and when he comes home, he's dead on his feet and I feel bad asking for help."

I didn't understand the pressures of raising three children alone, but I understood the feeling of being overwhelmed with doing stuff alone. "I'm sure he doesn't mind helping."

She sat alert. "Oh, I couldn't possibly complain about Ibrahim. Well, I probably could," she joked, "But he does the most he can. You know how he is. He always tries to put a smile on my face, even when I want to set the world on fire."

My thoughts went back to the first shift I worked with him when he started our little game. Ibrahim was a kind man. "Can I ask you a question?"

"Anything."

I tried to think of the best way to phrase the question without making her worry. I just wanted to know if I was justified in having worries about Yousef and this new female colleague. Eventually, I asked, "Do you mind me and Ibrahim being friends?"

This was a slightly different situation because Ibrahim and I never spoke outside of work. I wasn't calling and texting him unless it was work related. Even then I wouldn't be changing my phone password so my husband couldn't see.

Instantly, she shook her head. "Absolutely not! I have never once questioned your friendship. We live in a world where men and women speak freely. It would be impossible to expect Ibrahim to not know any females. As long as the boundaries of our marriage remained intact, I would have no problem."

"What boundaries do you mean?"

"I would hope he wasn't discussing our private life with you. I wouldn't like him talking to you late at night or excessively. I would hope you'd have enough respect for me as a fellow woman and wife and keep some physical distance between you."

"Of course! I would never..."

She smiled at me. "I know you wouldn't. There's a reason our religion teaches us to not socialise with the other sex. It's to stop that temptation, but unfortunately, the lives we choose to live don't take that into consideration."

Myra was right. I was jumping to conclusions. One conversation about kids and a phone call didn't mean Yousef was having an affair. That call could have been about anything. I would be foolish to dismiss it completely and at some point I knew I would have to ask him about it and let him know I wasn't comfortable. I wanted the same confidence in my husband as she had in hers.

"How do you make yourself so calm about it? How do you stop yourself from stressing about it?"

"It's simple. I trust my husband. I trust he loves me enough to not stray."

Her answer made me recoil back into my seat because I knew I would never have that reassurance. Yousef has already mentioned his wish for a divorce. Albeit in anger and retaliation, Yousef already showed me how easily he could kick me out of his home and life.

So how was I *supposed to trust my husband?*

Chapter Thirty-Five

"Did you check out the link I sent you?" I asked Yousef.

It was a Saturday night, and we were sitting in our room. I tired of the air and walls surrounding me. I needed to get out of there. I wanted to dress up and have some fun.

"I haven't had the time," he said ironically as he scrolled on his phone.

I wondered what he was doing. Was he texting her? *Stop,* I reprimanded myself. I would drive myself crazy if I kept fixating on that one thing.

"Why don't you have a look at it now while you're laying there? It's a really nice house and within our budget."

He dismissed me. "I don't have the money for a deposit right now. I told you I need time to save some more."

I raised my eyebrow. "You haven't even tried to get a mortgage yet. How do you know you don't have enough?"

As always, with discussing moving out, he slipped into a mood. "I just do."

"Then let's lower our budget."

"If you just wait a little longer, we can buy a house we love rather than settling."

"Fine," I snapped. "I'll go back to work and save my salary. That should make the process three times faster."

He finally gave me some attention. He looked offended at my offer. "I don't need my wife to help me buy a house."

My offer hurt his pride and ego. I could have laughed, but that would have only escalated the situation. Spending my Saturday in my bedroom was bad enough. If I argued with him, I would have to spend it downstairs with his family, which was worse. I was in no mood to gossip about others or fake smiles with my mother-in-law. For that reason, I dropped it.

"Let's go out."

His focus was back on his phone. "Where?" he asked, disinterested.

"Dinner. A walk. Literally anywhere but here."

He threw his phone down dramatically. His arms covered his eyes. "I'm so tired, Sumayyah. Work has been a killer with this new project."

By new project, do you mean your mistress? The irritation coursing through me almost let the question slip, but I held it back.

"It's only a few hours."

"Tomorrow."

I rolled my eyes, even though he couldn't see me. I was going out, regardless of him. "Well, can I go out then?" I expected questions about where I was going.

All I got was, "Fine."

With his agreement, I needed to find somewhere to go. Rani and Zoya both lived with their in-laws, so that was a no-go. My options were Halima or Ibrahim's house. It felt weird asking Ibrahim if I could come over last minute, especially when I knew Myra had three children to manage. With that in mind, I messaged Halima and started getting ready, anticipating her reply.

I wanted to feel good, so I put in extra effort. It took me twenty minutes to put on a light layer of makeup. I picked out a nice maxi dress and admired my reflection in the mirror. Gone was the miserable woman who usually stared back at me. This woman looked ready for a nice evening, even if it was just with one friend in her home.

"I'm off."

Yousef opened his eyes and stared at me with suspicion. "Why are you so dressed up?" He could have complimented me instead of asking that. He could have changed his mind and told me to wait up for him. *But no.*

"Hardly. I just don't look like a slob. Don't wait up for me."

"Don't be back too late!" he shouted, but I made no note of it.

Thankfully, Halima said it was okay to come over. I quickly stopped to get some sweets for Jannah and flowers and chocolates for Halima as a thank you for the last minute visit. I was practically bouncing around by the time I got to her front door.

"Hey!" Nazir greeted as he opened the door.

I don't know why I was surprised to see him when it was his home. I assumed he'd be out, as he usually was when we came over. Aside from dinner a few weeks ago, he always did a disappearing act when Halima had guests.

"Hi. I'm so sorry for intruding on your Saturday," I said awkwardly.

His smile was wide and reassuring. "Nah! Don't sweat it. You're always welcome here. Sit down. Halima is just in the bathroom."

I sat on the sofa and gave Jannah her sweets, which she was over the moon about.

"No sweets now, mummy," Halima scolded as she joined us. "It's almost bedtime."

With an apologetic smile, I said, "I'm sorry. I didn't even think about that."

Nazir swept his daughter into his arms and opened a pack of the jelly beans. "One or two won't hurt. Isn't that right, daddy?"

The little girl's eyes widened with excitement. "Daddy's the best."

Halima huffed as he left with his daughter in his arms. "Can I get you a drink?"

I patted the sofa. "It's only me! Sit down." My protests went unheard because Halima was already out of the room to get me a drink. As she walked back towards me, I looked at her with concern. "Are you okay? You're walking a little funny."

She shook her head. "I think I overdid it at the gym. My body is aching."

I frowned. "Do you want me to check you over? Make sure you haven't pulled anything?"

She placed the drink down on the coffee table. "Nothing a few painkillers won't fix." Grabbing the remote, she turned the volume on the TV down. "Is everything okay?"

Confusion held me hostage until I realised why she thought something was wrong. Most people didn't turn up to their friend's house this late into the evening unless they needed help. I smiled at her in reassurance. "I was just bored and Yousef is tired. Hope I didn't interrupt your plans."

Halima let out a soft laugh. "I have a five-year-old. My Saturday nights involve cleaning and being in bed by ten."

With the most serious face I could muster, I said, "I promise to be gone by then."

She playfully slapped my arm. "Don't be silly. Have you spoken to Rani or Zoya since the whole..."

"Disaster?" I finished for her. I shook my head. "They'll reconcile. Zoya was just upset that Rani attacked Idris like that in front of everyone. She said it was embarrassing for her."

With a shake of her head, she said, "Rani doesn't help herself sometimes. When will she learn it's better to keep your mouth shut sometimes?"

Rani's brazen tongue had got her into more trouble than I could count. Her fearlessness in standing up for herself was something I admired, despite others seeing it as a flaw. If I had more of that courage, then perhaps I wouldn't be as unhappy as I was.

"Idris is no better," I countered. "His mindset is so backwards. It's like he comes to these things looking to piss one of us off."

Once again, she disagreed with me. "I don't think he means to. It's just his beliefs. He comes from a slightly older generation to us and they're the type to say whatever they think. It's just the way he is."

That wasn't a good enough reason to throw words around carelessly. Words have more weight than people give them credit for.

I didn't want to get into a debate with her, so I hummed in agreement. "Well, Zoya said she wants an apology."

With a hundred per cent belief, she said, "She'll get it because we've been friends for twenty years and nothing will come between that."

A smile etched its way onto my lips at her certainty. "What makes you so sure?"

"Because at the end of the day, all we have is one another. It's the four of us against the world. We are as intertwined as those bows we tied on our wrists at our school prom. The four bows that represented hope, strength, courage, and resilience."

An overwhelming wave of emotion washed over me at her words. I squeezed her hand and echoed her words. "The four bows."

The evening turned out to be exactly what I needed: a friend, food, and a trip down memory lane. When it was way past her bedtime, Jannah stalked into the room with her stuffed bear in her hands and rubbing her eyes with tiredness.

Halima held her hands for her daughter. "Come here."

Too tired to climb onto the sofa, she slumped onto the floor and snuggled her rabbit. "Tired."

She let out a soft laugh. "Where's your daddy?"

"Phone."

With a tut, she stooped to pick her daughter up with a groan.

My eyes latched onto a dark purple patch on her lower back. It looked painful and explained why she groaned every time she shuffled around on the sofa. "Oh, my god! You need to let me check you."

Halima stared at me with wide eyes and shushed me. "I'm fine."

I stared at her in disbelief. "Did you drop a weight on yourself at the gym? What the hell!"

Halima grabbed my hand tight. She looked over her shoulder as if she was expecting someone to come barging through. When no one did, she turned back to me with a pleading look in her eyes. "Please. Just stop talking about it. Pretend you never saw it."

I was beyond confused. Why was she hiding that from Nazir? "Why don't you want to tell him?"

Wide eyes. Fear. Desperation. She clung to her daughter like her life depended on it. Tears brimmed as she pleaded with her eyes.

Realisation dawned on me, and my heart broke. Words failed me because the thought was unfathomable. Nazir was smart, witty, funny and loved his wife. He had doted on her since they met. How could he...

I couldn't even finish the thought.

"He did this?" I whispered.

Her hand covered my mouth to silence me. "You never saw anything."

"That looks like a serious injury. You need to go to the doctors," I pushed.

"No."

"Then let me check you. I'll be quick."

She shook her head. "It will heal on its own."

"How do you..." My choked sob came out as a gasp. "It's not the first time."

"Please."

"I can't just..." I shook my head. "I can't. You need to tell someone. Call the police. Family. Someone."

Her tears weren't falling like mine. Hers stayed in the brim of her eyes. "Nothing changes. Nobody hears. Nobody sees. I married him against my family's wishes. This is my burden to bear."

I looked at Jannah curled in the safety of her mother's arms. "What about her? What about showing her a better life?"

She looked down at her daughter, and a single tear fell. "A day will come when she learns the nature of men. I would rather her see it in my arms where I can teach her how to be strong. Nobody taught me. I learnt it myself when I was six and a man put his hands on me. And then again at nine. And then again and again and again. He's not the first, but he will be the last. I leave him and I'm back to being fair game to the vultures out there."

I tried to keep my voice low, scared of the consequences if Nazir heard. "Halima, this is not okay. It's not okay to be beaten by one man because there are others out there. You deserve to live a life free of abuse."

"Abuse is the life of women. What else do we know? My scars are physical. Yours are emotional. Rani's are invisible. Zoya's are psychological. How are our lives any different from one another?"

I had never viewed my marriage as abusive because Yousef had never put his hands on me. But he had broken me down until I became someone I didn't recognise. He had me begging for his love. His lack of support made me feel isolated. His actions recently had me feeling anxious and worried.

No matter how hard I shook my head, I couldn't get the image of her wound out of my head. "How am I supposed to forget?"

"You don't. You can't. But you get up the next day with renewed hope, courage, strength, and resilience."

As I left her home that late evening, I was filled with nothing but despair. How did this go unnoticed by us? How had we been so blind to it?

It was because we were all consumed by our own struggles. Halima was right; while different battles, our lives mirrored one another. I felt sick the entire way home, and I was desperate to ask somebody for some advice on what I should do, but I promised Halima to keep it to myself and I wasn't about to break my word to her.

By the time I reached my bedroom, I needed to be held before I fell apart. My heart was heavy, and I wanted Yousef to hold me close. But the room was empty because he had gone out.

I guess he wasn't tired after all.

Perhaps he was just tired of me and this marriage.

CHAPTER THIRTY-SIX

I SIGHED. "THANKS FOR giving me a ride home."

Ibrahim grinned. "I couldn't exactly leave you stranded."

Checking my phone again to see if Yousef returned my call, I was left with disappointment. "I don't know what happened to my husband."

My car was in the garage, so Yousef offered to pick me up after my shift. But he seemed to have fallen off the face of the earth. I'd been calling him for almost forty-five minutes when Ibrahim caught me outside and offered a ride. I couldn't stop my mind from wondering where he was, but more importantly, *who* he was with. He always answered my calls; that was one benefit of having a husband who was glued to his phone.

"It's fine. You're not that much out of my way. If you were, I would have charged you," he joked.

I didn't have the energy to pretend to be okay. I was just ... tired. Yousef offered no explanation of where he went last weekend. I didn't have the courage to hear the truth, so I never asked. It had been so hot and cold with him. One minute, he's the man I married. The next he's so cold I'm scared of getting frostbite if I get too close to him.

"Do you need to get home right now?"

Normally I would've answered yes, but I didn't have the energy to be in that house. "No. What did you have in mind?"

He pretended to think about it. "Three rowdy boys, a basic dinner followed by silence and a nice cup of tea. How does that sound?"

I hoped my smile translated how grateful I was for the offer. "Perfect."

Myra hugged me tight at the door. "This was so nice. Please come down like this again."

It was a much better evening that I could have imagined. Her boys were loud and warm at the same time. There was so much love in their family. Ibrahim and Myra had a fluidity between them that made it look easy. Where she cooked, he cleaned. She got the kids ready for bed and he tucked them in. It was a rare sight of equal partnership in a marriage.

Lasagne was on the menu, followed by the cup of tea Ibrahim promised. I laughed with them as I did with my friends. They brought comfort. Seeing him in his own element, I was happy that Ibrahim built the life he spoke about at university. His marriage was full of understanding and love.

"Don't tempt me too much," I quipped. "You'll never get rid of me otherwise."

"There's always a seat for you at our table. As long as you don't mind the mess of three young boys."

I hauled my bag back up over my shoulder as it slipped. "It was a pleasant break from the stiff perfection at my house," I said honestly. "May Allah always protect your family and its happiness."

She hugged me again. "May that same happiness find you again," she whispered.

"Let's go ladies! I might just fall asleep at the wheel."

With a last smile, I turned on my heels and made my way into his car. I checked my phone to see the numerous calls and messages from Yousef. I saw every one as they came through and ignored it. *Let's see how he likes it.*

The car ride was in peaceful silence, which I appreciated, knowing Yousef was going to disrupt the small comfort I found this evening. When he pulled up outside, I thanked him for the hundredth time.

"You deserve to feel the joy I saw on your face every day," he said.

"It's just a tough time right now," I defended.

Part of what made Ibrahim such an excellent doctor was his empathy. His smile was sad. "Ever since I've known you, you've always had this sombreness about you. I thought it was university stress, but now I realise it's because you're always trying to be more than you can."

I turned slightly and faced him. "What does that mean?"

"It means," he sighed. "It's time to live for yourself, Sumayyah. Becoming what others need you to be will never grant you happiness." He looked past me. "I think you've got company."

Turning around, I saw Yousef stood in the open doorway. "Thanks for the lift."

"Happiness. It's not permanent." His eyebrow arched. "It's also not impossible."

With those final words, I grabbed my bag and climbed out of the car. A weight rested on my chest the closer I got to the house.

"Upstairs. *Now,*" Yousef demanded as I passed him.

I did as he asked, wanting to be done with it. I was offering no explanation until he could tell me where he was. I dropped my bag onto the floor and patiently waited for him to break the silence.

"What were you doing with him?"

"I wouldn't have been with him if you picked up the phone. Where were you?"

"I was sleeping!"

The rage I thought I would hurl at him didn't make an appearance. I scoffed at him. "Alone or with someone else?"

There. I said it. I asked the question I wanted an answer to.

Yousef looked at me in confusion. "What the hell is that supposed to mean?"

I perched on the edge of the bed. "It means were you alone or with Maisha?"

The befuddled look on his face didn't waver. He genuinely looked surprised at my line of questioning. "Where did she come from?"

With a shrug, I said, "I don't know. Maybe it's because she texts and calls you all times of the day. Maybe it's because you changed your phone password. Maybe it's because you refuse to go out with me, only to disappear and come home in the early hours of the morning. Maybe it's because you know how many children this woman wants."

Like a stupid fish, his mouth opened and closed, but he couldn't think of a lie to feed me.

I pretended I didn't care. "You already told me you want a divorce. You've also kicked me out of the house once. I'm hardly surprised."

I waited for the moment he let his mask slip. The clock ticked in the silence as the second passed by. Yousef just looked at me and the longer he did, the anger joined us. The clogs were turning in his brain. He was trying to find an excuse to explain all my accusations away. I wanted to tell him to be a man and confess. That was the least he owed me.

And then it finally happened. The mask slipped, and he got defensive. "How could you accuse me of adultery? Is this your way of making what you did today okay? You think by saying all this bullshit, I'll forget you came home at almost midnight with another man."

I lifted one finger. "First, if I was having an affair with him, do you think I would be a fool and have him drop me right outside my husband's house?" I lifted a second finger. "Second, if anyone is trying to divert the conversation, it's you." I lifted a third finger. "And that brings me to my third point. I know you've been having an affair."

Yousef ignored everything else and latched onto my first point. "How could you think it was appropriate to have him drop you off this late when my parents are here? What would they think?"

I stood up. "Let's ask them, shall we? While we're there, let's ask them what they think about their son getting calls from another woman at all times of the day! Let's ask them if they think it's appropriate for their son to change his phone password so his wife doesn't see the filthy messages he's sending to his fucking mistress!" It felt like an out-of-body experience yelling at him the way I have wanted to since I got suspicious. I wanted to scream louder. I wanted to scream until my voice went hoarse. I wanted to smash everything I owned that reminded me of this godforsaken marriage.

"You are wrong! You have no idea what you're talking about."

I would have laughed at his stupidity if I remembered how to laugh. "Show me your phone."

"No."

"Show me your phone, Yousef."

He shook his head. "I won't even entertain this conversation."

My hands balled into fists. "Show me your fucking phone before I make you."

He took three slow steps away from me. "What is wrong with you?"

He was not going to gaslight me into thinking I was crazy. If he had nothing to hide, he would have happily shown me his phone.

I walked to our bedroom door and opened it.

"Run. That's all you know."

With a look of pity, I said, "I'm not running." Keeping one eye on him, I backed into the hallway. I screamed for my father-in-law. I called for him three times before I heard the footsteps. I joined Yousef in our bedroom again. "You could have kept this between us. I never would have betrayed you the way you have done me. But I'm fucking *done*. You can answer to the only people you actually respect."

"Kitha?" His dad shouted as he took in the sight before him.

I pointed at Yousef. "Tell your son to show me his phone."

"Why?"

My gaze fell back on Yousef. He begged with his entire body to stop, but nothing was going to prevent me from getting my answer. No amount of love could balance this betrayal. "Your son is having an affair."

"Baba! I'm not," he pleaded like a weakling. "She's saying all sorts of nonsense."

When the first few tears fell, I felt a betrayal to myself. My words were void of any emotions. "If he has nothing to hide and I'm just a crazy woman, he will have no problem showing me his phone. If he doesn't, I will have my answer and I promise, I will walk out of here and this time, *nothing* will bring me back. Tell him to show me his phone."

Sahil looked between us before a look of resignation overshadowed his face. "Give her your phone."

He held his dad's stare before he handed it over to me, unlocked.

"That will be all," I said to his dad, dismissing him.

He slowly came towards me. "Do you want me to stay?"

I gripped the phone tight and closed my eyes. As I wept, my shoulders quivered. When I looked at him again, I shook my head. "No matter what happens, he will always be your son. I have already disgraced him by calling you up here. Let me salvage what may remain between your father-son relationship."

He left the room, closing the door with a shameful look towards Yousef.

I sat on the floor with the phone in my hand. Yousef stood against the wall as I found their message thread. I scrolled all the way to the top and started reading. At first, the conversations focused on work. It then slowly drifted into arranging work lunches with a few of their colleagues. I tried convincing myself there was no cheating, but I knew the worst was coming.

I'll have to check with my wife first.

She sounds like a drill sergeant lol

A little haha

"Is this how you talk about me to other people?" I asked, appalled.

He sighed. "It was just a joke. She knows how much I love you."

"Uh-huh." I went back to reading the messages.

Somewhere along the way, the lines blurred, and the conversation became more about their day. Not long after that, there were 'good morning' and 'goodnight' texts. She would add a kiss at the end of some of her messages, but I noted he reciprocated.

My mum started going on about me getting married again

You don't want to get married?

Some day....

I'm just waiting to meet the right man

What is the 'right man' to you?

kind, loving, funny, thoughtful... and definitely older :)

"How old is she?"

As quiet as a mouse, he said, "Twenty-three."

I felt sick but carried on the reading the conversation.

how much older?

At least six or seven years...

guys my age are soooooo immature

Where are you looking for this 'man'?

"At least you could admit to her you regretted the choice you made."

Yousef closed the space and sat opposite me on the floor. "I have no regrets."

I pushed his hands off me. "Don't ever touch me again."

He tried to grab the phone out of my hands. "Please stop doing this. Whatever you want to know, I'll answer. Don't put yourself through this."

I wanted to stop reading. But I knew this was my only chance, as he would erase everything once he had the phone back. They say ignorance is bliss, but I would've slowly died if I didn't know what else was said.

you should know that men talk

???

I didn't think one word could break me so deeply. *Unhappily.* He had told her he was unhappy with me, with our life, with our marriage. He had basically given her a free pass at him. This young girl heard the woes of this older, handsome, successful man and naively though she could make all his problems disappear.

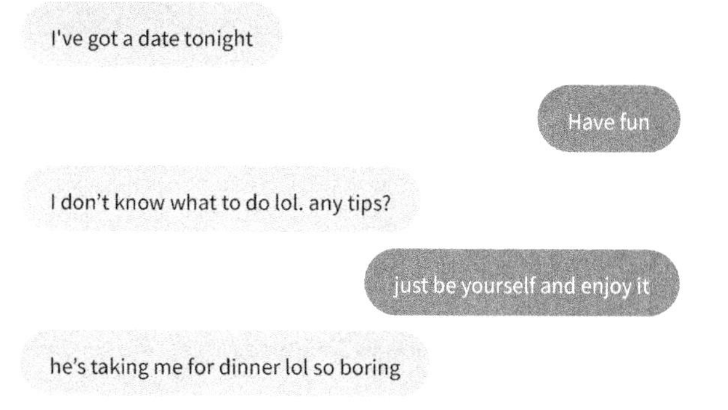

where do you take your wife? or has that honeymoon phase passed?

usually dinner. we like to stay in

boring!!!!

"Were you jealous?"

"Of course not. Why would I care? She was just asking me for advice because she was nervous."

My palms tingled him as the urge to slap him came full force. "She was trying to make you jealous."

"The fact that I didn't see that should prove that this was all nothing."

The edge of doubt faded as I continued reading the conversation from later that night.

Bile rose up my throat. I grabbed the bin and heaved into it, but the nausea never passed. I looked at Yousef in disgust. "You talked to her about our sex life?"

"It was a general statement. Everyone knows that couples have less sex the longer they're together."

I shoved him, needing to get out some of my aggression. "You. Are. *Disgusting.* You are *nafakh.*" *Dirty.* "Get away from me. You make me sick. You..." I couldn't get any more words past my sob.

Yousef grabbed my arms. "Sumayyah, please. Just stop reading."

I pushed him off me. "Did you have sex with her?"

He flinched. "No! I would never touch another woman."

I let out an incredulous laugh. "No, you just text them when you're laying in bed all sad, alone and horny because your drill sergeant wife went to work. Did she send you any pictures of her in bed?"

"No!"

"Has she seen how your penis looks? Was she blessed with a dick pic?"

Yousef shook me. "Stop it!" he bellowed. "Stop talking like this!"

"Why?" I screamed at the same volume. "Does it make you sick hearing your wife talk about you sexting another woman? Does it make you feel like ripping your skin off? Does it make you want to scrub your genitals raw? Because that is how I feel!" I roared.

He began to cry. "I'm sorry. I never did anything more than *talking* to her."

I wiped my tears and gave him the coldest look I could muster. "Why did you stop there? Does that make it any better? Is that supposed to stop my heart from feeling like someone set it on fire? What, Yousef? Should I fall to your feet and thank you for not fucking another woman? Should I be grateful you didn't send a picture of your dick to another woman? Should I worship you for keeping your infidelity to slagging me off and fantasising about fucking a younger woman?" When he never answered, I screamed, "Fucking tell me!"

My head fell back and rested against the bed. The wave in my chest rose and I *finally* let out the loud sob that had been keeping me hostage. I wailed, not caring that everybody in the house could hear me. Every bone in my body crumbled and my heart shattered. Everything that I knew and loved was all lies. He was laying in our bed and texting another woman. He was talking to her as I laid next to him and spoke about our future. He was texting her once I was asleep. He was talking to her before our date nights. Even when we were on our weekend away, he couldn't stop talking to her.

Yousef cupped my face and begged me to look at him. His regret and pain did little to soften the blow of my heartache. "I'm sorry. Let me make it up to you. I will spend the rest of my life making this right. Please Sumayyah. Please don't leave me. Forgive me."

I zoned out of reality. I couldn't see anything past my tears. When I spoke, it was in a trance. "I've been killing myself, trying to make you happy. I've been killing myself trying to give you the baby you want. I've been so *unhappy.* But I thought our love would survive anything. It turns out I've been on the battlefield alone."

"I'm here," he begged. "It was a mistake."

I looked at him. "What was? Talking to her or marrying me?"

Chapter Thirty-Seven

My eyes stung from the tiredness mixed with the tears. I had been sitting in the same spot for two hours trying to absorb the reality of my marriage. It was like my brain couldn't comprehend Yousef doing such a thing, but I had seen it with my own eyes. Every time I closed my eyes, all I could see were their messages back and forth. I tried to imagine what the phone calls were about, but I felt sick at the thought. Yousef sat opposite me on the floor, unmoving and silent.

"Why?" I croaked out. "Is it because I wasn't fucking you enough? Were you bored with fucking this old, infertile woman?"

His lip quivered. "Stop talking about yourself like that. It was never about sex."

I looked at him. "Then what?"

"You were so distant from me and it felt good to be... wanted."

My soft laugh ached me. "So, it's my fault? I didn't pay enough attention to you. I didn't instigate sex enough. I didn't tell you just how horny I was."

"*Sumayyah*. Please stop talking like that. It wasn't a physical thing. I'm not attracted to Maisha at all."

With the coldest tone, I said, "Don't ever utter that name in my presence again."

He took a deep breath. "I was just lonely, and she was there paying all this attention to me. She reminded me of you when we first met."

I covered my face with my hands to muffle my laugh. "Could you get any more cliched? I don't recall ever texting like that. I couldn't even talk to you about contraception before we got married. *You* couldn't even tell me you didn't want to use a condom. *That's* the Yousef I married. He had morals and shame. The one before me is immoral."

His back stiffened. "My messages to her were not explicit."

"I was looking forward to tonight, but my wife fell asleep. I guess it's just me again," I said, repeating one of his texts. "Maybe not explicit, but definitely suggestive. Did you touch yourself in our bed, or did you go to the bathroom with your phone?"

"I never did that," he forced out.

"When we were being intimate, were you thinking of her?" I wanted him to make a final stomp on my heart. I wanted him to crush whatever was left of my soul so I could leave with no doubts plaguing me.

With a pointed stare, he said, "No."

My eyes didn't waver from his face. My gaze trailed over his face, and it almost felt like I was looking at a stranger. How had I missed this? The messages dated over six months ago. Had I become that indifferent to my husband that I never saw the fear and worry of being caught in his eyes? When his phone pinged, how did I miss his smile at her messages? When we laid in bed and he was engrossed with his phone, why didn't I question it? *Because you loved him and with love comes blind trust.*

There was only once I noted his worry – the day I overheard the conversation with his mum. I told him I didn't want him to look at other women, and for just a moment, he panicked. I assumed it was because he thought I overheard. But the truth was so much worse.

"So, why? Make me understand why you would do this to me? To our marriage? Was it really that bad?"

He struggled to get his words out. "This was a long time ago and if you read the last messages, you will see that I told her it was inappropriate and that we should stop speaking. I ignored her messages and calls. I stopped all contact with her, even at work. She's not in my life anymore because I realised how bad I fucked up. I was stupid and made the biggest mistake of my life. I stopped long before you found out."

He was right. He told her she should stop messaging him. His call log was proof that her calls went unanswered. But one point remained.

"If it was over, why did you keep the messages?"

Once again, Yousef struggled to answer. "I just ... I forgot about them."

"I think you're lying. You kept them for one of two reasons. Actually," I backtracked, "Maybe it's both. You kept those messages because you wanted them at hand to go back and read. When you were angry at me or upset, you went back to them to boost your little ego. They served as a reminder that there was someone who would satisfy you more than me. And the second reason is the obvious one. There was a part of you that wanted me to find those messages."

"Why would I want that? I have been begging you to let me fix this."

"You already told me. You just don't have the guts to do it. You want me to do it for you."

"What?"

Like it was obvious, I said, "Divorce."

My mum was sitting on her bed mending the button on one of my dad's shirt. I entered her room slowly. It felt like I was young Sumayyah again as she prepared to tell her mum about Ibrahim. But I wasn't that young girl anymore. I was a woman who life had ripped apart.

"Amma?"

"Did your dad's appointment go okay?"

I took my dad for an MRI just to be on the safe side, as he still complained about twinges in his back. Despite my need for solitude after last night, taking in the fresh air was refreshing. Being outside reminded me that life continued, even if it felt like I was paralysed.

"Fine. Can we talk?"

"What's wrong with you now?"

I sat at the foot of her bed. With as much confidence as I could muster, I said, "I want a divorce."

She was so stunned she dropped the button and didn't even try to look for it. "Astagfirullah. What are you saying?"

She needed to see I was strong about this, so I bit back my cries. "I can't do it anymore, Amma. I can't live with that man."

"What did he do?"

There was no way to have this conversation without telling her the truth. If she knew about his affair, even if it was just emotional, she would understand. She would be the one to demand a divorce for me. Not only as a mother but also as a woman.

"He cheated."

There was a flicker of disappointment before it was gone. She climbed off the bed and started looking for her missing button. "With who?"

"A girl at work."

"Just the one?"

"Does it matter?"

"How did you find out?"

"I saw the messages."

She found her button and resumed her seat and sewing. "Is there a baby coming?"

I scrunched my brows in confusion. *Where was her rage? Where was her pain?* "No. He never ... he just messaged her."

My mum let out an exasperated sigh. "Why did you say affair then?"

Maybe she misunderstood, or I downplayed it. "Amma, these messages were not good. They were dirty."

She waved me off as if I told her I lost a penny. "These things are normal. Don't worry about it."

My Dadi walked in at that moment. "Worry about what?"

Please don't say it.

"Your granddaughter wants a divorce because her husband messaged a work friend."

Disbelief was an understatement. How could my mother not support me in this? Yousef's mum would obviously support her son even though he was the guilty party. The least my mum could do was show some understanding.

My grandmother waved me off. "What's wrong with that?"

"It's wrong! It's *haram*." *Forbidden.* "If that was me, you would have all killed me."

My grandmother took a seat next to me. "Listen, these things happen. That is men for you. They can't control their urges. Do you think you're the first woman to have a husband with a wandering eye? It's in their nature."

I felt ashamed that another woman, let alone my own flesh and blood, had such a cold, evasive stance on this. How could she justify infidelity because he was a man?

"That doesn't make it okay."

She tutted at me. "Your grandfather was known in our village. He even made one his second wife and made me live with her. Did I complain?"

"This isn't back in history. I won't tolerate my husband speaking to another woman because he's sleeping alone."

My mum scoffed. She addressed my grandmother. "Now we learn the truth."

I stood. "What's that?"

"Why wouldn't he go for another woman when his wife is parading around hospitals all night? This is why your *hori* said what she did back then. Men don't like their bed to be empty." She went off on a ramble to herself. "I told her dad not to educate her too much. I told him she doesn't need to become a big doctor, but *no*. He wanted his daughter to have a big name. What do I know? I'm just the house slave."

I wanted to shake some sense into my mum, but I was more hurt than anything else. "You're blaming me?"

"Not blaming, but this is life."

"If I did what he did, my name would be slandered. The world would talk about the woman who cheated on her husband. But because he's a man, it's justified? The blame falls on me? He doesn't have to take any accountability?"

My grandmother looked at me with irritation. "You British girls are too much; always complaining when life gets a little hard. This is what marriage is. Tell him to say sorry and finished. Back in my day, we wouldn't even dare to ask for an apology."

I couldn't stand there and argue with them. I had no tears left to cry. I went, hoping I would have support in getting a divorce. If my mum as a woman couldn't understand why I couldn't get past this, going to my dad was hopeless. He too would justify Yousef's actions. He'd probably blame my work, too. He'd tell me I wasn't a good enough wife, hence why my husband was led astray.

A good wife keeps her husband satisfied. She keeps his bed warm. She keeps him from straying.

I failed in all of those areas.

I failed in my marriage.

With no support from my side, getting a divorce was impossible.

With nowhere else to go, I got back in my car and drove back to Yousef with a list of demands.

Chapter Thirty-Eight

The candles and dimly lit restaurant didn't make this feel any more romantic. It was details I overlooked because it felt more like business than a couple out for dinner.

Yousef was dressed in a powder blue shirt and smart trousers. Normally, his groomed appearance would have earned a compliment from me. I would have told him I loved this colour on him because his grey eyes shone brighter. But he didn't get more than a look of indifference. In contrast, he showered me with compliments. His belief that it would compensate for his mistakes was far from reality. The only way forward was his agreement.

Betrayal to myself stung in my blood. I didn't want to make my marriage work, but it was my only choice. The thought of having him touch me made me feel sick to my stomach. I had been sleeping in the spare bedroom on our floor. It was a small space with only a single bed and dresser. But at least I could breathe. Being near him made me want to cry. I wanted someone to blow air directly into my lungs because I couldn't breathe. It was a blend of anger and pain.

There was a part of me that wanted him to grovel until this weight disappeared. But the other part never wanted to look at him again. Perhaps I could overcome this. Maybe that was my only option.

He looked up from his menu. "The ribeye looks good." He sounded so normal. He was acting like nothing happened and I couldn't tolerate that.

"Did you ever take her out for dinner?" *That burst his bubble.*

He sighed. "Do we really have to do this now?"

"Yes."

"Why are you torturing yourself?"

I rolled my eyes. "That's a yes then. Good to know." When he tried to speak, I said, "Just shut up and order your food."

Tension settled between us. The waitress came and took our order. Her smile lingered too long on Yousef. He smiled back. *Was he attracted to her?* I wanted to take my steak knife and stab him in the back, so he knew how I felt. I wanted to twist the knife in his heart and then turn it on myself. I never had trust issues before. I never doubted Yousef. When we were out, I never thought to wonder if he found other women attractive. Now it was all I could think about.

Once she was gone, he placed his hands on the table. "How is work?"

It was no surprise that I avoided him by working extra long shifts the past two days. I was happy when Ibrahim wasn't on the same shift as me because he could see right through me and I needed to be invisible. I wanted to become a ghost.

"Does she look like our waitress?"

He took a deep breath. "Is this how it's going to be anytime we go somewhere?"

"Until you earn my trust back."

Yousef let out a breath of relief. "I'll take it because it means you haven't given up. What will it take?"

I don't know what it said about my character that I felt smug about his desperation. Our entire marriage has been *me* begging him for love and acceptance. It was *me* desperately trying to make him happy. At that moment, I felt powerful. I finally felt in control for the first time in my life.

With a polite grin, I said, "I'm glad you asked. Let me set something straight; you don't get to make the decisions anymore. There are no more demands from you. I don't care if it makes you feel emasculated. You *should* feel like that because a real man wouldn't fantasise about a young woman. Is that understood?"

Like a puppy following the trail of a treat, he nodded. "I'm going to prove how much I love you. I will do anything for you." He had said that before, but it was a lie.

"Let's get the obvious out of the way. She is dead to you. You don't text, speak or even look at her. As far as you're concerned, she doesn't exist."

Another nod. "Okay. I've already made that clear to her. Avoiding her at work might be a little harder," he said honestly.

Thankfully, I had a solution to that issue. "That's fine, because you're going to quit your job. Tomorrow hand in your resignation."

He completely stilled. He watched me as if I was about to laugh and tell him I was joking. "You're being serious?"

"My demands are non-negotiable. You *will* quit your job."

"That's unreasonable and unrealistic. I have bills to pay."

I shrugged. "You should have thought about that before you found yourself a little play thing at work. You can explain to your parents and brother why they will have to cover the household bills for the time being. But you will not work there while she's there. I have no right to tell her to leave, but *you*? I have every right over because you may have forgotten, but I am still your wife."

The begging started. "Sumayyah, please. I've been with that company for eight years. I worked hard to get myself to my position."

A laugh ripped out of me without warning. "Where have I heard that before?" I feigned contemplation before meeting his gaze. "Oh yeah! When you begged me to put this marriage above my career and I tried to make you understand. I studied, put myself in debt and then gave up my career to make this marriage work. Fat lot of good it did me," I ended sarcastically.

"I never wanted you to quit your job."

"Not in those exact words, but you were the reason. And I did it because I needed you to see the sacrifice I was willing to make for us. Are you incapable of doing the same?"

He met my challenging stare. He closed his eyes and nodded. "What about buying a house?"

Time to dig the knife in a little harder.

"I'm going back to work full time. I will save for our house and when I'm ready, we *will* be moving. No more excuses. No more bullshit. You can stay home and look after your parents. You can learn to cook and clean. I expect you to be home every single day, being a good house husband."

The sadness in his eyes was hard to look at. It made me lose some of my confidence. But one reminder of his messages, one memory of being alone in that house, brought it all right back.

"You want to punish me."

I shook my head. "No. I want you to understand what my life has been; what you stripped me down to. You've had it all for the past six years. Now live in my shoes and maybe you'll understand a fraction of what it means to be the wife and daughter-in-law."

He resigned into his seat. "My notice period is three months."

Our conversation came to a pause as our dishes were brought out to us. The waft of my steak and creamy mash didn't make my stomach rumble. It just added to the nausea. I pushed my plate away, more focused on this conversation.

Once we were alone again, I continued. "Your location is to be shared with me. You go straight to work and come back home. There are no more outings with your boys. We're going to buy an Apple Watch and connect it to your phone. I want to see every message that comes through to you."

He briefly wondered if all these new rules and regulations were worth it. Whatever he saw on my face made him accept his new reality. "Okay," he whispered. "Whatever it takes. However long it takes."

My heart raced in my chest. I expected him to resist more. I expected demands of his own. But this Yousef was defeated. He wasn't even trying to get his own way. I should have been elated. I needed this to prove he wanted to make this marriage to work. *So why was I disappointed? Why didn't I feel as good as I expected?*

Because you wanted to him to disagree. You wanted to fail. You wanted him to leave.

My subconscious was right. She knew none of this would make me happy. Too much had happened. Too much was said. The damage was done and the rose-tinted mirror had shattered. No amount of false promises and pretty lies would make it whole again. I could never heal from the wounds of my marriage.

I wanted out.

But I couldn't make the first step. This culture would never accept me. My family would never accept it.

So this was my only choice. I had no choice but to find a way to survive in this marriage. It wasn't living. It was barely existing.

"Is there anything else?" he asked.

"One more. If you ever lie to me again, I will leave. Any lie, Yousef. I won't forgive you again."

I knew it was a lie. I would have to forgive him because I was trapped.

There was no way out for me.

Chapter Thirty-Nine

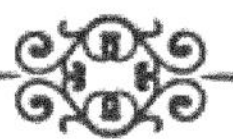

I stormed into the clinic with purpose. It had been another month since Yousef provided a second sample and his results were yet to be given. I worried they had lost his sample again. If they had, I intended to write a lengthy complaint to the governing body.

I was offered a laparoscopy, but I wasn't going to put my body through that if there were issues on Yousef's side. My doctor had formed me that some women with endometriosis can conceive. It is harder, but it was possible. That made me wonder why it hadn't happened for me and Yousef. There was two viable answers; one: my endometriosis caused too much damage to my ovaries and tubes, but I had gone without symptoms or pain, which made this unlikely. Two: there was a problem with Yousef's sperm. Either way, we needed his results before taking the next step.

IVF was the recommended route, which sounded ideal to me because making a baby the normal way was the last thing I wanted to do. I decided if I was stuck in this marriage, I would do everything I could to have my baby. I needed some love in my life.

"Excuse me," I called for the receptionist's attention. "Can I get the follow-up results of a sample that was provided weeks ago?"

She smiled at me. "Yes. Could I get the date of birth?"

"Twelfth of June 1987." I impatiently tapped my finger against the desk as she clicked away at her laptop.

After confirming a few more details, she looked at me, confused. "Those results were sent out almost six weeks ago."

It was my turn to look befuddled. Yousef never told me he got his results. If what she was saying was correct, it meant he got his results before he provided a second sample. Did he miss the letter or email?

"How was it given?"

"An email was sent, but I can also see Mr Hasan came and spoke to Dr Li about his results."

Cold spread through me. *He lied to me.* What was in those results that he wanted to hide from me?

I put on a polite smile to hide the red I was seeing. "My husband must have lost the papers. Could I get a copy of his results, please?"

She saw right through my sweet tone. "Unfortunately, GDPR laws don't allow us to provide those documents unless it's the patient requesting it. If Mr Hasan would like a new copy, he would have to come down with some photo identification and request it."

I knew she was right. It was the same laws I followed as a doctor. "But I'm his wife," I deadpanned. "I just passed all of his identification questions. I'm a doctor myself."

With an apologetic smile, she said, "I'm sorry, Mrs Hasan. There's nothing else I can do."

It wasn't her fault I felt like disobeying the oath I took as a doctor and murdering someone, but the snide comment came out. "It's not *Mrs* Hasan. I'm *Doctor* Rahman." With that, I left the clinic and drove straight home.

I stormed straight upstairs and paid no attention to a half dressed Yousef. When he said hello, I ignored him and starting rummaging through our draws for his letter from the clinic. I pulled most of our clothes out and swept every draw, but I came up empty.

"What are you doing? What are you looking for?"

Still ignoring him, I checked his bedside draw and then mine for safe measure. I opened our wardrobe door and checked every pocket, but still found nothing.

He must have thrown it away.

I turned to him. "Give me your phone," I demanded.

"Why?"

"Because I said," I snarled.

He looked at me with wary before putting his phone in my outstretched hand. "What are you looking for?"

I took a seat at my dressing table and started with his messages first. There was no message from the clinic. I checked his email next. I typed the clinic name into the search bar. When it loaded zero results, I threw his phone on the bed.

"Where is it?"

His eyes widened. "What are you talking about?"

I stood up and stalked towards him like my prey. "You've made me the biggest fool in the world. To my family, to yours, to my friends. I went to your clinic today."

His face paled.

"I was ready to scream at them for losing your sample again. Imagine how idiotic I looked when she said you got your results *weeks* ago!"

He said nothing.

"Tomorrow you're going to get a copy of your results. It better be on my dresser before I get back at six. Understood?"

"I can tell you what it said."

"Do you think I'll believe a word that comes out of your mouth?" I stood up. "Get the papers." I quickly changed out of my clothes and got into a fresh set.

"Where are you going?" he asked.

"To get a fucking break from you and your lies."

🎀🎀🎀🎀

The group hug was tighter than usual. I squeezed my friends tight, needing to feel some love.

"All is right in the world again," Zoya said.

Rani holds onto Zoya. "I've missed you."

With a shake of her head, she said, "It's forgotten."

My eyes fell on her growing bump. "It feels like your bump has grown overnight."

She groaned as she lowered herself onto the sofa. Once she was comfortably nestled against the cushions, she said, "I don't know what it is about this pregnancy, but I am really feeling it. Maybe it's my age because my body can barely keep up."

Halima winced. "Don't say that! You're making me question if we should carry on trying."

Rani gasped. "You're trying again?"

With a sheepish smile, she said, "Yeah. We only decided a few weeks ago. Jannah is in school, so it feels like the right time."

As Zoya warned her about the jump one from child to two, I looked at my friend with worry. Why would she choose to have a baby with an abusive man? *Why are you trying to have a baby with a man that lies to you?* I recoiled at my own rhetorical question. With Yousef, it was different. He didn't make me fear for my life. *No, he just makes you feel unloved.*

"Is Nazir excited?" I asked.

With a look of silent pleading, Halima implored me to keep quiet. "Yeah. He really wants a boy."

"Aw! That would be perfect. A mini Halima and a mini Nazir."

Would Nazir raise his son to be like him? Would he teach him to raise his hand on a woman?

"What are you having? Do you know yet?" Halima asked Zoya, changing the subject.

Our friend cradled her bump as if she was trying to protect it from the world. "A girl," she said softly.

We all cheered with joy. None of us noticed the frown on her face.

"Women for the win!" Rani said with a fist bump in the air. "Isn't it crazy that she's all tucked inside her mum, unaware of the love that awaits her?" There was a wistfulness in her words.

"Has someone changed their mind about children?" I teased.

Her eyes narrowed. "No. I just think it's crazy that she's in there, getting ready for the big, wide world. Who knows what she's going to become or who she will meet in her life. The world is at her feet and we get to see her take her first step."

As a joke, Halima pretended to check Rani's temperature. "Are you okay?"

We all laughed.

Rani smiled. "I guess I'm just feeling grateful for you girls. When we met, we were just children and now we're all settled into our lives. We're on completely different paths but still tied together. How many people are that lucky?"

I felt emotional at her soft tone. "You're right. We are the lucky few to have a friendship that turned into sisterhood."

Zoya fanned her face. "My hormones run my body and you guys are making me cry. I love you guys. My baby girl is so lucky to have you guys as her aunts. She will look up to you. You are going to be the best role models for her."

"So will you. Her mum is so strong."

Zoya looked down at the ground. "No, I'm not. I've spent my whole life letting others tell me what to do, and I've never found the strength to push back. I never want my little girl to see me as a role model."

Halima sat in front of Zoya and squeezed her knee. "Never sell yourself short. She is so lucky to have you as her mum. None of us are perfect. We all have our shortfalls. It's down to us to make our children learn from our mistakes. We teach them what we were never taught. We build them to be stronger than us."

"Yeah," I added. "If we look back at our lives, none of us can say we did it all right. Mistakes are part of life. We just have to learn from them. We need to promise ourselves to never make the same mistake twice."

It felt like the word hypocrite was tattooed on my forehead. I hadn't learnt from my mistakes. I was so afraid of disappointing those around me; I continued making the same error. I forgave Yousef one too many times. What part of my life had I done right? I was living for everyone else. I killed myself to study and become a doctor. I got married before I was emotionally ready. I gave up work to make my in-laws happy. When would I realise that my actions would be fatal?

"You speak like you don't have a story worth telling," Rani said with a frown. "But you do. Your story is filled with equal parts struggle and strength. Look at the life you have built. You were forced to write a story with characters and a setting you didn't want. But you made it work and one day when your little girl comes and asks for advice, you'll know exactly what chapter to turn to guide her. Isn't that what motherhood is about?"

Zoya wiped away her few tears. "I love that. A story worth telling."

We held hands, reminiscent of school days. The four girls who were afraid of the scary world.

"We all have a story," Halima said. "And we all deserve a happy ending."

With determination, I said, "We will get the ending we deserve."

Rani shuddered. "Great, now I'm crying. I love it. The story of the four *bous.* The four women that are going to break tradition."

I smiled. "The four wives that are going to live for themselves."

"The four daughter-in-laws that will stand up for themselves."

Halima shook her head. "Wrong. We're the four *bows.* We are those young girls who, at sixteen, were forced into the world. We were beaten, bruised and forced to live for our families. Not anymore. We're not just a *bou*. We are *women.* We forged a bond with those ribbons. We tied the knot with our own hands. Our stories are not the ones where we belong to *them.*"

The determination in her face made us feel *fierce*. It made us feel *empowered*.

"Why should our story be tied to them? Our lives started long before them. It started when we were sixteen and tied the only bond that never let us down. We're The Bows: intertwined, strong and forever-lasting."

Chapter Forty

I STARED AT THE white envelope sitting on my dressing table. Yousef had done exactly as I asked and picked up a copy of his results. He was out with his parents. The weight of my future rested in that envelope. Deep down, I knew what that paper said. I just wasn't ready to face the consequences.

Changing out of my scrubs and into my pyjamas, I took a seat in the middle of my bed. My fingers held onto the envelope. With one final deep breath, I tore it open. My eyes honed in on every word of his report, and with that, my heart shattered. I could have handled the results. I would have stood with Yousef, forging a path together. Yet, he went out of his way to lie to me. He said his sample was lost. He lied about attending another appointment. He tried to hide this from me.

Was it because he thought I would see him as less? Just because he was ready to leave me didn't mean I would have done the same thing. He had no belief in me. After all I had done for him, he still didn't trust I would stand by him.

I don't know how long I sat in that position; cross-legged, teary-eyed, and that paper in my hand. It could have been minutes or hours. I didn't move until Yousef entered the room.

He stilled by the door. He looked at me, but I couldn't look at him. What was I supposed to say? How was I supposed to get over this? It seemed to be one problem after another, and I was helpless. I didn't know what else to do. *How much more was I supposed to take?*

The door clicked shut.

"Doctor Li said there are things we can do to increase the sperm count."

I didn't care about any of that. "When were you going to tell me?"

He walked into the room. "I was just trying to process it. I was going to tell you."

I looked at him. "I don't think you were. I think you hoped that Doctor Li was going to give you the solution to your problem. You were okay with letting me think this was all my fault. You could have lifted this burden off my shoulders and shared my pain, but you *chose* to save yourself. You chose yourself."

The bed dipped as he took a seat at the edge, facing me. "That isn't true. I just needed—"

I cut him off. "What *you* needed. That is all you care about; what Yousef needs. What Yousef wants. What about what *I* want? What about what *I* need? You tried to save your face. That is the only reason you hid this from me; because you were *ashamed*." I spat the last word at him. "You thought I would abandon you the way you wanted to abandon me."

"If I was going to abandon you, I would have done that. I stayed!" His temper raised. "I stood by you."

I threw the letter at him. "You stood *behind* me like a fucking coward! You let me take every hit in this sham marriage."

He punched the bed. "You have never appreciated me. It's like you choose to ignore everything I have done."

I pushed off the bed. "What have you done for me? Go on! List five things you've done for me that didn't serve you." I wanted to laugh when he struggled to list one thing. "Did you say anything when people asked question after question about why we didn't have children? Did you tell them it was a private affair? Did you tell them your wife was doing *everything* she could? Did you?" I screamed.

"I had to answer those same questions," he said defiantly.

"Why are you stopping your husband from being a father? Haven't you worked enough? How much education do you need? Have you seen a doctor? Have you tried to lose some weight? Have you tried putting on some weight? Have you tried this diet? If you don't want children, why would you get married? You're ruining his life along with yours." My voice cracked. "Are those the questions and comments you have had to face? Tell me," I begged.

"I can't control what other people say."

It was a pathetic answer.

"But you can control what you say. When your mother begged you to get a divorce, what did you say?"

"I don't know what you're talking about." The lie slipped off his tongue so easily, as if it was second nature.

If he lied, he would do so while looking into my eyes. I rounded the bed and stood before him. "Don't lie to me. I heard it with my own ears. I was in our bed and you were out there," I pointed to the door, "and she told you to leave me and start over because I couldn't carry your child. What did you say? For once, be honest with me."

He met my stare. "I told her I needed to try first."

His words felt like a bullet straight into my heart. I backed away from him, holding my chest because it felt like my heart was going to bleed out. "Let's see if she gives me the same advice."

"Sumayyah!" He called out after me. "This is between us."

I stopped mid-way down the stairs. "Nothing in our marriage was between us." I ran down to the ground floor where Anjuman and Sahil were sitting. "I want to ask you something."

She glanced away from the TV. "What's wrong now?"

"Your son is the one who cannot provide a child. What should I do?"

Yousef pulled my arm to drag me out of the room, but I shook him off.

"What is she talking about?"

"When I'm talking to you, address me!" I shouted. "Tell me! What should I do? My husband cannot provide me with a child."

"What did the doctor say?" my father-in-law asked.

I turned to face him and spoke at a lower volume. "He can't have a child. He knew about this and *lied* to me. He hid it from me. So tell me, what should I do? When your wife found out we were struggling and assumed it was me, she told your son to divorce me. As a mother, she couldn't bear to see her son unhappy. Now I'm unhappy. Am I deserving of the same understanding?"

He turned to his wife in disbelief. "Is this true?"

She shared a look with her son before defiance came over her. "I said what I said."

I knew she wouldn't regret her actions. "As a daughter, as a *woman*, I am telling you I have never been this upset before. Look at what your son has put me through!" Those were the same words she used when she pleaded with her son to see sense and leave me.

She recognised the words immediately. "You'll get over it. You always do after making a big drama."

Anger like never surged through me. This was the consequences of always coming back to him. "Your son didn't want children because he was too busy having an affair. What did that affair get him?" I asked, still twisting her own words. "Did it give him happiness? Did it give him children? All that searching for another woman and it's *his* body that is ruined."

With a scoff, she said, "Does that mean there's nothing wrong with you?"

"There's still a chance for me. Islamically I have the right to leave a husband that cannot provide a child. This life isn't enough for me. He won't be able to make me happy. I'll leave and start over. It's easier for a divorced woman to find a husband than it is for a man who is infertile." Every word hit her where I wanted. I wanted to ask how it felt for the tables to be turned.

She looked down at me when she thought I was the problem, but now that it was her son, she only held sympathy.

"Let's go."

I turned to Yousef. "Go on! Defend my honour! Stand up for me. Tell her how miserable you make me. Tell her how much you make me wish I was dead! Tell her how this marriage was the biggest regret of my life!"

With force, Yousef pulled me into his arms and held mine down as I struggled to get away from him. "Stop it. Please stop. Stop saying this stuff."

I punched his chest until I was breathless, and he let me. My forehead rested on his chest as I sobbed. "I want to die. I want to die. I can't live like this anymore. Just kill me."

"If you want to go, then go." His mum spoke in the coldest tone I had ever heard.

I wiped my tears and turned to face her. "How does a woman treat another woman in such a way? What did I ever do to you?"

She stepped closer. "Do you think you are the first woman to have a hard time with her mother-in-law? Your father never let your feet touch the ground. He treated you as you do a son. A woman should learn how to handle these relationships."

"If you understand my hardship because you went through it, why would you wish that on someone else? Did you not learn from her mistakes?"

"I paid my dues."

"You have a daughter," I reminded her. "A daughter who will also become a daughter-in-law. Is this the life you want for her? What would you do if your daughter came to you crying for this very reason? Would you tell your daughter to forgive the husband who has an affair?"

"I would tell my daughter this was the test Allah gave her." She was unbelievable. She didn't have a heart.

"You once said there was a reason Allah never gave me children. Maybe you were right, but He gave you children as a lesson. It's a shame you believe a man can do no wrong. A man is perfect, even with flaws; something a woman can never be. It was easy for you to accept your son's infidelity, but unable to accept a woman that works. No matter what sins he commits, it is permissible because he is simply a man. A woman cannot be held in the same regard in your eyes. Perhaps that is why you were given a son who failed in all aspects of being a true man. He was given to you because your lesson was that men are weaker than women. They aren't a higher being. They are flawed. They deserve the same punishment as a woman. And you were given a daughter for one reason. She's going to pay the dues you owe for being the mother-in-law you are. There will come a day when your daughter will come to you, on her knees, begging and pleading for you to show her a way out. When that day comes, I hope you remember me. I hope you wipe her tears and carry the burden you placed on her. The pain you have inflicted will come back on you. I hope it leaves you feeling helpless, alone and terrified."

"How dare you curse my daughter?"

I shook my head. "My curse is on you. You were so desperate to have your son to yourself. He's all yours now. Have him. I don't want him," I spat at her. "We might not see the world eye-to-eye, but we should have stood together. Men have ruled the world for as long as mankind has existed. It's down to us women to fight against them. You said my father raised me like a man. You are so ashamed to be a woman that you fought *for* them. What does that make you?" I didn't wait for her to say anything else and finally left.

Yousef was hot on my tail up the stairs. As soon as the door shut, he asked, "Did you mean what you said? Are you going to leave me?"

"Give me one reason to stay."

He cupped my face. "Because I love you."

It's just words.

My tears stopped falling. I stepped away. "That's not enough."

"You want to move out? Let's go. I'll put a deposit down by the end of the week," he rushed out.

After months of begging to move out and a flat out refusal from him, his offer was just desperate. If I agreed, he'd find another excuse to delay it. "Where did the money come from now? Or have you been lying to me all this time? Do you secretly have millions in the bank? I wouldn't be surprised. Lying comes so easily to you."

"I'll borrow the money. We can rent somewhere. Let's just go. Let's find somewhere new to start over. We can find who we were. I'll get you to fall in love with me again. We'll do it right this time."

"That's the thing, Yousef. I did it right. I did everything right. My whole life, I've never settled for anything less than perfect. I did everything I was supposed to do. It wasn't supposed to end this way for me." I just felt ... empty. It was like I had spent my whole life pouring water into everyone else's vase, and there wasn't enough left for me to blossom. I was just a sad, dying flower.

"I know. I know," he cried. "Let me prove myself this time. I won't let you down. Please, Sumayyah. I need this. I need you. Our marriage has to work."

I sat on the edge of the bed. The silence we were becoming accustomed to fell upon us again, but this time he was the one that was crying. I sat emotionless while his pain poured out of his eyes. I wanted to ask him where this determination was all this time? Why did he half-ass our marriage? Why did he search for comfort in another woman? *What changed?*

Then it hit me.

"You stopped speaking to her when you got your results." I looked at him and knew I was right. "You knew she wouldn't want you if she knew the truth. It had nothing to do with an epiphany about our marriage. The timings match up." The more I spoke out loud, the more sense it made. "You were interested in her. Maybe you even fell in love with her. The young woman who wasn't stopping you from becoming a father. She was much better than the wife who could barely stand to try for a baby anymore. The young girl was more joy to be around than the wife who kept turning up with negative pregnancy tests. She made you feel good. She didn't make you feel emasculated."

"That's just a coincidence."

"Nothing in life is a coincidence. You were looking to take your mum's advice. You wanted a divorce. You just didn't have the courage to ask for one."

Yousef grasped for the only bow in his quiver. "How is she any different from Ibrahim?"

"I never spoke to him outside of work, except that one time when you and your family were present. We never text or call. That is not the same thing."

An ugly green jealousy shadow came over him. "But I told you I didn't like your friendship with him. You never stopped speaking to him. I could call that cheating."

"I never spoke to him about our marriage. I never whined about sleeping alone. I didn't tell him about our sex life. I didn't slag you off and call you names."

"Fine! I did that because it was how I felt and if I felt like I could speak to you about it, I would have. I turned to another woman because my wife made me feel like I couldn't come to her for comfort. You were never here! You were always at work, or at your parents' or out with your friends. I felt invisible in our marriage. So I made a mistake and spoke to her."

I looked at him with nothing but pity. "A mistake is once. You made a choice. Every message, call, flirty look ... it was a choice *you* made. I am done answering for your choices. It's not for me to fix or accept."

He kneeled before me. His eyes were bloodshot from crying. "Then make the choice to forgive me. Let us draw a line and start this again. We can't give up. We can't fail."

Fail.

My biggest fear; to fail my exams, to fail university, to fail securing a job, to fail to meet everyone's expectations. I was never allowed to fail. It was unacceptable. *Number one.* That was what my dad had always taught me. But I was tired. I was shattered. I was done.

In trying to meet everyone's expectations, I had let myself down. I let people treat me however they saw fit, and I stayed silent because that was what a good woman does. She bows her head and accepts whatever comes her way. I've worked extra hard my whole life because I was the daughter my dad didn't truly want. I had to be the proof that something good comes from having a daughter. I had to stop being the daughter he dreamed, to become the daughter-in-law and wife that Yousef needed. I had to be the proof that he made the right choice by defying his mother and marrying me.

Along the way, I stopped being a person. I just became a tick box on the list of how to be perfect.

I didn't want to be number one anymore.

I didn't want to be perfect anymore.

What did I want?

I wanted to be happy.

And I would never be happy here. I tried everything to make this work. I sacrificed myself for this marriage. There was too much heartbreak in this part of my story. Every line I had written with Yousef felt like a lie. What I needed was a fresh start. I needed to end this story and start writing one where I got to choose who Sumayyah was. This Sumayyah was just an echo of what others wanted. And it wasn't enough anymore.

Yousef was clinging onto my hands like his life depended on it. Marriage is meant to be a life sentence, but I needed to pull the trigger because he was too scared. He wanted to live because he finally believed we were equal. His infertility meant we were worthy of each other.

But I wanted this Sumayyah to die. I needed her to die.

So, I requested the very thing that Yousef lacked the courage to do. I pulled the trigger and let the bullet rip through my heart. I felt the heartbreak pour out with my blood. While one part of me died, another finally came to life. She breathed a sigh of relief. She unshackled her chains and ran towards her freedom.

I made one final demand.

"I want a divorce."

Chapter Forty-One

No one in the room noticed I wasn't fully there. I was sitting in a daze as they spoke amongst themselves. Nafisa struggled to get Aila asleep and ignored the parenting advice my mother and grandmother were giving her. She rolled her eyes and rejected their suggestions, reassuring them she knew what was best for her child.

My mind focused on the feeling of suffocation. The last two days were filled with Yousef's begging and tears. I thought I would cry, but for once it was him who fell to his knees and fell apart. He was the only one crying. I was numb. I was just existing. I moved into the single room next door to our bedroom. Despite his pleas, I had made my decision.

Last night I heard him arguing with his mother, blaming her for where his marriage had ended up. I wanted to correct him and tell him it was him who did this. While it didn't excuse her behaviour, she thought she was protecting her son. He was the one who let me down and his rescue came too late. There was nothing left to save. Sumayyah was gone. She was dead.

"I want a divorce." The words blurted out of me. I don't know if I shouted it because all eyes landed on me.

"What?" Nafisa said.

I looked at her. "I want a divorce."

I knew it would be difficult, especially given Yousef's newfound dedication. A divorce in my culture was taboo. But this was the only way I could survive. I remembered the day of my Nikkah when Masuma said I could come to them if I needed to. I remember the sinking feeling of discussing divorce, but here I was.

"This again?" my mum said with a huff. "What did I tell you the other day? These things happen."

"He lied to me. He never told me he can't have children." I don't know why I thought that would grant me any sympathy from my mother.

"Who told you that?"

"The doctor."

"I'm sorry," Nafisa sympathised. "Is there anything that can be done or is it a definite no?"

I shrugged my shoulders. "It doesn't matter. He lied to me. He hid it from me. He's known for weeks and only told me because I caught him in a lie." I should have stopped there because I didn't want to drag his name through the mud, but I needed all the proof to convince my parents to support me. "He was cheating on me with a woman from work. He caught feelings for her. He wanted to divorce me and marry her."

Nafisa handed Aila to my mum before taking a seat next to me. She took my hand in hers and gave a squeeze. "Why didn't you call me?" She was the first person to show any softness.

I wanted to sob into her lap, but kept myself composed. I needed to be strong. "I told mum and Dadi and they told me this is what men do and I should accept it. If my own mother couldn't understand, who else did I have?"

She looked outranged at our mother. "Did you really say that?"

"He didn't even do anything with her. Friends can text. What's the big deal?"

I was done feeling hurt. I was angry and wanted to roar. "Okay, then shall I text my male friends and tell them I'm lonely in bed because my husband fell asleep? No?" I asked rhetorically. "Why? Is it only permissible for a man to do it?"

Her eyes widened, and she spat air at the floor. "Listen to what you're saying."

"You listen to what you're saying!" I shouted. "You are telling me, your *daughter*, to accept a man that has strayed. You are telling me to lower myself and accept a man that has been unfaithful. How can you do that?"

"This is what men do! They have always been selfish!"

I climbed off the bed to make myself feel stronger. "Why do we accept it? Why do we tolerate being treated like a second-class citizen in our relationships? Why is it so wrong to want better for ourselves?"

My grandmother intervened. "Women don't dare to want. You are so lucky to have more than what we ever dreamed of. Your grandfather would have slit my throat if I ever disobeyed him."

"Time has passed, but our culture has stayed the same. Despite being raised in this country, how has my life been any different from yours? I studied, yet my life became about cleaning and cooking. I wasn't allowed to marry for love. I'm supposed to accept that my husband can disrespect me just because he can. My life should have been different, it should have been better than yours. We raise our children to have a better life than us. Why don't you want better for me?"

My mother's eyes filled with ice. "Ungrateful. I've raised an ungrateful daughter. What haven't we given you? Your dad gave you everything you wanted. I fed you, clothed you and raised you. You married someone of your choice. Did I even see your dad before I married him? I saw his face after my Nikkah. I let you talk to him on the phone without saying anything. You worked and had your own money. Did we ever ask your for a single penny?"

"You just asked for my life instead! I broke myself trying to make you happy! Was it ever enough? No. I'm still a failure to you. Everything I did, you always wanted more."

"Whatever I did, it was for you. Only a mother would understand the sacrifices I made."

Nafisa stood in front of our mum as if it would block her words, but they were out there. They hung in the air and blared like a siren. "Abba is downstairs. You don't want him to hear this,"

"Let him. I'm sure he would love to join in and tell me how I failed because I couldn't give him a grandchild."

My mum sat on the bed and began crying. "I told your dad to keep within reason. I told him not to get greedy. All this success for a woman is never good. Allah had to take something from you. You were given the status of a man, so Allah took the thing that made you a woman. A woman doesn't stay out late at night to work. A woman's place is the home. You never understood that."

"No, Amma," I said quietly, "I understood that very well. I just didn't want to live your life; unhappy and incomplete. I wanted something for myself."

"Nothing in this world is belongs to a woman," my grandmother intervened again. "Not even our children. A son is his father's, and a daughter belongs to her husband."

I shook my head. "Not me. Not anymore. I've been abused in that house and I'm not going back."

"Afa, maybe you just need to take a break from it. Why don't you stay somewhere else?"

My stony stare turned to my sister. "Would you take Junaid back? Would you go back to a house where you have to hear snide comments about yourself?"

"It's hard, I know—"

"Hard?" I cut her off. "It's death by a thousand cuts. Every day in that house slowly takes a part of my soul. Every moment I'm worried about what's going to set her off. When my husband gets a notification or leaves the house, I feel sick to my stomach that it's another woman. I lay in my bed and I want to scrub my skin raw. I can't trust a word that comes out his mouth because he's lied to my face before. I've tried! Why can't anybody understand that all I have been doing is trying and it's not fucking enough! I can't do this anymore! I either get out or I die! Those are my only options!"

My shouts left everyone silent. My grandmother settled at the foot of the bed. My mother held Aila as she quietly wept at the embarrassment of having me for a daughter. My sister held sympathy for me but said nothing to support me.

In the quiet, my dad's heavy footsteps came up the stairs. When he entered the room, he took a second to absorb the scene. "What is all this shouting?" he asked.

At first nobody answered, but then my grandmother said, "Your eldest daughter wants a divorce." She didn't let the shock settle before she twisted the knife she dug in him the day I was born. "You so proudly said that your daughter will do everything a son could. You made sure you raise her like a son. Today she's done worse than a man ever could. Even a man would never have the courage to ask for a divorce."

"That's because a man never asks for anything," I said. "Men just do whatever they want. The world is at their feet and as women, we wipe it clean for them."

She pointed her finger at me. "I'm not your mother. You will show me some respect."

"What respect can I give to a woman who only ever favours men?"

"Sumayyah!" my dad shouted. "Chup!" *Be quiet.*

"Why?" I asked in English. "I said nothing untrue. This family, this *culture*, has never understood a woman's struggle or pain. We are expected to give and give. In the end, what do we get? A life of misery. When have I ever asked for anything? Whatever you said, I did. I followed your plan and where did it get me? Where is the happiness you said would come?"

"You aren't finished!"

"Yes, I am! I am done! This is the end for me. I don't want a life with him anymore!"

"Why not?"

"Because I'm not happy! I tried, Abba!" The tears I held back flowed. "I have tried, and nothing works. He spoke to another woman. He wanted a divorce."

My dad looked surprised at the admission. He only let it show for a moment before he concealed it with reassurance. "He only did that because you couldn't have a baby."

He justified it. He just gave Yousef the perfect excuse.

"His happiness means more to you than mine. As that's the case, then accept this divorce and let him live a happy life with someone else."

The father I knew always pushed me, but he was never cold. When he spoke, he was trying to hurt me. "Do you understand the *shame* that would befall this family if you got a divorce? People are already talking because you've failed to produce a child. When they hear whispers of a divorce, they'll know its because he wanted children."

"Let them talk because I will tell them he is also the problem. Our inability to have a child was not just me."

"Do you think people will care?" my mum said, finding her voice.

"Then why should I care? Let people talk! Why does it matter so much? People talk even when you do good. That's the toxic society of this culture. A woman can never get it right. We are judged so harshly against standards that are impossible to meet!" I pinched the bridge of my nose in frustration. "She's too dark. She's too fair. She's too tall. She's too short. She's too skinny. She's too fat. She's too educated. She's too dumb. She can't cook. She can't clean. She lives off her husband. She works too much." I stopped to catch my breath. "What is this culture? Why do we hate women so much?"

Nafisa wrapped her arms around me. "Nobody said that about you."

I pushed her arm off me and stepped away from her. "Yes, they have! And even if they hadn't, are you saying nobody has said that about you? How many times have people commented on your skin? How often did mum curse you out because you couldn't cook a chicken curry? Why is it men are never judged against these standards? Why aren't these expectations forced on them? Why does he not have to answer?" My loud questioning left everyone silent.

"It's different for them," my dad said.

I stared at him. "Was Yousef a good son-in-law? Did he ever call you? What has he ever done for you?"

"He doesn't need to!" my grandmother shouted. "A man doesn't serve his in-laws!"

"And I don't serve mine! I am not a slave, but I did my part. If I was being a good wife, I failed as a sister. When I was being a good daughter, I failed as a daughter-in-law. Where does one win? I can't make anyone happy!" My words came out rushed and intertwined with my sobs.

My dad's eyes widened with rage. "Bangla bol!" *Speak Bangla*.

I almost laughed, but instead I cried harder. I continued in English. "Why, dad? Isn't this what you wanted me to become? The perfect, educated, high-status daughter of an immigrant? Wasn't this your dream for me? *Education! Education! Education!* After school tuition. Weekend classes. Extra GCSEs. Academic a-levels. All that just for the chance to become the doctor with a title. You were so ashamed to be an immigrant who could barely speak English. You lost the status you had in Bangladesh, so you made sure I earned it here. You wanted me to be accepted by those who rejected you. You wanted my peers to be the children of those who never saw you worthy of ranking amongst them. You equally hated and envied them, but you still wanted me to be one of them because you had to prove *you* never failed. You wanted to prove that a daughter was enough. So I did it. Only for *you*. But it wasn't enough because I was a woman and I still had two-thirds of the dream left. A husband and children."

His resolve broke and the father I had known joined us in the room. "Life is hard. It is a test. You can't fall so easily."

My vision blurred. "Do you think I want this? Tell me, Amma," I looked at her, "Does a woman so easily ask for a divorce?"

My dad answered instead. "Whatever he has done, he will say sorry. These things happen in a marriage."

"Why wouldn't it happen?" For the first time, I saw my mum stand up to my dad. "You made her into a doctor and she was working nights. Would you tolerate that as a man?"

He was lost in thought before saying, "We'll tell him she won't work nights anymore. Finished."

I didn't have anymore energy to repeat the conversation again. It felt like I had exhausted every hypothetical scenario to make them understand nothing could ever justify such a betrayal. He was my husband. We made a vow before God to honour the sanctity of marriage.

"That's not enough!" she snapped. "She needs to stop working altogether. Let her sit at home and maintain her house."

"I'm not going to do that," I defied. "I won't go back."

My mum turned to me and pleaded, "Go back to your husband. A daughter doesn't return to her family."

The look on my dad's face had betrayal stinging in my blood. "Go home. Forget about all this."

"What about children?" I asked. "What about a family of my own?"

He grew frustrated with me. He wanted this conversation to be swept under a rug and forgotten about. "Will you get that with another man? If you both have problems, then what choice do you have? Some dreams are meant to remain incomplete."

He wasn't talking about my dream because my dream was simple: happiness. It was his dream that remained incomplete. Despite having the job and husband, I was still a failure for not fulfilling the dream.

When I glanced at him, a hint of sadness lingered. I mostly felt anger. "Did I not become everything you wanted me to be? The perfect daughter, wife, and daughter-in-law. I wanted to be all those things because that was what was expected, but I couldn't be the thing I wanted most: a mother. Maybe it was God's will, or maybe it's a blessing in disguise. Whatever it is, in your eyes, I'm also now the perfect failure. My life was just a checkbox to you. So add another checkbox to your list. You can't see how much pain your child is in. You raised me with your own hand. As my parents, you should have protected me and my honour. I'm bringing shame upon you by asking you to save me from this pain. Why is he not being held accountable? I was made to answer for my shortfalls. I was forced to make sacrifices. Men are not shamed for their shortfalls. Why should they be when the woman is held accountable for their failures? I tell you my husband committed such a grave sin, and your response is to accept it because that is what happens. You blamed me for his infidelity. I wasn't doing enough. But this is all I have left. I cannot conform to your expectations because no one can ever be perfect."

CHAPTER FORTY-TWO

THE HOTEL ROOM'S SILENCE offered no solace for my mind. Neither of my parents tried to understand why I desperately needed to get out of my marriage. They couldn't see how it was hindering me. Their only concern was others' opinions. To them, Yousef was a good husband. When I gave examples of when he wasn't, they found any excuse for his actions. I couldn't get them to understand how every small incident led to this. No matter how hard I tried, I couldn't forgive him for his relationship with Maisha or for hiding the truth about his fertility issues.

After leaving their home, I couldn't get myself to go back to Yousef's house. Every explanation to my parents was a reminder of all the small heartbreaks I was forced to patch up. But those weak stitches had come undone and no treatment would fix it.

I got myself out of bed and freshened up. Nafisa's text said she would be here in fifteen minutes and I had spent the last ten laying in bed replaying the events of my marriage. When she knocked on my door, I let her in.

She hugged me tight. "Did you get some sleep?"

I shut the door. "A little," I lied. "Where's Aila?"

"With her dad. I thought we could talk properly. Yesterday was ... a lot."

Just like when we were children, we sat cross-legged on the bed.

"It went exactly how I thought it would. I thought I would have garnered some sympathy from them, but I should have lowered my expectations."

She pursed her lips. When she spoke, it was with reason. "They were surprised. You have to understand that divorce for that generation is a monster they don't talk about. It is forbidden. They come from a time when you make your marriage work, no matter the consequences."

"But *why*? What do we get from that? How are we still living like that? If divorce was forbidden, then Islam wouldn't have a process for it. Tell me, what would you do if you were me?" I begged. I needed someone to tell me I wasn't over-exaggerating.

She sighed. "It's hard because while I understand why you're hurt and angry..." She paused. "I don't know if I could give up on my marriage like that. People make mistakes. I'm not saying it's okay, but he's human. I think if he actually went and slept with her, it would be different."

I remembered Halima talking about how women only knew abuse. She pointed out that physical abuse was the same as emotional abuse. "An affair is an affair. Just because it was an emotional one doesn't make it different from a physical one. In fact, it's worse. If he slept with her, I would accept their argument that men are men. He wasn't getting enough from me, so he wanted to fulfil his urges. It doesn't make it okay, but it would support their argument. But this..." I shook my head. "It's harder because he didn't love me enough. He had some left to give someone else."

With a frown, she said, "You were going through a tough time. Maybe he gave up then, but he's trying to make it work now, right?"

"Only because he can't have children. He wanted to leave when he thought *I* was the reason we couldn't have a baby. He's not fighting, he's settling."

"He's accepted that you are enough for him."

"You know, I asked him to move out. I was so unhappy in that house and I told him I needed that space in order for our marriage to work. He couldn't give me that. He's had so many chances to prove he would fight for our marriage, but he failed. He couldn't give me anything. There's no point fighting when the war is already over."

Lost in thought, Nafisa gazed downward. I knew she came here on behalf of my parents. They wanted her to relay something, and I was waiting for her to find the courage to say it.

"They want to sit down with Yousef and his family to sort things out."

My back straightened. "I'm not doing that. They're going to blame me and this side will accept all the blame because it's automatically my fault."

"Afa, you have to accept some of the blame. You have to accept that some things were driven by you."

"I do. We both hurt each other, but no matter how much pain I was in, I never did what he did. I had every chance, but I remained faithful. I was honest with him about my medical issues."

She looked afraid to ask her question. "Do you want a divorce because he's the one that can't have children?"

Subconsciously, my thumb brushed my wedding bands. "I wouldn't have cared because I loved him. His results weren't the end of the road. I would have tried everything to make it happen."

"Then why don't you do that? Try to start your family. Everything might fall into place for you."

I shuffled closer and held her hands in mine. "I pray you never know how it feels to be me. I am so happy your marriage is filled with love and happiness that you can't understand this feeling of hopelessness. I can't see a way out of this. I have tried. I spend every moment asking myself what it would take to make this work. But there's nothing. I have no faith in Yousef. Everything he does for me now would be the actions of a man who is helpless. He told me he wanted a divorce almost a year ago. Do you want to know what I did?"

"What?" she whispered.

"I sacrificed my happiness to convince him to stay and love me. That isn't marriage. I'm not enough for him. All I have wanted to be is enough for someone."

"They'll cut you off," she warned. Tears brimmed in her eyes. "You'll be dead to them."

I brushed her tears away. "Mourn for me. Grieve for your sister because she's already dead. Everyone took and took and there's nothing left."

"How's mum and dad?" Yousef asked when I entered the bedroom. He rarely asked about my parents, but I knew he was trying to make conversation after the little interaction between us since I asked for a divorce.

"They know I want a divorce," I said harshly.

"What?" he said. "Why would you do that?"

"Because I meant what I said. We're getting a divorce."

He grabbed my shoulder and forcefully turned me around. His eyes housed anger and betrayal. "No, we're not. We're going to sort things out."

Shoving his hand off me, I took a step away. "We're not having this conversation again."

He closed the distance between us. "I've been looking for a house. We can view some of them."

I rolled my eyes and started separating my whites from the colours in my hamper.

"We're going to go on a holiday to get a break and reset. We can go back to Bali. We haven't been since our honeymoon. We're going to fix this."

"There's no fixing this. What's done is done. My parents know."

"They won't accept this either," he said with confidence.

"I told them out of respect. I don't care if I have to do this alone. I've suffered in this marriage alone."

"Sumayyah, please just stop. Let's just try one more time. Please, I'm begging you."

I was glad my back was turned to him because I didn't want him to see my tears falling. "You said you'd never ask me to choose between you and my job. But now you're asking me to choose between you and me. I'm sorry, Yousef, but for once I'm choosing me."

Chapter Forty-Three

The room looked bare now that my things were packed into suitcases and boxes. I made the bed, dusted the surfaces and vacuumed before taking a moment to get a last look at the space where most of my marriage took place. Everything came rushing back to me. I looked at where Yousef and I stood on our wedding night, half-dressed and with so much hope. I could hear my giggles and sighs of pleasure from the times we were intimate in our bed. The echoes of hours-long conversations and laughed filled me. I remembered the exact spot we were in when we took our first pregnancy test and Yousef hugged me when disappointment filled me. These walls were witness to some of the best and worst times of our marriage. They heard every time I sobbed quietly, afraid that his family would hear me. They saw me beg Yousef for more. They saw Yousef beg for more. This room held so many memories for me. When I imagined leaving this cocoon, it was with the dream of moving out with my husband, not because of him.

Yousef said nothing when he entered. He stared at me with sadness.

I cleared my throat. "I've changed the bedsheets and vacuumed. The toilet has been scrubbed but don't flush it for another hour or so because I've put something in to clean out the pipes. Your clothes have been ironed and hung up."

He stepped closer, and I swallowed hard.

I avoided looking at him. "I'm pretty sure I've got everything. If you find anything after I've gone, then just put it in a bag and I'll send Abdul or Mahmood to come and pick it up."

"Sumayyah," he cried, taking another step closer.

"You'll need to take the bins out. I forgot to do that before I showered. The bathroom one is quite full because I threw away my toiletries."

"Stop," he begged.

A lodge formed in my throat. I forced it down. "I've moved the extra bedsheets from the bottom of the drawer to the other side of the wardrobe."

"That's your side." His voice cracked.

"Everything else is pretty much in the same place. The dressing table has been cleared. I'm not sure what you can use that for. You can throw it out if you want."

His arms wrapped around my waist from behind. "That's where you get ready and I sit on the bed and watch you. I tell you that you don't need makeup because you're already so beautiful."

The first tear fell. "Do you remember the pin to the safe?"

His face tucked into the crook of my neck. "It's got your stuff. Why do I need it?"

I caught my sob. "I've left my wedding gold in there. Whatever was gifted by my family has been packed. Everything else ... it's still there. Ask your mum what she would like to do with it."

His body shook as he sobbed like a child into me. "Those were gifts from me. Our wedding. Our anniversary. It's yours."

Through my tears I forced out, "I don't want a reminder of this."

He held me in a tight vise. "Please. Please don't leave me. Please don't go. Please, Sumayyah. Stay. Let me fix this. Choose me again."

I couldn't take it anymore. I let out my sobs. "I can't."

We stood in the middle of our sanctity and cried. We cried for all we had and then all we lost. We cried for our broken dreams. We cried for all the wrongs we did and the pain we inflicted. We cried at the ending that was never supposed to be ours.

"I can't live without you."

"Go and live your life," I begged. "Go and find happiness and love."

His hands found mine. He intertwined our fingers. "I already found it. Our names were written long before we existed."

My hands clenched into balls as I felt doubt attack me. "Our names were written in two different stories. Please let me go."

"I can't."

I let myself feel his embrace for one last moment. And then I let go. I let go of all the anger, resentment and pain and stepped away. "I need to go. Abdul will be in touch about the divorce."

He shook his head. "I won't do this."

I believed him. I looked at him. "If any part of you loves me, you'll do this for me. You'll let me live a life I deserve."

"Why can't we do this together? Why can't we just start fresh?"

"Because a story that was meant to be a tragedy can never become a love story. You weren't all bad. I know that and I thank you for the happiness and love you let me feel. But I can't be this anymore. I can't be confined by what others need. I can't be unhappy."

"I'll change. Whatever you want ... please."

I grabbed my suitcases. "I'm sorry."

He stood in the doorway. "Where are you going to go?"

My parents made it clear I wasn't welcome in their house. I was being forced to pave my own path in life now. "Yousef."

"Just stay until you find somewhere else." He was desperate. "Maybe you'll change your mind."

"I won't," I said with a strength I didn't feel. "Please let me go. You're hurting me by keeping me chained here."

Perhaps he saw something in me because he moved out of the way. I carried my bags down the stairs one last time. I placed them by the front door. I swallowed hard and went into the living room where his parents sat.

His mum looked at me with a look I couldn't decipher.

"I'm leaving. I wanted to say goodbye."

Haniya stood up, already crying. "Bhabi. Please, just stay. We'll be better."

I hugged her. "You were the perfect little sister. I wish you happiness in your marriage."

She didn't let go. "I need you. I need a Bhabi to get me through this. Nobody else understands me."

Pulling back, I smiled at her. "You are so strong. You'll be okay."

Younes and Amina remained silent. Disappointment was evident on Younes' face. Amina looked at me with understanding.

I looked at Sahil. "Maaf khoro," *forgive me.* "I couldn't bear the burden of forgiveness, but I hope you can. I'm sorry for the pain and trouble I brought into your home."

"I asked you to stay. I'll make sure you are okay," he promised.

"I am no longer my father's daughter. Your responsibility to him has ended. You owe nothing to me."

He stood and hugged me. "I feel shame. Today, I feel shame."

I wiped my tears and turned to the last person.

Anjuman continued to watch me, but said nothing.

"I was never what you wanted. I hope you find a daughter-in-law that will be enough. I hope she fulfils your wishes."

"My son married for love," she simply stated.

"In this culture, there is no room for love. It's filled with duty and toleration."

"I spoke to you as a mother does to her daughter. The things I said never came from a bad place. You were so hurt by me, you're leaving my son."

I shook my head. "There was a time when I had two sets of parents. Today, I'm dead to both. I have no anger towards you. You protected your son. It was my husband who didn't protect me."

Her voice wavered. "My son will die."

"I already have," I whispered. I glanced at their faces once more before exiting.

Yousef was standing in the hallway. He stared in a daze at the front door.

I took my keys out of my bag and unhooked the house key. I held it out to him, but he made no move to take it. "Yousef."

He looked at me. "No."

I took his hand in mine and forced the key into his fist. "Look after yourself." I grabbed my bag but stopped when something caught the light. I stared at my rings. With the last bit of strength I had, I pulled them off. My finger felt incomplete. I walked back over to him. "These belong to you."

He stared at them and then at his own wedding band. "Taking those off doesn't stop you from being my wife. You're still mine and I'm still yours."

When he made no move to take them, I left it on the entrance side table. I couldn't hash this out again. He would eventually have to accept the truth. With my bag in my hand, I left the house that I once welcomed as my home. I could hear Yousef calling for me, but I couldn't face him anymore.

I kept walking, and I didn't look back.

CHAPTER FORTY-FOUR

THE ONE-BEDROOM FLAT WAS much smaller than what I was used to. The volume of my boxes outweighed the limited furniture in the living room. I had spent the last two days slowly unpacking, but started with my clothes because I had booked myself back-to-back shifts for the next few days. It felt weird sleeping alone on a double bed. There were moments when I found myself waiting for Yousef to come to bed or I grabbed two plates instead of one.

Nafisa had called to see how I was doing. My parents didn't want to know. Yousef had been calling me non-stop. Haniya sent message after message. When I went out next, I had to remember to pick up a new sim card.

When my phone rang, I almost ignored it until I saw it was Zoya. I broke the news to my friends yesterday when I invited them over. They cried with me, but ultimately they stood with me.

"Hey," I said after answering.

"Hey. How are you?"

"My back is aching. I just finished putting all my clothes away. Is everything okay?"

"Yeah. I just wanted to make sure you were okay."

My heart clenched. At least I wasn't completely alone. "I'm okay."

Her soft breathing could be heard through the line. "Are you really okay? I mean ... do you have any regrets?"

It would be a lie to say I never questioned whether I made the right choice. When I sat alone, I wondered whether this loneliness was better than the life I was so desperate to leave. It wasn't what I wanted for myself, but I had to believe it could only get better from here.

"No," I said honestly. "When you know you've given it your all, and you tried your hardest, there's no room for regret. I didn't fall at the first hurdle. I picked myself up and tried to make do with what I had. It wasn't enough. I deserved better."

A weight burdened her thoughts. "How did you do it? How did you leave?"

Worry filled me. "Why are you asking?"

She sighed. "I'm having a daughter. I already know the life that has been written for her and I don't want this for her. Unless I get her out, she'll be exactly like me. They'll mould her to be weak and obedient."

Goosebumps rose on my skin. "What are you saying?"

Zoya went silent for a few seconds, but when she spoke, it was with clear determination. "I need to protect her. I need to get out of this prison."

After too many nights of no sleep, my eyes stung from tiredness, but I couldn't leave this mess on my floor. Nafisa was kind enough to pack up the few belongings I had at my parent's house. With limited storage space, I was forced to get rid of the things I held onto from my childhood. I laughed to myself as I read through the notes my friends and I passed during class.

When I found the ribbon we wore on our prom, I felt a surge of strength. That night, I felt overwhelmed with worry about the future. I had no idea what would happen. But I still ventured into the world with hope in my heart. It was scary, but I did it.

Those same anxieties fills me tonight, but I am no longer the young girl who was chained. I've escaped and broken free as a woman. I have the chance to start my life the way I want.

As people, we spend our whole lives trying to appease others. I've strived to be a successful student. A hardworking doctor. A good daughter. An attentive daughter-in-law. A loving wife. An aspiring mother.

But above all that, I am a woman and it's the heaviest title someone can bear. Because a woman must be strong. She must be tolerant. She must be worthy. She must be perfect.

When I think about the women in my life, they have constantly fought to be seen. We have to scream to be heard. People don't see the invisible battles we fight daily. My infertility was to never be spoken about. I was so ashamed because I thought it made me less of a woman.

Being a woman extends far beyond that. My infertility doesn't make me less worthy of love and acceptance. It's not a battle I should have been silent about. It's not a scar I should be ashamed of. Being a woman isn't about carrying a child. It's not about people what other people need.

A woman is fierce. A woman is strong. A woman is resilient. A woman is courageous.

My culture makes being a woman feel like a burden.

But why?

Because of the expectations that are tied to us?

Who set that precedent? Who said a woman can't be enough on her own? Who said being a divorcee or childless strips you of your womanhood? Who said we aren't worthy?

Because we are.

And we will no longer settle for less.

I won't settle for less.

I stand up and tie the green ribbon onto my bedpost.

I smile.

The bow isn't symmetrical. The bow isn't equal.

But my smile still doesn't falter.

Because a bow is never meant to be *perfect.*

The end.

Sumayyah, Zoya, Rani and Halima will return.

Upcoming books in The Bow Series:

The Obedient Bow

The Modern Bow

The Silent Bow

Afterword

Thank you to everyone who has made it to this point in the book. The choice to write and publish a book where the main characters shared the same heritage as me was an easy one, despite knowing it would not commercially succeed compared to my other published works. But anyone who knows me will stand by me when I say, I never started this venture of my life to make money. I aimed to create stories that readers could connect with and learn from. So, I do not mark my success using monetary value. Success to me is if this book resonates with my readers, even just one person.

There is a recurring theme of 'choice' throughout the book. The Perfect Bow was never written to promote divorce. Sumayyah's ultimate strength came from finally deciding to make a choice that she wanted, regardless of the consequences. As the book ends in present tense, we leave Sumayyah at a point in her life where the decisions haven't been made for her. The world is at her doorstep and she's ready to embrace it. She is no longer telling the story that others have written. She firmly holds the pen in her hands, unknowing of the adventures that await her.

This book, and others within The Bow Series, is not a hate campaign against men or my culture. It is simply to highlight the injustices and expectations that are forced on us as women. I hope that publishing it will start conversations that can no longer be ignored. The Bow Series is an interconnected series that runs along the same timeline. As Halima said, while different, their lives mirror one another as each of them fights to escape the stereotypes that have been forced upon them. Their journeys are ones of breaking tradition and women's empowerment. I hope you see parts of yourself in all, or at least one of our four female leads. They each harbour a strength that deserves to be recognised and I cannot wait to delve into the three remaining stories.

Like Sumayyah and many of my readers, people have judged me against standards that existed long before the generations before me. Whether that be my appearance or life choices. But I learned that we are the authors of our stories and it's down to us to write a story we'd be proud to shout from the rooftops. When I envisage an older Samirah, I hope she doesn't skim past the chapters of her life, but proudly stops to absorb all the things she's achieved. I know for certain she will be proud of this moment.

Details for upcoming books in the series will be shared via Instagram *(@szaman.author)* and TikTok *(@samirahzamanauthor).*

ACKNOWLEDGEMENTS

I would firstly like to extend my gratitude to all the women who shared their stories with me. Reading through your responses broke me in ways I will never be able to explain. It was your honesty and willingness to share your reality that allowed me to write an authentic story. I hope you all found some strength and courage in Sumayyah's story.

A special thank you to my cover designer, @_brints who I'm also lucky enough to call my friend. Every element on this cover, spine and blurb was hand drawn. She exceeded all my expectations and was the easiest person to ever work with! And I am so happy to share she is the official cover designer for the rest of The Bow Series. I'm excited for all the magic we're going to create together.

Rem, your excitement for this book and series will always astound me. There is so much I could thank you for in my life, but pertaining to this book I want to thank you for sharing all your knowledge and experience with endometriosis. Many of our catch-ups were spent discussing fertility issues and for that I thank and apologise!

To my Suto Bhabi, thank you explaining the education and training process for doctors to me about a million times. Your willingness to sit with me and explain the struggles / pros and cons helped me to adapt the early chapters of the book into something much more realistic and develop the depth of Sumayyah and Yousef's issues.

My blurb fairy, I'm going to have to copy and paste your acknowledgements into all my books at this rate. I can't thank you enough for turning the first terrible version of the blurb into the work of art it is now. You always do such a phenomenal job – even though I never tell you any details about the book!

As always, thank you to my Brianna. You have and always will be my rock in life. You are the one who pushes me to keep going when I feel hopeless. You never fail to listen to my long rambles and calm me down when I go into a meltdown. Your belief in me will always make my heart feel fuzzy and warm.

And last, but certainly not least, thank you to you – my readers. Your continued support and love allows me to continue writing and publishing. I hope to write many more stories that will have you feeling every range of emotions. I can't promise a traditional HEA every time, but I can vow that it will be a story that will remain with you; one where you find strength and hope.